In Antares' Darkest Dawn

"Now we are invincible in battle. Now the potent force of the Witherer is with us. He will waste away our enemies. Long and long have the Hawkwas waited for this time. And now it is here.

"There is more. The army from Hamal landed to the south of Vallia has gained a great victory. The hosts of the emperor are withered away, his warriors strew the ground in windrows, their blood waters the dirt. This is a further sign! The Witherer is with us and nothing can stand in our path.

"Our own fleet of airboats will fly us south. We will join with our friends from Hamal. We will march upon Vondium and take that great city and utterly destroy all who stand in our path! All hail to the Witherer! All hail to the Hawkwas!"

"MARCH, REBELS . . . TO BURN THE CAPITAL!"

"The lupal projection writhed in my bedchamber."

CAPTIVE
SCORPIO

by
Allan Burt Akers

Illustrated by
Josh Kirby

DAW BOOKS, INC.
DONALD A. WOLLHEIM, PUBLISHER

1301 Avenue of the Americas
New York, N. Y. 10019

Published by
THE NEW AMERICAN LIBRARY
OF CANADA LIMITED

First Printing, August 1978

1 2 3 4 5 6 7 8 9

PRINTED IN CANADA
COVER PRINTED IN U.S.A.

TABLE OF CONTENTS

LIST OF ILLUSTRATIONS

A NOTE ON DRAY PRESCOT

Dray Prescot is an enigmatic figure. Reared in the inhumanly harsh conditions of Nelson's navy, he has been transported many times through the agencies of the Star Lords and the Savanti nal Aphrasöe to the beautiful and brutal world of Kregen, four hundred light years from Earth. A coherent design underlies all his headlong adventures; but so far the pattern remains indecipherable.

His appearance as described by one who has seen him is of a man above middle height, with brown hair and level brown eyes, brooding and dominating, with enormously broad shoulders and powerful physique. There is about him an abrasive honesty and an indomitable courage. He moves like a savage hunting cat, quiet and deadly. On the exotic and perilous world of Kregen he has fought his way to become Vovedeer and Zorcander of his wild Clansmen of Segesthes, Lord of Strombor, Strom of Valka, King of Djanduin, Prince Majister of Vallia—and a member of the Order of Krozairs of Zy. To this plethora of titles he confesses with a wryness and an irony I am sure masks much deeper feelings at which we can only guess.

Prescot's happiness with Delia, the Princess Majestrix of Vallia, is threatened as the notorious Wizard of Loh, Phu-Si-Yantong, seeks to destroy Delia's father, the emperor. Together with their friends Delia and Prescot save the emperor from a poison attempt by other factions and return him to power in Vondium, the capital. But their comrades are scattered over the face of Kregen. Now, blood-splashed from the last fight in the palace, Prescot is determined to seek the whereabouts of his daughters, alienated from him during a forced absence on Earth. But the brilliant world of Kregen under Antares will always challenge Prescot with new problems and adventures. **Dray Prescot knows only too well that he must continue to struggle against himself as well as the malignant fates that pursue him in the mingled streaming lights of the Suns of Scorpio.**

Alan Burt Akers.

Chapter One

Before the Dawn

"Oh, yes, it is common knowledge," said Travok Ott expansively, leaning back, sipping his light white wine with a most delicate air. "Delia, the Princess Majestrix, is continually indulging in affairs. Why, her latest inamorato is this muscular wrestler, Turko. Oh, yes, a lovely man. Who can blame her?"

The perfumed currents of warmed air moved caressingly about the group of men sitting in the ord chamber of the Baths of the Nine. The chamber presented a comfortable, modish, relaxing atmosphere. Young girl slaves carried wine and parclear in glazed ceramic flagons, and bronze trays of sweetmeats and tempting cakes. No lady bathers were allowed here, their establishment was separated off by a stout masonry wall. The scented air cloyed.

"Surely, this is just rumor, Travok?" said Urban the Gloves, popping a paline into his mouth.

"Hardly." Travok Ott, a slender man with the brown hair of Vallia cut into a curled bang, sipped his wine with a knowing smile. He, like them all, was naked, covered only by a small yellow towel. "Have you seen this Turko? A Khamorro, so I am told, from somewhere outlandish deep in southwestern Havilfar. But a lovely man. Oh, yes, beautiful—"

"I hold no brief for the emperor," cut in the overfed man with the three chins and swag belly, all quivering as he shook his head warningly. "But he'd have your head if—"

"Of a certainty, Ortyg—perhaps!" Travok cast a sliding glance at the shadowed alcove where a yellow towel draped down from the arm of a bronze faun, prancing, abandoned, garlanded with loomins. "But I mean him no disrespect. He understands business, and that is good enough for me."

They were all businessmen here, traders, merchants, shopkeepers to whom war and country-wide distress could bring profit, for they were shrewd in the mysteries of bargaining and gaining a corner and of stocks and the human frailties of supply and demand. This particular establishment of the Baths of the Nine stood at a crossroads in the southern part of the great city of Vondium, the capital of the Empire of Vallia. It was not one of the enormously luxurious first-rank establishments; but its entrance fees were high and it catered to a certain clientele of the middle rank, merchants and traders who could afford to pay for a night's comfort.

These men were habitués of the place, they knew one another, had been coming here for years to relax and gossip. The fellow who sat somewhat removed from them along a marble bench on pink and yellow towels smiled and nodded and joined in the conversation and listened with due respect; but he was a stranger. So the talk was more circumspect than normally the case in these secluded, sybaritic and seductive surroundings.

A beautifully formed Fristle fifi glided forward to refill Travok Ott's glass, for he found the flagons tiresomely too heavy. The Fristle's fur was of that deep plum color that limned her lissom form, made of her a sprite of beauty in that place. Travok grunted as the wine reached a whisker below the rim, and trembled, and stilled. Had the Fristle spilled any it would have gone hard for her.

"I've always stood by the emperor," Travok went on. "Did I not give thanks to Opaz when he recovered from his illness? Did I not put up the shutters on my shops when those Opaz-forsaken chyyanists went on the rampage with their Black Feathers? Have I not a son at sea?" The wine gleamed on his lips. "Vallia is built of men like me."

"You say this Turko is the princess's inamorato," said Ortyg. "But is she his inamorata? That is a conundrum."

A low, fruity chuckle ran around the circle of men lounging in their chairs or on the benches, warmed and caressed by the scented air.

"The princess owns men's hearts—but I wager Turko has his own little inamorata tucked away somewhere safe in Valka."

Ortyg leaned a little forward, his belly bulging. "The princess does not own my heart."

The shrimp of a fellow in the corner where the warmest breezes blew puckered up his lips, his little tuft of goat's beard blowing. His brown Vallian eyes were deeply sunken under sandpapery brows. He hitched up his yellow towel and said: "Of a certainty, Travok, Vallia is built of men like you—and of Kov Layco."

The words might mean what the listener cared to put into them. This Travok Ott construed them as a compliment.

10

"Kov Layco Jhansi is the emperor's right-hand man, Vandrop, true. It is said he slew Ashti Melekhi with his own hand. The guards—"

Ortyg laughed, waggling his chins. "Those guards will not be seen in Vondium again."

"All the same, he, too, is aware of the Princess Majestrix's infidelity. She is becoming notorious—"

"And this shaggy clansman, her husband. He knows nothing?"

"He knows nothing of Vallia, that is sooth, by Vox!"

They appeared to be in general agreement about this.

Vandrop put a hand to his shaggy tuft of goat's beard. He stroked reflectively. "This shaggy clansman is shaggy. It is said he has a beard to his navel."

A young fellow on the other side of Travok shouted: "And that's quite long enough for a barbarian."

Travok nodded. "By Vox! A great hairy clansman from far Segesthes has the impudence to barge in and carry off our princess like a graint or a cramph or a leem—"

"But," persisted Vandrop, "was he not there, in the palace, last night? The stories are confused, garbled, but—"

"He was there, Vandrop," Ortyg told him. "I had the news red hot from my freedman who got it from the palace—a shishi there who saw much—and this Dray Prescot was in the palace. How he got there no one knows. But Kov Layco saved the emperor from Ashti Melekhi—"

A babble of voices broke in, and so Ortyg was persuaded to tell them the story as he had heard it. He made the most of it, how the Vadnicha Ashti Melekhi sought to poison the emperor and of how Layco Jhansi had slain her with his dagger. There were dead guards and blood everywhere; but Ortyg's information offered no explanation for them, even though, it was whispered, they were Jiktars of the Chulik mercenary guard—aye—and their Chuktar, also.

The talk wended on in the scented air. With the long night to get through men and women sought rest and relaxation before bed at the Baths of the Nine. Soon these men would rise and then, each to his whim, either dress and go home or partake of the Ninth Chamber. Strangers might elect to sleep in the establishment in the tastefully appointed hostelry. The stranger, a well-built young man with hair darker than the normal Vallian brown, would probably sleep in. Vandrop yawned.

"By Vox!" he said, his goat's-beard tuft quivering. "What

11

you say about Delia, the Princess Majestrix, is hard to believe. I think I shall not believe it."

"You always were a credulous old fool, Vandrop," bellowed Ortyg, slapping his gut, reaching for his towel.

"Anyway," said Travok. "When Queen Lushfymi gets here she will soon find out—"

"—Aye, a sharp queen, that," said Urban the Gloves.

"—And she'll have this Turko's head off and the princess packed off back to Valka, or Delphond."

"D'you think Queen Lushfymi will marry the emperor?"

"If she has any sense, Urban."

They spoke of the Queen of Lome as Queen Lushfymi. The emperor had intemperately threatened to have off the heads of all those who blasphemously called her Queen Lush.

With two strangers present in the ord chamber these men spoke with more restraint than usual. Without clothes their allegiances were not at once apparent, and their words hid what they did not wish revealed. As middling tradesmen and merchants they were probably of the Racter party, some perhaps of the Vondium Khanders, those who looked to the business community for combined strength. The Racters were the most powerful party in Vallia, formed of aristocrats and nobles, and the merchants looked to them for the continuance of the status quo and a stable economy. But without the colored sleeves, without symbols and favors, they were simply men, naked in the flesh, so much alike and each one different in his own personal ways.

They spoke with a caution. But they had said a great deal, also. They were of the general opinion that it was high time the emperor married again and got himself a son to carry on the line, if the prince could hold in his hands what would come to him, and dispatched his daughter Delia and her grizzly graint of a clansman husband back to the Great Plains of Segesthes. One or two even said the Prince and Princess Majestrix could even go to the Ice Floes of Sicce for all they cared.

In these last moments before they left they talked again of the interests most pressing to them, as businessmen do; the prices and sources of supply, trading prospects, the cost of money, the laziness of slaves, the prospects of renewed war with the Empire of Hamal, the hedging against future disasters.

They even spoke of Income Tax; but obscenities found little favor in the Baths of the Nine—at least, of that kind.

Travok Ott, genial, yawning, looked across at the stranger.

12

"You put up here tonight, Koter? You have not told us your name."

"Yes, I think I shall. And my name is Nath Delity."

The others nodded. Their thoughts were transparent. A provincial, seeing the sights of Vondium, the greatest city of Paz.

Nath Delity half smiled. "I am from Evir, and I find Vondium a trifle warm."

They laughed at this, proud of their city, half-contemptuous of any provincial place and particularly of Evir, the northernmost province of Vallia.

"You should have been here when the emperor lay dying, or the chyyanists were rampaging or the Third Party was active, Koter Delity. You would have been more than warm then."

Vandrop tweaked his goat's-beard tuft and looked across at the alcove where the yellow towel lay draped across the bronze statue of the faun. "And you, Koter," he spoke civilly, smiling. "You have said not a word. We would not wish you to think we are unsociable here. It is just that we know one another so well. Your name, Koter—if you wish to tell us."

Some of the others had already risen to leave and now while some pushed on, laughing and shouting, others hung back to listen. No doubt they wanted reassurance. Perhaps, their thoughts probably went, perhaps they might have said something less than wise. Spies from anywhere and serving any cause could cause troubles. . . .

"My name is Jak Jakhan," I said, speaking smoothly and just quickly enough so that they would not know I lied. "From Zamra. And I have enjoyed your conversation, Koters."

"Zamra?" said Travok Ott.

"Zamra?" said Ortyg. His three chins wobbled.

"Zamra is, I believe," said Vandrop, "a Kovnate of the Prince Majister's?"

"Oh," I said. "I have not been there since I was a child—"

They visibly relaxed at this. I ought to have said I was from some damned Racter province, or, better still, have said nothing of my origins. Anyway, I am fond of Zamra.

As we went out through the different doors, some to debauchery, some to a night's sleep, others to the many amusements afforded to the night owls of Vondium, I fell into step beside Vandrop. We entered the robing room together and I

13

hung back, for I did not wish Vandrop—just yet—to see my clothes.

"Is it true, Koter Vandrop—about the Princess Majestrix, I mean?"

He squinted up at me.

"I have never seen this Dray Prescot—well, few of us here would have, although Travok claims he was within spitting distance of him at the wedding—still, that is like Travok. But as to the Princess Delia, the Princess Majestrix—I do not know. There are rumors—"

"And who would have told Travok Ott?"

Vandrop edged along to his locker with the key handed to him by the robing slave in attendance on him.

"By Opaz, I do not know. He likes to keep abreast of things."

The slave unlocked the cabinet and began to fuss around Vandrop, whereat he pushed him away and dressed himself in his evening clothes. Typical of Vallia, a lounging robe in a dark rich hue of plum color, with silver embroidery, the clothes at once gave him a dignity, a measure of command, more in keeping with his character. It is said that clothes make the man. I looked at the favor pinned to his left breast. It was not black and white, the colors of the Racters, nor white and green, the colors of the Panvals. Shaped like an opened book, with an ancient abacus and a writing pen, it was stitched in white, green and yellow. The favor was that of the Vondium Khanders.

He saw my glance.

"I believe we businessmen must stand together. You may be a Racter, for all I know, Koter Jakhan; but the Racters will hold for themselves, for the nobles, I think."

"And the emperor and his family?"

He frowned.

At once I said: "I have overstepped the bounds of common usage, Koter Vandrop. Put it down to a stranger's uncouthness."

His frown remained and he sighed, "No, no, Koter Jakhan. Rather, put it down to the evil days that have fallen on Vallia and Vondium. Once, we would all have shouted for the emperor. And for his daughter. But there are forces at work—you may know of some, and there are others I know nothing of, but can sense, can feel. I am almost a hundred and seventy-five. So I know about these things. Put it down to this strange and unpleasant new world in which we live."

The slave handed him a belt with a few tasteful jewels

studding its length, and with lockets from which swung the long thin dagger of Vallia. He bucked up the belt, sighed again, and said: "If you are not staying the night, here in the Bower of the Scented Lotus, perhaps—?"

About to say I would walk with him for a space, I checked.

I had things to do. The blood had been washed away. But I still had things—urgent things—to do before I could rest.

And, could I ever rest?

In Zair's truth, could I ever rest?

I said: "Could you direct me to the house of Travok Ott?"

His goat's-beard tuft quivered. But he said: "He is a good man, Koter, do not forget that. He has labored hard for what he has, here in Vondium. He is an ivory merchant, and may be found in the Souk of Chem."

"I give you thanks." I turned to go and, as Vandrop moved away, said: "Rembree, Koter Vandrop."

"Rembree, Koter Jakhan."

I caught a quick glimpse of the stranger, Nath Delity, going past as Vandrop went away to his respectable bed.

The robing slave—he was a little Och and his middle left limb was withered—fussed over me as I reached the cabinet assigned to me and unlocked it. My suit of decent Vallian buff looked the worse for wear. It had come from the wardrobe I kept up in the Palazzo of the Four Winds in Djanguraj. But I shrugged it on, philosophically, and drew on the tall black Vallian boots. The weaponry was rolled in the cloak. I held the cloak and did not unroll it, standing ready to leave as I had entered here, after the fracas at the emperor's palace.

When the Och saw I gave him a silver stiver he babbled his thanks; but I merely nodded and stepped out along the marble floor, over the geometric tessellations, to the doors. Outside, the night of Vondium pressed down, and wayfarers were only too pleased to hear the link men's calls of: "Loxo! Loxo!" and see them come hurrying up with their torches and lanterns.

One of the lesser moons of Kregen went hurtling past, low, casting down a thin scattering of light. Shadows lay heavy and dark, pierced by lanterns at corners and the winking sparks of the link men's torches as they guided their customers home—or, given the nature of a Kregan's desires and expectancies of the good life—to the gaming halls, the theatres, the dancing places, that would carry on right through to what on Earth would be called the small hours.

15

The palace of the emperor dominated its island between the canals and the River—She of the Fecundity. I passed along, not caring to employ a link man, moving fast. The emperor was safe now. Kov Layco Jhansi, the chief minister, had slain Ashti Melekhi who had sought to kill the emperor, and that particular plot had misfired.

Of course, there would be other plots against the emperor.

That was natural.

But the old devil was now possessed of a thousand years of life, because he had bathed in the sorcerous waters of the Sacred Pool of Baptism. I did not think he knew that fact. Not yet. But the thought had made me laugh, which is a rare occurrence, Zair knows.

A little wind flickered awnings half-seen in the erratic light. Leaves scuttered across the pavings. Vondium is indeed a magical city, fit to be the capital of an empire. The palace reared ahead, a monstrous pile, and I was comfortably aware that I would now be able to enter freely, instead of either having to creep in by a secret stair or bash my way in by brute force, as I had been constrained to do up until the events of this very night.

The guards let me pass. I noticed that the numbers of Chuliks had materially reduced. Just how Jhansi had contrived that I did not then know; but the guards were still alert, and halted me, and then, obsequiously, let me through.

It is a strange and observable fact that most wizards prefer to have their chambers in a tower. One would think they would prefer the deepest cellars, since most of them appear to have truck with the powers who are alleged to lie in that direction, rather than those in the other. But it is so.

High up the winding stair of the Tower of Incense lay the bronze-studded door. No guards were posted here. Some folk say a Wizard of Loh needs no human guards; but although that is a popular belief, it is not so. The Wizards of Loh are famed, feared, formidable; but they remain still mortal men.

A coldness appeared to cling about that door. I say appeared to cling; this was an irrational feeling and I brushed it off testily and bashed the door open with my boot.

Dimly lit, hung with macabre artifacts, the chambers of the Wizard of Loh lowered down. A lamp burned in the corner beside the skull of a risslaca. The skeleton of a chavonth had been wired in a leaping posture facing the doorway. Solemn black drapes swathed the walls. The arrow-slit windows were swathed in long blood-red curtains. A sturm-wood table supported weird objects—human heads, animal bones,

"You come hard upon your fate, rast!"

bottles of blood, fetuses, jars of colored powder, strangely shaped instruments.

This whole mish-mash was designed to impress the credulous.

This anteroom resembled the working chamber of a common sorcerer. I had never met a Wizard of Loh who put much store by this kind of rubbish.

The Wizard of Loh at the court of the Emperor of Vallia had been Deb-so-Parang; but he had died some seasons ago. The Wizard of Loh who had taken his place was, so I was led to understand, some kind of sibling, and was called Deb-sa-Chiu.

He looked up from a table in the inner room. A thing writhed and screamed on the table, and Deb-sa-Chiu's hands were green.

He frowned.

The shadows threw my face into darkness, and so my form bulked in the doorway, startling him.

"You come hard upon your fate, rast!" he said. He spoke with that harsh Lohvian hiss that some of the redheaded folk of Loh cannot control. His hands flew up. Whether or not he could fashion a spell to blast me, turn me into a toad, do anything particularly unpleasant, I was not prepared to find out. Men credit the Wizards of Loh with supernatural powers and, by Vox, I have seen a few weird happenings in my time on Kregen.

So, quickly, I said: "Lahal, Deb-sa-Chiu. I have come to talk privily with you, San, and to seek your assistance."

He dropped the green-oozing thing onto the worktable.

"You try my patience—"

"Then let me try to untry your patience, San."

I gave him the honored title of San—dominie, sage, master—for although already I had my doubts of this one, I did not wish to prejudice my chances of finding out what I must know. Time was wasting. Perhaps I ought to have come here directly instead of going to the Bower of the Scented Lotus to wash away the blood.

He peered under his hand at me, and then motioned me to stand to the side so that the samphron oil lamp's gleam might fall upon my face. His own face was smooth, unmarked, crowned with that red Lohvian hair. His eyes were wary. He affected the black moustache arranged in two long drooping tails down the sides of his mouth, a fashion I find ludicrous and offensive, for all the chill menace it invariably creates.

Moving to stand where he might see me plain, I said in a

18

voice I knew grated out harshly: "You would do me a favor, San, if you will tell me the whereabouts of the Princess Majestrix."

His smooth and knowing face lifted at my tone.

"And who are you who seeks this knowledge? I have warned you that you try my patience at your peril. I shall see you cast down to the dungeons. Naghan the Pinch will show you the error of your ways—"

He stopped speaking abruptly.

The light fell upon my face.

For a moment he stood, unmoving, his eyes black buttons revealing his thoughts. Then: "I have seen the court portrait of you, hung in the Gallery of Princes. What you ask—"

"I have beforetime asked a Wizard of Loh to go into lupu for me and to discover the whereabouts of Delia, the Princess Majestrix. My regard held him transfixed. "I have not asked them to go unrequited for the service."

If I admit to a guilty twinge of conscience here over the Wizard of Loh Que-si-Rening of Ruathytu in distant and hostile Hamal, it was surely merited, for I had done precious little for him in recompense for his assistance in tracking down Saffi the golden lion-maid. I brushed the thought away and glared at this Deb-sa-Chiu, prepared to be extremely nasty to him if necessary, although heartily wishing that unpleasant necessity would not arise.

"It is said that the Princess Majestrix and a great crowd of her friends left Vondium secretly and in a great hurry."

"It is said?" I forced myself not to mock him. "Surely a mighty Wizard of Loh has sources of more precise information?"

"We have, we have. But information is not cheap."

So ho, I said to myself. A greedy one. Well, we know how they may be manipulated.

I could not smile; but I tried to make myself relax. This would take a little time, for when a Wizard of Loh goes into lupu it seems the very forces of nature are distorted, denied, turned aside from their normal courses to the ends of wizardry.

"You must know I have means of recompensing you."

He inclined his head—a fraction, by a fraction only, for they are haughty and proud in their wisdom—and said: "Then let us come to an arrangement." He gestured with a finger and thumb touching, his other fingers stiffly outspread. "For there have been apparitions within the palace, appearances, specters—"

19

"Tell me."

"You have the honor to receive the assistance of Khe-Hi-Bjanching. He has made himself a power among the Wizards of Loh who render assistance to princes. The emperor, who is honored to be favored by my assistance, speaks highly of him. You are indeed fortunate."

I said nothing but simply glared.

He went on a little hurriedly.

"Khe-Hi-Bjanching has discussed with me a certain Wizard of Loh who seeks to maintain an observation upon you—"

"Phu-Si-Yantong."

He swallowed and moved away toward a side table of sturm wood upon which stood glistening flagons and linen-covered trays. He busied himself pouring wine. I shook my head when he lifted an eyebrow at me. If he wanted to go through this flummery and play-acting, all very well; but my patience was running out.

"Phu-Si-Yantong. A most powerful, most puissant Wizard of Loh. His appearances have been observed in the palace. I myself have seen them. Khe-Hi-Bjanching, also. We are concerned."

"So am I. What has this to do with the whereabouts of the Princess Majestrix?"

"She returned alone from wherever she had been." As he said this, Chiu's face shadowed and he took a quick gulp of wine. I knew the fellow knew where Delia had gone with our friends. Aphrasöe, the city of the Savanti, the Swinging City—that was where Delia had taken the emperor to be cured of the poison administered by the bitch Ashti Melehki—who was now dead—and I knew, further, that the Savanti nal Aphrasöe threw a most dread horror into the hearts of even the greatest of the Wizards of Loh.

So I said: "She returned. I wish to know where she is *now*!"

He smoothed down his silk robe, liberally embroidered with symbols and runes, archaic signs that would daunt the credulous who sought his help. He paced across the chamber, careful to place his curled brown slippers upon the rugs and carpets and not upon the harsh stone. He carried the wine in one claw-like hand. At last he stopped and eyed me.

"I will go into lupu for you, prince, and seek the whereabouts of the Princess Majestrix. The price—"

Almost, I smiled. That was a crude word for so haughty a fellow.

"Name it."

As must be clearly evident to you who listen to my story as the tapes spin through your heads, I reasoned that after all my friends had been flung by magical power back to their points of origin about Kregen, Delia would have been hurled back to Vondium. Knowing her, I knew she would instantly take flier and hare off back to Aphrasöe to find me. But, I had the sense to realize she might have gone to Valka, to the east, first. I did not wish to fly all the way to the island of Ba-Domek, in which stands Aphrasöe, and miss her. And I did not wish to waste time flying to Valka if she had not gone there. I wanted—I hungered—to know where she was at this precise moment.

"Gold," said Chiu, and allowed a smile to crimp that thin mouth of his. "Wizards of Loh are always in need of gold, for we have not so far unravelled the secret of its manufacture." He waved airily. "But gold is only a small part of the price."

He was telling me nothing that was not generally known over Kregen. I looked at him, and he went on quickly.

"The Vadnicha Ashti Melekhi has been foiled in her plans to slay the emperor—"

Here I cut in brutally, rapidly growing tired of his procrastinations. "And no thanks to you. Your duty was to warn him. Why should he clothe and feed you if you fail him?"

He drew himself up at this, a flush creeping under the smooth skin of his cheeks. He looked savage. "You should speak with more care to a Wizard of Loh, prince. Do you forget—"

"I will forget that you failed in your duty to the emperor if you instantly tell me where the Princess Majestrix is. As to payment—gold, you may have gold." I let the swaddling cloak unroll, letting the covered weapons glint suddenly in the samphron oil lamps' gleam as they came free. "And as for further payment, I fancy that can be arranged."

His face looked murderous. But he nodded, as though coming to a decison. He squatted down on the floor. There was no need to aquaint him with the person whom he sought; he had met Delia in the palace. He put his hands to his eyes and began to rock backwards and forwards, keening a note that rose and rose until it shrilled into an unheard vibration.

Clearly, Chiu was a very powerful wizard, or he knew more than he had said. He had started on the third phase of going into lupu, bypassing that first long silent struggling with the bonds of the spirit—the ib—when the constraints are

21

loosened and reality and the forces beyond reality strain and merge.

He stood up. His hands dragged away from before his face. He began to rotate, slowly at first, his arms outflung, then faster and faster. There are different disciplines within the Wizards of Loh, and adepts go into lupu in different ways. But the results are very similar. I knew that the ib of Chiu had broken free from his corporeal body, was drifting, was seeking the whereabouts of Delia.

Abruptly, he dropped to the ground, crouched, his hands pressed flat against the rugs. He threw his head back. His eyes slowly opened, and once again I saw that drugged, eerie, *knowing* look.

I waited.

"Yes, prince," he breathed. He spoke chokingly. "Yes. The Princess Majestrix rides an airboat. The wind blows. She flies west."

"Across the Sunset Sea?"

"No."

"Across Vallia?"

"Yes."

So she *had* gone to Valka first, then. . . .

"Tell me more."

"The Princess Majestrix flies to Vondium. I feel the wind. The air cuts. She is alone."

I jumped at this. I didn't like the sound of this at all.

Then this great San, this puissant Wizard of Loh, this Deb-sa-Chiu said: "She is in great distress. And there is a shadow—I see a shadow, dark, hovering—" His drugged eyes opened wide and he clasped his hands together, lifting up from the rug. He glared at me and the knowingness on his face sickened me. "Phu-Si-Yantong! He it is. . . . It is he. . . . But the powers fail, the ib grows fragile and must return—Phu-Si-Yantong's kharrna overbears all—"

The wizard clutched abruptly at his throat, choking. His eyes rolled up and this time they did not show white half-moon crescents as he went into lupu, rather they showed the awful terror of a man being strangled. I took a step forward and grasped his shoulder, roughly, and shook him.

"Chiu! Chiu! Wake up, man!"

He shuddered and writhed away; but I held him, and shook him again, shaking a potent and devilish Wizard of Loh as one might shake an angry willful child.

Then, seeing this was doing no good I hooked my fingers inside his and dragged his clutching hands away from his

22

throat. So stiffly did his arms move, so much like sere winter branches, I thought they would snap off. But I forced his hands apart and wrenched away those lethal fingers. He choked and blubbered and whooped in great draughts of air. Tears ran down his smooth cheeks. He closed his eyes and a shudder wracked his whole body. He shook in those fine silken clothes with the runes of power embroidered in gold thread.

Presently he had recovered sufficiently to take a glass of wine. He gulped. Then he looked at me over the crystal rim, shaking still; but gathering command of himself.

"Phu-Si-Yantong," he whispered. "The power! The power!"

"All right, San. Tell me."

"The strength of his kharrna overpowered all my lore, my arts, my own devices. I would have choked myself to death— at his command."

"I saw that."

Truth to tell, the notion was eerie and mind-wrenchingly scary; the idea that a man a great distance away could so control another that he would take his own life. It was frightening. I still clung to that scrap of knowledge I had gathered, overheard as I felt by the command of the Star Lords, that Phu-Si-Yantong would not order my assassination. He would have no need of paid assassins, stikitches out to earn their gold by stealthy murder. Ashti Melekhi had set her assassins on me and I was not free of them yet. But Phu-Si-Yantong—then the thought occurred to me that perhaps one had to be in lupu to be thus attacked at a distance. I sincerely hoped so.

"And you can tell me no more?"

"You have saved my life, prince. But I wonder how long I shall retain it, if—"

"Yantong has no quarrel with you."

He gave me a long pitying look, recovering his composure, getting back to the serious business of being a Wizard of Loh. It is strange but true that these famous Wizards are seldom called merely wizards; usually they are given their full name of Wizards of Loh. The other wizards of Kregen, also, favor those from Loh with the full name. It is a measure of their importance in the eyes of other sorcerers.

"The Princess Majestrix will arrive in Vondium when the suns rise." He puffed out his cheeks, getting his color back. "Now, prince, we must talk about the balance of your payment to me."

I glared at him. I should have listened. I should have

waited for him to say what he wanted. It might have saved a few thousand lives, saved a torrent of blood, saved a few burning, looted towns. But, onker that I am, I said bluffly: "As to payment, San, you may have your gold. But I think if you believe I have saved your life you are fully requited and I no longer stand in your debt."

Anyway, at the time it struck me as fair.

But fairness and justice do not go hand in hand with expediency and cleverness and the saving of pride. So, onker of onkers that I am, I nodded to him, scooped up the weapons in their cloak, and stomped out.

Get onker!

I can say that, now, looking back. I was, indeed, still very much of an idiot in those days.

But, of course, as you will perceive I was in a turmoil of fear for Delia. If that bastard Phu-Si-Yantong was up to more mischief, and my Delia flying all alone—I sweated and shook and went off running toward the high aerial landing platform where her airboat would touch down.

Any sensible fellow would have waited. I had been up and about for a long spell. I had fought a combat in the emperor's bedroom that some would put down as a jikai, although I did not vaunt myself that far. The Chuliks who had come to slay the emperor had been dealt with by me, and their employer, Ashti Melekhi, had been stabbed to death by Kov Layco Jhansi. I was tired. But tiredness is a mortal sin.

So I rousted out the guard and yelled and bellowed and acted like a high and mighty prince and secured an airboat and went leaping away into the star-studded night.

Due east I headed, on course for Valka, trusting that Delia's flier would be on the reciprocal of my course, and I would see her airboat in the bright star glitter. She of the Veils, Kregen's fourth moon, was hidden by cloud but as I flew on eastward of the great circle of the city so the clouds dissipated and cleared and pink and golden moonshine flooded down. I could see better then. The land fled past below. The wind buffeted my face and roared in my ears. On and on I flew, searching the heavens for the first glimpse of the airboat.

As I flew on searching the sky for that flitting sharp-prowed form, Deb-sa-Chiu's words recurred to me. I puzzled over one word. He had said: "kharrna." I did not know what that was. I would have to ask my own Wizard, Khe-Hi-Bjanching.

Then I checked.

24

After my friends had dipped the emperor and themselves in the Sacred Pool of Baptism on the River Zelph in far Aphrasöe, the Guardian of the Pool, Vanti, had dispatched them all willy-nilly to their places of origin. That meant that Bjanching was somewhere in Loh, that veiled and mysterious continent to the southwest of Vallia. It meant that Seg Segutorio was back home in Erthyrdrin, the mountainous promontory at the northern tip of Loh. It meant that Inch was home in Ng'groga, in the southeast of Loh. Odd how they all came from Loh, a fact I had been barely conscious of. And my other friends, all my comrades on the expedition, were back home. Gloag was in Mehzta. Hap Loder was back on the Great Plains of Segesthes. Turko the Shield in Herrelldrin in distant Havilfar. Tilly, Oby, Naghan the Gnat, back in Hyrklana. And Balass the Hawk in Xuntal.

There was no help from them in the coming struggle.

Many of these friends had made a new home for themselves with Delia and me in Valka. I made up my mind I would make the most strenuous efforts to assist them if they wished to return, as I felt they would—as, indeed, knowing the comradeship between us, I was absolutely certain they would.

But, first things first.

By the wheeling movements of the stars and the onward progression of She of the Veils I counted the passing hours. Each bur is roughly forty terrestrial minutes, and as another of the little catapulting lesser moons of Kregen vaulted across the sky I knew the burs were rattling away. The good graces of Five-handed Eos-Bakchi, that chuckling Vallian spirit of luck and good fortune, were passing me by, too.

When I reached the point at which it was fruitless to hurry on farther I slowed the voller in its headlong rush. If Deb-sa-Chiu spoke the truth and Delia was due to reach Vondium at dawn, then she must have passed a circumferential line around the capital city by now. So I had missed her.

She was vectoring in on a different approach line.

Instantly, I swung the voller about and slammed the speed lever over full. It jarred against the stop. Well, as you know, that was a bad habit I'd been getting into more and more of late. As to whether or not driving a voller at top speed all the time through thin air materially affected its performance, I did not at the time know. I cared. Airboats still broke down at distressingly frequent intervals in Vallia. We bought our fliers from Hamal, and they continued to sell us inferior models, that broke down, despite the drubbing we'd given them at

25

the Battle of Jholaix. I brooded as the night wind whipped at my face, hurtling back to Vondium under the Moons of Kregen, brooded on the mighty and proud Empire of Hamal and what must be done about that place and its mad and cruel Empress Thyllis.

So many schemes and mischiefs needed attention on Kregen. Four hundred light years from Earth, the planet of my birth, Kregen is a marvelous world, peopled by wonderful beings, filled with light and clamor and furor of life lived to the hilt. But Kregen has its darker side, where horror and terror batten on innocent people, where sorceries rend reason, where injustice denies light.

Yes, there was much still to be done on Kregen.

I am but a simple, ordinary, mortal man—despite that I have been vouchsafed a thousand years of life—and although my shoulders are accounted broad, they can only seek to bear the load I can carry. I was despairingly conscious of all those things I had left undone. But, by Zim-Zair! I would do them. Aye, by the Black Chunkrah, all of them!

The hurtling headlong pace of the voller faltered.

The wind-swept spaces of the sky extended all about. The star glitter above, the pink wash of moonlight, the drifting shadow clouds, all coalesced.

The flier was falling.

Screaming with wind-bluster the flier fell toward the dark earth below.

Many philosophies and religions of Kregen seek to give guidance and reassurance to those at the last ontremity. I have spoken little of these things. Each to his own. If I turn to Zair—because I am on Kregen—and, also, to Opaz, this is only natural. Djan, too, holds importance in my scheme of things. If I was to be denied a last long lingering look at my Delia before I died I would curse and rave and then, at the end, perhaps accept that harsh decree. Certainly, I'd do my damnedest to claw back up out of my coffin to bash the skulls of those rasts in Hamal who sold us faulty vollers.

The wind blustered at me, screaming past the fragile wood and canvas of the little two-place flier. She twisted and turned, toppling through the air. Down and down we went, headlong, screeching for the final impact.

The controls appeared to be useless. I juggled the levers and then, intoxicatingly, fancied I caught a spark of response. The cover ripped away over the silver boxes that upheld and powered the voller in flight. I probed in, trying to figure out what the damage might be. If the silver boxes had turned

26

black then that would be the end, for their power would all have leached away. They gleamed dully silver back at me. I began frantically to search back along the linkages of bronze and balass, the orbits that controlled the movements of the two silver boxes, the vaol and paol boxes.

The flier lifted a little, flew straight. I stood up with the wind in my face, gasping, and the flier lurched and slid sideways.

In the pinkly golden rays of the moon I saw another flier, below me, heading west. She was a largish craft, with an upflung poop, and so I knew she was not Delia's voller.

The moonlight ran glittering along her coaming, sparkling from ornamentation there. Flags flew, mere featureless tufts of cloth in that erratic light. My flier lurched again, and slid sideways, and then, recovering, skewed the other way. We wallowed through the air like a reveler reeling from a tavern in Sanurkazz, celebrating the capture of a Magdaggian swifter.

More frenzied bashing of the controls brought me up level again. But it was a mere matter of time before my voller gave up completely and down to the hard earth we plunged, to make a pretty hole in the ground of Kregen.

The flier below flew parallel, surging on surely. By her lines she was a first-class Hamalian-built vessel. I could see no sign of life aboard her; doubtless her passengers were asleep in the cabin aft and her crew snugged down along the bulwarks.

There was a chance.

A slender chance—true; but it was all I had.

I let my voller down as gently as I could, gentling the controls now, handling her like a fractious zorca, light on the bit.

Sink me! I said. Was I not an old sailorman? Did I or did I not have the skill?

Putting my trust in myself is no new sensation for me; but always I do so with a trembling uncertainty. I can never be sure. With a muttered prayer to Zair—and to Opaz and Djan—I let the voller drift down, fighting the controls, feeling the rush of wind, feeling the sinking bottomless sensation of the gulfs of emptiness under me.

Down we plunged, down to a chance in a thousand.

In a thousand?

In a million. . . .

Chapter Two

An Aerial Reception

That chance in a million came off, of course, otherwise I would not be here to tell you of it.

The crippled voller responded lurchingly to the controls. There was little time left as I brought her in over the flier's foredeck. Judging distance was tricky. I was for a crazy moment reminded of the time when I swung from a long rope slung to a corth whose wide wings beat the air above me, swinging down to land clawingly on the tower of Umgar Stro. So, now, I swung the airboat down and hit the deck and bounced. We nearly went over the rail. The wind tried to lift us off, and then was miraculously stilled, so that I knew this large flier was of that kind that creates its own little biosphere in which the wind has no power to force an entrance.

The stillness settled and I took a deep breath and put a leg over the wooden coaming of my airboat.

Now, I own my sudden arrival was unceremonious. Out of the night sky a voller had come swooping in to land on this airboat's foredeck. Kregen is a world where abrupt actions of that sort almost invariably herald mischief. So as I jumped down to the deck I called out in a most pleasant voice.

"Llahal!" I called, using the double L of the familiar greeting for those one does not yet know. "Llahal. I crave your indulgence for my flier—"

I was allowed to go no farther.

The airboat was not deserted, as the stray thought had crossed my mind. As though conjured magically from the sleeping decks men sprang up, hard and dark against the last of the moonlight. The bright wink of weapons ringed me in.

Those weapons drove forward with purpose, unhesitating, sword and spear points aimed at my heart.

As I say, my arrival had been unceremonious.

But, even so, even on Kregen, a little of pappattu might have been made, a little time taken to sort out the situation, to understand why I had dropped out of the night sky.

But no.

The spears lanced toward me, the swords flashed down.

With the instinct a fighting man must needs have or perish very quickly I was leaping away, my rapier whipping out, the main gauche flicking up out of its scabbard.

These sudden devils trying to degut me were Chuliks. Their oiled yellow skin glistened in the radiance of She of the Veils. Their upthrust tusks glinted. They bore in, silently, ferociously, and I had to skip and jump and beat away those murderous brands.

"Listen, you bunch of onkers!" I yelled, prancing away, scrambling across the deck, around my voller, flicking and flashing swords and spears away. "I'm no stikitche! I haven't come to assassinate anyone!"

But they bore on silently. I own their very silence gave me pause; even a Chulik will give vent to a war cry every now and then, when he fights.

The rapier and left-hand dagger flamed under the moon and I had to exert myself smartly. So far I had not spitted any of them or slit anyone's throat; but they pressed and the cramped conditions hampered free movement. Pretty soon now someone was going to get his fool self killed, and I did not intend that someone to be me. And then, when the explanations followed, there would be a pretty pickle.

"Listen, you stupid onkers!" I bellowed, and slid a blow and my rapier winked out of its own accord, or so it seemed, and I had the devil of a time merely slicing down the Chulik's cheek instead of his throat. He staggered back, and I kicked his companion betwixt wind and water, and bellowed again. I was beginning to become annoyed.

One of them rushed in headlong, attempting to overbear me by sheer bulk and speed. I bent. He went over me, his arms flailing, letting out no sound, no surprised whoofle, simply somersaulting on to fetch up with a rib-cracking thunk against the bulwarks.

These fellows wore dark harnesses, black belts and leathers, and I could see no signs of favors of insignia, no colors. Their swords and spears were the badges of their trade.

A light bloomed from the poop rail. The radiance fell on the man holding up the lamp. He was a Fristle and his cat's face showed hard and angular in the light. At his side stood a bulky figure clad in a black cloak, with a bronze helmet jammed on his head, a bronze helmet with a tall cockscomb of gold and white feathers. Only the deep-set eyes of this person glittered out over a fold of cloth, drawn up over the face.

"Do not kill him!" The words were harsh, fierce, with a

29

rattling, hissing viciousness. They commanded immediate respect from the Chulik mercenaries. I saw the way the swords twitched in the yellow hands. They would use the flats, now. . . .

"Take him alive! The rast who kills him will be flung overboard."

Again the words battered the mercenaries. The man in the concealing black cloak and face cloth clearly handled these Chuliks with the proverbial rod of iron.

Two Och bowmen on the deck of the poop lowered their bows. They might have done for me had they loosed on me unawares. Now they would not chance a shot, under the interdiction of their lord, even though the bows were mere small flat short-bows. I leaped away from the coming attack and bellowed up at the black-cloaked figure.

"Tell these nurdling rasts of yours I come as a friend! I am not—"

"What you are and what you are not are of no concern of mine," came the hoarse, hissing, rattling voice. I fancied I heard a distant resemblance in that voice to a scoundel I had known on the inner sea, the Eye of the World; but I could not be sure. And what with keeping the swords away from me and skipping about and bellowing at them to desist, I thought no more about it at the time.

How that little scene would have ended I do not care to dwell on—or, rather, how it should have ended with the lot of them pitched overboard—but in the event the black-cloaked figure turned abruptly half-about. He stood in a strained, attentive, silent pose for a moment and I surmised he was listening to someone whom I could not see. After a moment or two in which I came perilously close to sinking the rapier between the ribs of a Chulik who wanted to finish matters, the man stand back.

His hard outline bulked against the last of the moonglow, for She of the Veils sank into the west and flooded the flier with a roseate light. So we had turned in mid air and were heading east. Why, I did not know. He flung up a commanding hand, and something about the gesture, some awkwardness, tugged at my memory.

"Hold!" he bellowed. Then: "Take the flier down. Let that man stand free, do not harm him."

The swords glittered as they lowered.

"Well," I said. "By Vox! You took your time."

The flier slanted toward the shadowed earth. The tableau held. The eeriness of it was not lost on me. If anyone of

30

those Chulik mercenaries made a wrong move, this time he might not be so lucky, and might, indeed, take six inches of good Vallian steel through his guts.

The airboat touched down. A tiny pre-dawn wind sang in the trees. The shadows loomed. The land spread, dotted with tree clumps, with not a light in evidence anywhere.

"Over with you!" shouted the man in the cloak. He pointed with his sword at my voller. "Throw that after him."

The Chuliks stood back, for they were fighting men and the volmen of the flier would handle details like casting a voller over the side. These sailors of the skies were men like me, apim, some of them; others were Brokelsh and Womoxes, diffs whose racial animosities were not too blatant. There were no Fristles that I could see apart from the one on the poop with the lantern, for as a rule, although not always, Chuliks and Fristles do not get along too easily, one race with the other.

My voller was incontinently heaved up and chucked over the side. I heard the breaking and splintering of wood, the ripping of canvas.

"By Vox!" I yelled. "Who's going to pay for that?"

That harsh hissing voice carried not the slightest trace of amusement. "You are a man with much gold. The trifle of a smashed voller will not trouble you."

He said voller, which is the word for an airboat most often heard in Havilfar, where they are manufactured.

I said: "And do you then know me?"

"Aye."

I pondered. He was very sure of himself, then. . . .

He turned his head again, and listened, and when he swung back to face me he held the cloth even higher so that only those dark, narrow, widely set eyes glittered out upon me.

"Now go. Take yourself off. And give thanks to your gods that you still live."

Pondering, I walked to the rail. Of course, I could have bounced up the ladder onto the poop, taken him by the throat, choked a little politeness into him. I might have cowed the crew and done something along similar lines with the mercenaries. But my first concern was Delia, and as these thoughts sprang into my head I saw a light go on half an ulm away. That would be a farm awakening to the daily labors. There I could find transport.

It would take more time than I wished to spare to deal with these rasts and commandeer their flier. All the same, I was conscious of the indignity—no, that is not true. Dignity

31

and I share little in the harsh realities of life. Pride had nothing to do with it. The cardinal rule for me upon Kregen has been and remains always the concern for Delia. Only she concerned me.

At the rail I started to jump over, then turned. A Chulik stood near, lowering down on me. Many apims say, with a casual laugh, that they cannot tell one Chulik from another. They say this about Fristles, and about many other of the wonderful races of people, called diffs, upon the world of Kregen. I saw this big bulky fellow and I would know him again. I saw his sword. It was a rapier, for he was in Vallia, and the hilt and pommel were fashioned into the likeness of a mortil, very fancy. I nodded to him as I went over the side.

He did not speak.

None of the confounded Chulik mercenaries had spoken or cried out.

I had taken a bare half-dozen steps away from the flier before it lifted up, quickly, going low over the ground toward the east. It vanished past a copse of trees. Wherever that cramph in his concealing black cloak and the person from whom he had taken his orders were going, they were going there in the devil of a hurry.

I set off for the farm.

That mysterious lot had been flying west when I'd first seen them and managed to land on their deck. Then, during the fight, they'd changed course a hundred and eighty degrees. Now they had taken off, going low, heading east. I fancied that they had kept low so that once out of my sight they could turn again and head back onto their original course.

They were flying to Vondium. And they had not wished me to know that.

Then I banished them from my thoughts and walked up to the farm and thundered on the door.

Half a dozen stavrers started barking.

"Quiet you famblys," I said, making my voice as soothing as possible.

The stavrer with his fierce wolf-head, his eight legs, the rear six all articulated the same way, with his stumpy tail, is an enormously loyal watchdog of Kregen. He can put in a sudden charge that will leave a chavonth standing for sheer acceleration; but the loyal stavrer has no long-distance legs to him. In a dash to take the seat of the pants off importunate strangers at the door he is hard to fault; but if they get a head start they can usually get away scot-free. I just hoped

32

the stavrers at this farm were all securely chained up for the night.

Lights showed at the windows and the door was cautiously opened. There had been troubles in Vallia of late. I saw the gleam of weapons beyond the edge of the door so, quickly, I sang out: "Llahal and Llahal. My airboat has broken down and I would crave your help, Koters."

After that it was relatively easy. I was in the Vadvarate of Valhotra, of which Genal Arclay was Vad. The province lay immediately to the east of Vondium and, most sensibly, was always held by a family loyal to the emperor. It was rich farming land, filled with fat cattle and good, fruitful earth, bringing forth abundance. I knew Vad Genal as an easy-going likable fellow, with a weakness for riding sleeths in fast races on which he would bet far more than he should. But these people made me welcome, offering refreshment and the use of their best airboat—indeed, their only airboat. She was an ancient craft, much used, and very much a symbol of the farm's prosperity in the surrounding district. The farmer, Larghos Nilner, and his wife and family were clearly loyal to their Vad and through him to the emperor.

I reflected that not all of Kregen is vicious and hostile, and not all of Vallia made furtive and strenuous attempts to get rid of the emperor. He had his friends.

Making proper arrangements for the use of the flier, I bid them Remberee and took off, heading back to Vondium.

The colors of Valhotra are red, brown and green, with a diagonal slash of white. They were painted up on the airboat in the private style, to indicate that the airboat's owner was a Valhotran but not of the retainers of the Vad.

Before the ancient airboat reached Vondium the suns rose.

I took deep breaths of air, the sweet, limpid air of Kregen. Bursting over the horizon, filling the world with light and glory, the Suns of Scorpio drove away the shadows and drenched all the marvelous world of Kregen in light and color. Zim, the great red sun, and Genodras, the small green sun, poured down their floods of radiance. I basked in the warmth and brightness. Over in Havilfar they call Zim Far and Genodras Havil. The suns have many and many names over Kregen. But they remain the Suns of Scorpio, Antares, blazing, superb.

So, if Deb-sa-Chiu had spoken the truth, Delia would be settling down to a landing on the high platforms of the palace at this moment. I fancied she would quickly learn I had returned. But I did not relish the idea that, further learning I

33

had taken a voller, she would at once start the long journey to Ba-Domek and Aphrasöe. I drove the flier on mercilessly; but she was a slow old tub at best and we made poor progress. So I raved and cursed, as is my wont, and attempted to calm myself, as always, and, as nearly always, lamentably failing.

Below the trundling flier the ground passed in a swirl of greens and browns and blues, with the silver-glittering canals of Vallia cutting their lordly way across the landscape. Magnificent are the canals of Vallia. True, their water is a nasty poison to anyone not of the canalfolk. In Vondium there are many canals fed by the waters of the Great River, and these canals are safe for ordinary folk, not of the canals.

The canalfolk of Vallia are a people apart. As far as I knew up to that time they had kept themselves strictly separate from the intrigues and struggles for power within the Empire. Now that the emperor was assured of a thousand years of life, vouchsafed him because his daughter Delia possessed the courage and fire to take him to the Sacred Pool of Baptism, he was most firmly seated on his throne. He could outlast his enemies, and guide and control those who followed after. Oh, yes, there were still plots against him, and factions seeking to topple him. But he had only to last out the current crop of troubles, and then, by Vox, he was safe.

So I thought.

As for myself, after my own problems, I was concerned to discover who it was who had been controlling Ashti Melekhi.

Some shadowy figure of great power had been giving her orders. She had attempted to poison the emperor and been foiled. Then she had brought Chulik guards to slay him, and been foiled.

Now that she was dead the menacing shadow at her back would have to find fresh tools for his nefarious purposes.

I knew, as I winged back to Vondium the Splendid in the mingled steaming radiance of the Suns of Scorpio, that I was in for a few hectic bouts of action. And, so I was. As you shall hear.

Poison is not often a favored instrument of murder on Kregen and the abhorrence of just about everyone concerned at the imminent death by poison of the emperor gave a true indication of that kind of morality. But death by hired assassin—well, now. . . . In that department of murder the stikitches of Kregen have few peers. Which, I suppose, reflects badly upon the morality of those who employ them. My friends and I had been set upon by stikitches, and we had

34

tumbled them into a handy canal; I recalled the promise Ashti Melekhi had made and knew her promise would be kept. Her stikitches would be after me, still.

In that, thinking that her malignance persisted from the grave, I misjudged the niceties of protocol and honor of the stikitches of Kregen.

In the growing light the land spread bountifully. Truly, Vallia is a rich and rosy island. Away on my right hand the lofting twin pinnacles of rock spearing up from the land showed me Vondium was very close. That curious double formation of rock and crag is called Drak's Seat. From its slopes ice is brought down to the city.

The Great River—Mother of Waters, She of the Fecundity—glimmered ahead. And Vondium—ah! Vondium, the proud city. I have spoken but little of that splendid city, and to think of it now brings a pang. The slanting mingled rays of the suns smote full upon the serried array of domes and towers, of spires and roofs, caught gleams from the gilt, struck sparks from the ranked windows. The long granite walls ringed the city, and the buildings spilled out beyond their ancient circumference. Here and there the dots of early fliers spun up into the morning brightness. Across the long-reaching arms of the aqueducts the clear, clean water flowed down from the hills. Smoke from breakfast fires coiled into the limpid air. The boulevards already thronged with people and carriages, a steady traffic that would continue all day. Narrow boats and barges glided silently along the canals. Movement, color, life—all were spread below me as I slanted in over the seething metropolis of Vondium the Proud, heading for the palace of the emperor.

A number of tributaries of varying size and importance empty into the Great River at or near Vondium. Combined with the meanderings of the River at that point a couple of tributaries contrive to isolate a section of the city, with the adjacent canal forming an aloof enclave. This is the Old City, called Drak's City. A warren, festering in places, sumptuous in others, it attracts both disreputable elements and free spirits, artists, poets, thinkers, students, and provides them with a kind of security. I say a kind of security, for Vondium herself offers that kind of security a man of the cities can understand.

As I sped toward the palace I gave but scant thought to Drak's City, for I then knew little of Vondium. In Ruathytu, which I knew much better, the Sacred Quarter in its way served for the purposes of Drak's City in Vondium. But the two were not the same—very far from the same.

Old and ancient and steeped in the mysteries of its past is Drak's City. Here men first built their camp when they came to the Great River, gradually enlarging their buildings and walls, until what is now the Old City dominated the surrounding countryside. The light picked out the colors along the tall walls of the higher palace. Each fluttering from its own flagstaff every province flag of the empire flew. The long rows of flagstaffs and their gorgeously colored treshes passed below as I turned to slide in for a landing.

Drak's City sank from sight as I lowered in the air. The Old City completely surrounded by the modern metropolis carried on its own life, had its own mores, gave scant attention to what went on in Greater Vondium. The flier touched down.

The guards were duly obsequious. The Vallian Air Service patrols above had let me through because the Valhotran colors marked me as a friend. Unmarked boats would be challenged.

Because she understands me passing well, Delia had waited for me. The moment she learned I had returned to the palace and of the collapse of the latest plot against her father, she had said something—which I will not repeat—and had gone up to the landing platforms with a picnic basket and a good book. How she does these things amazes me still.

So, clad in my worn and travel-stained old buff, I stomped across the platform.

She looked up and marked her place in the book with a slim finger—I know that gesture well. Then she saw who it was. The book went up in the air. The picnic basket flew the other way spilling palines and delicious fruits and sandwiches and bottles of wine. She flew at me.

Time after time I have come home to my Delia. It is always the same and it is always different. Close, we held each other, close. My Delia—my Delia of Delphond, my Delia of the Blue Mountains!

Chapter Three

Barty Vessler, Strom of Calimbrev

I hitched up the huge brown beard on its silver wires over my ears, and smoothed down the golden plates of the helmet. I turned to let Delia see me.

She lay on an elbow, her white gown voluptuous in its curves and lines, and started to laugh so that the little gilt sofa shook.

"Dray! Dray! You look—"

"I look like a shaggy graint of a clansman. If that is the way the good folk of Vondium imagine me—then that is the way they can see me."

Much had happened since yesterday, when Delia had met me on the high landing platform. Now we prepared in our own private apartments for the great thanksgiving ceremony. Much of what had happened was talk. There were other things; but they remain between Delia and me. Now we put on fine fancy clothes, readying ourselves for the dismal prospect of a state function.

"But you can't go out looking like that."

"Why not?"

"Well—for one thing, you're hardly recognizable and absolutely not respectable."

I laughed at her. "True. And two more admirable qualities I have yet to find. I do not wish to be recognized, and if ever I was respectable, I fancy I'd—"

"I know you, Dray Prescot. If you were respectable you'd die of boredom."

"True."

She sat up. Those soft red lips pouted at me.

"Very well. Wear the beard. But at least have Tilly trim—oh!"

"Yes. Our friends are scattered all over Kregen. Tilly will be back in Hyrklana."

"We must help them—I'm sure Tilly would wish to come home. Valka is her home now."

"We will. As soon as the emperor has given thanks to the

Invisible Twins through Opaz the All-Glorious, we can start."

A shadow passed across that face, that face that is the most beautiful in two worlds.

"What is it, my heart?"

"Dayra—"

Now I frowned.

"We have lost our daughter Velia—" The pang this caused both of us had to be endured; neither of us could forget Velia. I went doggedly on. "Our three sons are making their ways in the world. But our daughters, Lela and Dayra—do you know, since I returned from—" Here I checked, and stammered.

"Yes?"

I had been about to say "from Earth." But that would mean nothing to Delia, and I had not yet nerved myself to explain to her that I was born on a world that had only one sun, only one moon, and had only apims as people. So I fished around and then said: "Since I had to leave you on the island of Lower Kairfowen—"

"In the village of Panashti—"

"Yes. I've spent most of the time in the Eye of the World. We have managed to save your father. But in all this time I have not seen my two daughters."

Delia made a small, not so much helpless as resigned, gesture. "It is a matter for the Sisters of the Rose. I have told you much. Lela is very much the grand lady now. She goes her own way. She stubbornly refuses all offers of marriage."

I nodded. "If she gets married and I'm not there, I'll—"

"You no doubt would, you great grizzly graint. But Lela is like Drak. They are twins. Drak can run affairs while you are—away—"

"I know. They call him the Younger Strom and me the Old Strom, in Valka."

"He does not want Valka. You know what he has said. He is a fine man now, my heart. As for Zeg, you did well when you made him the King of Zandikar, and Queen Miam will be good for him."

"I didn't make him. Miam did that."

"That may be. And our third son, Jaidur—"

"Jaidur." Jaidur, sometimes called Vax, Vax Neemusjid, was Dayra's twin. "He hasn't made up his mind about me, yet. But Dayra—"

"Jaidur and Dayra. They were born when you were away. It was a hard time for me."

I could not look at her. The Star Lords who had callously

38

hurled me back to rot on Earth for twenty-one years had a great deal to answer for. I ploughed on.

"Jaidur still doesn't believe I can possibly be his real father—yet, I think, he does know and will not acknowledge it. If I were a true Vallian father I'd take a whip to him if he continued on that tack."

"But as you are a savage and barbarian clansman, you will not."

"So Dayra hates my guts. Well, that is fair. I deserve that. But I shall find a way of making her see—I have to—as I owe it to you and the children."

"She ran away from the Sisters of the Rose. I saw the—I saw the necessary people there and smoothed things over. But she joined up with a rascally gang. Seg and Inch found out about them, or as much as they could. Seg's daughter, Silda, was also mixed up with them at one time. But Seg was there and he sorted that out."

I had turned to look at her and as she spoke a flush mantled up onto her cheeks, and she looked away, and went on speaking very quickly, very quickly indeed.

"And as Inch couldn't wed his lady Sasha from Ng'groga for some reason connected with their taboos he was making further investigations but it was all very difficult and kept most secret and I can say that Dayra fancied herself in love with this man who calls himself by any name that takes his fancy and as the whim strikes him and no one knows who he is although I expect Dayra does." She finished a little bitterly, on a sigh.

I felt the fury mounting.

Calmly, I said: "And this was the problem you had to go away to attend to? You and Lela?"

"Oh, no." She looked up. "That was settled. Well, more or less. Dayra has been led astray. That is what I meant when I spoke of her when you talked of going to Hyrklana to fetch Tilly and Oby and Naghan the Gnat."

"Aye, and we'll bring the others. But I see." I took off the ridiculous golden helmet and scratched the false beard. "We must find Dayra first—and this fellow, what's-his-name—and then we can see about our friends."

"I think—Dray—I think— yes."

"Well then, Delia my lovely, we must dress ourselves up and attend the emperor and see your father right. Have you any idea where we should start looking for Dayra?"

"They used to go around smashing up the taverns."

"Right."

39

"And Barty Vessler is here in Vondium and desperately unhappy, wanting to help."

"Who," I said, "in Zair's name is Barty Vessler?"

Delia shook her head so that those gorgeous chestnut tints in her rich brown hair caught the light, dancing, enchanting.

"You knew the old strom, Naghan Vessler? Strom of Calimbrev?"

"Oh. Oh, yes. So this Barty Vessler is the Strom of Calimbrev. How does he come to be so desperately unhappy?"

But I could guess. Calimbrev is an island of about the same size as Valka situated off the southeast coast of Vallia, just to the southwest of Veliadrin. If this Vessler was unhappy and wanted to help it could only mean he and Dayra had been friends. Probably the loon wanted to marry her. I cocked an eyebrow at Delia, and she smiled, and confirmed the suspicion.

"He is a charming young man. Very well thought of. You mind you are nice to him."

"And he has nothing to do with Dayra's running off? Her running with this wild bunch? He's just a good friend?"

"Yes. I am sure. He had a struggle to hold onto the stromnate when his father died. But he did."

"Well, good for him."

All my hackles had risen at the thought of a man sniffing around my daughter. I thought of Gafard, Sea Zhantil, the King's Striker, who had wed Velia, and I sighed. . . .

"If he's half the man Gafard was then he'll do, I suppose, providing you approve."

"For the sweet sake of Opaz, my heart! It is not as definite as that yet. Not by a long way."

So, bristling more than a trifle, I set about putting on all the ridiculous fancy clothes a state occasion warranted. As was often my custom I deliberately loaded myself down with bright gew-gaws, lengths of cloth-of-gold, brilliant silks, tasselled scarves, bracelets, necklaces, and under all a shirt of that marvelously supple mesh-steel they manufacture down in the Dawn Lands of Havilfar.

The mazilla was a thing of wondrous beauty or downright irritation, depending on your point of view. Truth to tell, as it jutted up at the back of my head, gaudy with feathers and sensil and gold, it was both. Only the noblest may wear an aristo-sized mazilla. So, adding this to my calculated insult in the whole stupid finery I wore, my mazilla towered, flaunting, arrogant, insolent.

I stroked the luxurious brown beard and felt that, at the

40

very least, should upset more than a few of the best-born of Vallia.

Which seemed to me a delicious and highly desirable achievement.

Delia—well, Delia was simply superb.

Dressed in white, with discreet jewels, with feathers and sensils, she floated like a—well, I will say it and be damned to all and sundry—she floated like a goddess as we sallied out to take our place in the procession.

A long Vallian dagger with the hilt fashioned from rosy jewels swung from golden lockets at her side.

As for me, I belted on a veritable armory, well-knowing the frowns such wanton display would provoke. How Delia put up with my contempt for the nobles of Vallia escaped me.

Besides a rapier and dagger I belted on a clanxer, a djangir and a small double-bitted axe. Over my back and hidden by the crimson trimmed cloak and the feathers of the mazilla, went my Krozair longsword. I drew the line at a Lohvian longbow. After all, there are limits, and to push beyond them would have been counter-productive.

The procession was gorgeous and immense. Everyone was there. The nobles lined out in order of precedence and a splendid array they made. The whole sumptuous proceeding went off well. Due thanks were offered up at various temples for the safety of the emperor. He, the old devil, strode through it all with a face like a granite block, hard and yet haughty, lapping up the plaudits of the crowds, conscious of the looks and feelings of those who fawned on him, sorting them out in his shrewd old head, those for, those against, those who might be bought by gold.

The stinks of incense blew everywhere. Perfumes covered the smells that might have proved intrusive. The noise blossomed as the crowds huzzahed and screeched. It was all a terrible ordeal, yet an ordeal that had to be gone through so that Vondium might witness that the emperor was safe and in full health.

Those of my few friends among the nobility—like the Lord Farris—knew that on these occasions I was like a graint with a thorn in his foot, and so they merely acknowledged my presence and smiled and went on with the business. As for my enemies, they ignored me, which suited me.

Kov Layco Jhansi, the emperor's chief minister, was there and looking mighty pleased with himself. High in favor, now, Layco Jhansi, after his valiant defense of the sacred person of the emperor. I nodded to him, and then turned away, and the proceedings ground on.

When they were over and I headed off at once for the palace to strip off the ridiculous outfit, Delia held me back.

A young man, slender, supple, his brown Vallian hair stylishly though decently cut, wearing ornate robes—as we all did—approached. His face looked freshly scrubbed, bright, cheerful, yet with an anxious dint between the eyebrows he manfully tried to conceal.

He wore the colors of gray, red and green, with a black bar, and his emblem was a leaping swordfish. By these I knew he was of Calimbrev. So this must be Barty Vessler, the Strom of Calimbrev.

He made a deep obeisance. Delia gripped my arm. She knows how I dislike this crawling and bowing; but we were still in public and were watched.

"Majestrix, Majister," said Strom Barty.

"Strom, how nice to see you," said Delia.

We stood on a marble platform with the crowds yelling below and the pillars and statues of the Temple of Lio am Donarb at our backs. Lio am Donarb, although a minor religious figure attracting a relatively small following, was considered worthy of a visit of thanks. To one side a group of nobles prepared, like us, to take to their palanquins or zorca chariots to return to their villas set upon the Hills. Among all their blazing heraldry of color the black and white favors showed starkly, proud, defiant, arrogant.

I nodded at the group who watched us avidly.

"You do yourself no good with the Racters by talking to me, young Barty. But you are welcome."

He looked up, quickly, taken aback. He must have heard what a crude clansman I was; he had not expected this. And I piled on the agony, despite Delia's fierce grip.

"The black and whites would like to tear down the emperor and his family. And whatever I may feel about the emperor, he is my father-in-law. You would run a similar risk?"

The flush along his cheeks betrayed him; but he spoke up civilly enough—aye, and stoutly.

"I am prepared for much worse than that, prince. My concern is only for the princess Dayra."

I did not say: "Well spoken, lad," as I might have done in the old days.

He would have to perform deeds, and not just prate about them, if he aspired to the hand of my daughter.

When Delia invited him back to the palace I had no objec-

42

tion. On the journey—and we took a zorca chariot with Sarfi the Whip as coachman—Barty indulged in polite conversation, inquiring after all the members of the family. Drak must be in Valka still, for Delia had seen him there when she'd raced there to find me. Her distress, which Deb-sa-Chiu had so graphically described, had been all for me. She had by now become a little used to my disappearances and was prepared to search across to Segesthes, aware that in the past she had found me against what must have seemed to her all odds. Barty inquired after Jaidur, and Delia told him that that young rip had decided to return to a place he knew well and where he would visit his brother Zeg. So Jaidur had gone back to the inner sea and a few casual questions elicited the unsurprising fact that Barty had heard of the place but that was about all.

Our youngest daughter, Velia, was well and thriving, looked after by Aunt Katri, who was also caring for little Didi, the daughter of Velia and Gafard. Lela, well, she was about her own life in Vallia. And Dayra. . . ?

"I have had some news, princess," said Barty, hesitantly, as the zorca chariot rounded the corner past the Kyro of Spendthrifts.

Delia leaned forward. I frowned. Barty sat opposite us and he shifted about, nerving himself. At last he got it out.

"She was seen traveling through Thengelsax. A party left the Great River and hired zorcas. She was recognized by a groom who once served in the palace and had returned home to a posting station in the town."

I held down the instant leap of anxiety—an anxiety akin to fear. The whole northeast of Vallia resented being a part of the empire, still, although their animosity was being fanned by agitators. They raided down, real border raids, and one of the towns around which their activities had centered was Thengelsax. Its lord had complained bitterly. Was my Dayra mixed up with these border reivers?

That did not seem likely; but it was a possibility and I could not discount it, much though I would have liked to.

"Nothing else, Barty?"

"Nothing, prince. The troubles of the northeast are well known. The lords up there do not like us down here."

"It is more likely," said Delia, with calm firmness, as when she demanded one take a foul medicine, "far more likely that Dayra has gone up there with her—friends—to stir up trouble. It pains me to say that; but it is sooth."

43

Barty threw her a reproachful look; but he knew enough of Dayra to understand the truth of the remark.

"Listen, Barty." I paused and looked at him, whereat he grew red in the face and his eyes widened. It is odd how a simple calculating look from me will change a person's appearance. Most odd. "I've had dealings with the Trylon of Thengelsax. He was there today, as squat and bluff and foul as ever. Ered Imlien—he nurses a grudge against me because I broke his riding crop. He had told me what you are telling me now—only he was less tactful."

Delia was looking at me. Barty swallowed.

"If Dayra is mixed up with this Liberty for the Northeast rot, then, all right, so be it. We will *hoick* her out of it and if I have to tan her bottom for her, that I will do." I took a breath and saw the streets passing, the wink of sunlight from a canal, the bunting and flowers and brilliant shawls. "Do you know I have never even seen my daughter Dayra?"

"You are being rather—hard—on her, prince." Barty spoke slowly, softly; but he did not stammer and he came right out with it. I warmed to him.

"Of course I am. That is natural. It does not mean—"

I stopped speaking and threw my arms around Delia, hurled her to the floor between the seats.

"Get down, Barty!"

The long Lohvian arrow quivered in the lenken wood pillar where it had split the crimson curtains and severed a golden tasselled cord. The feathers were all shivering with the violence of the cast. Those feathers were dyed a deep and somber purple.

"Keep down! Sarfi the Whip!" I bellowed out at full lung-stretch. "Give the zorcas their heads! *Gallop!*"

The chariot lurched and bounced on the leather straps of the springing. The sharp, hard clitter-clatter of the zorcas' polished hooves on the flags of the street beat into a staccato rhythm. With Delia safely on the floor and Barty off the opposite seat, I could peer up. People were leaping left and right as we careered along. Sarfi was wailing away with his whip, sharp cracking flecks of sound through the uproar. We hurtled past a shandishalah booth and the stink whipped past to be swallowed by the fishy smells from the next stall.

"Where the hell are you taking us, Sarfi?"

He didn't answer; but plied his whip. I looked back. A train of destruction lay wasted in our wake for Sarfi had belted the chariot left-handed off the main street and taken us hell for leather down a narrow souk. Overturned stalls, spilled am-

44

phorae, crates and boxes splintered and strewing their silver-glinting fish across the flags, torn awnings and smashed awning-posts, and people—people crawling away, people staggering about like Sanurkazzian drunks, people dancing with rage and shaking their fists after us.

The smells, the sounds, the colors were wonderfully zestful to a man who has just had an arrow past his ear.

Whoever had loosed at us had had no chance of a second shot—and then I checked my foolish thoughts. This was a Lohvian arrow. Before I'd yelled, before Sarfi had ever laid a single strand of his whip to the zorcas—a practice I abhor and will not tolerate—a Bowman of Loh could have loosed three shafts—Seg Segutorio could have loosed four and possibly five.

So the one arrow had been enough.

Delia said: "I will resume my seat now, and then we can look at the message."

Barty and I helped her up—a quite unnecessary act for she is as lithe as an earthy puma or a Kregan chavonth—and we pulled out the arrow and unrolled the scrap of paper wrapped around the shaft.

Sarfi slowed down. The uproar subsided and we turned right-handed into the Boulevard of Yellow Risslacas and so sat staring at the message written on the paper. The writing was in that beautiful flowing Kregish script. A cultured hand had penned those lines. But the paper was ordinary Vallian paper, of good quality, yes—but it was not that superb and mysterious paper made by the Savanti nal Aphrasöe.

The message was addressed: "Dray Prescot, Prince Majister of Vallia, Hyr Kov of Veliadrin, Kov of Zamra, Strom of Valka."

I give all this gaudy nonsense of titles because they at once afforded two clues to the identities of those who had had a bowman deliver the message.

One: the island of Veliadrin was called that and not Can-Thirda, which had been its name until Delia and I changed it in memory of our beloved daughter.

Two: only Vallian titles were listed. Not one of the razmatazz of titles in the rest of Kregen I had acquired appeared.

The salutation read: "Llahal-pattu. Prince Majister."

Llahal with the double L is the usual greeting for a stranger—the usual friendly greeting, that is—and when written the pattu is appended because Kregish grammatical and polite conventional usage demand it.

The message went on: "You, as the kitchew in a properly

45

drawn-up and witnessed contract, the bokkertu being ably written and attested, are appraised of an irregularity. It is needful that you, Prince Majister, have an audience of Nath Trerhagen, the Aleygyn, Hyr Stikitche, Pallan of the Stikitche Khand of Vondium."

"By Vox!" exploded Barty. "The nerve of the rast. I have heard of him. Nath the Knife. Quoting his spurious and stupid titles at us!"

"Stupid they may be, as most titles are," I said mildly. "But spurious? I doubt it. Is he not the most renowned assassin in Vallia?"

A Pallan is a minister or secretary of state, and this assassin—a high and mighty assassin—was the chief man of his khand, or guild, brotherhood or caste. I guessed he had some fugitive lawyer drafting out this rhetoric for him.

I was to meet him at a tavern called The Ball and Chain (as I have said, Kregans have a warped sense of humor which can greatly infuriate those not attuned to its niceties) and this unsavory hostelry was situated a stone's throw from the Gate of Skulls.

"The Gate of Skulls," said Delia. "Well, you aren't going there. That is inside Drak's City."

"I've never been there. It might prove instructive."

"But, majister!" said Barty. "You can't just go walking in on a bunch of rascally assassins just because they send an invitation! It—" He spluttered a little, his cheeks red. "It just isn't done!"

Delia was looking at me with that look upon her face that gets right inside my craggy old skin, coiling in my thick vosk-skull of a head, itching me all along my limbs, making the blood pump around fast and faster. But she knew.

"I think, Barty . . . No—I know—that there is nothing you can say. The prince is going and that is all there is to it."

That was not all, and well she knew it. If Delia said to me you are not going, I would not have gone. But, all fooling aside, we both knew that there were weighty reasons for acceptance of the summons from the assassins. Had they wished to slay me the arrow would have driven straight.

"Well, prince," said young Barty, and his fist gripped around the hilt of his rapier. "In that case, I shall go with you!"

So ho, I said to myself—maybe Dayra has found herself a man here. Well, the proof of that would not be long delayed.

Chapter Four

Knavery in Drak's City

There are many Naths on Kregen, partly because of the affection felt for the myth hero Nath, who bears to Kregen much the same kind of physical prowess as the terrestrial Hercules does to us here on Earth, and among that number are good men and rogues, heroes and cowards, ordinary folk and men with the charisma about them that transcends goodness and evil. Also, among the many Naths there are many called Nath the Knife.

This particular Nath the Knife bore a reputation at once unsavory and yet respected, a blemished fruit, feared, of course, and yet still remaining very much the man of mystery.

As, indeed, he must. No assassins are going to put on fancy uniforms with favors proclaiming their trade and go off about their business. The community into which one such came with the avowed intent of committing stealthy murder would get together to deal with him. If anyone of the community refused, then it would surely be reasonable to suppose he had hired the damned stikitche in the first place. So, once that was established, the community could dispose of them both. I say reasonable. Of course, it might be the case that the community would not be sensible, or be frightened, or for some reason or another not collaborate. But that would scarcely happen on Kregen, where folk are hardier than most despite the weaker ones and the revolting aspects of slavery and all that that entails, no matter what pundits speculate may occur on other less-favored planets.

In the event I managed to persuade Barty to remain at the Gate of Skulls. I put it to him that he was on watch. He fingered his rapier and shuffled restlessly. We were both dressed roughly, with old brown blanket-coats, our weapons hidden. Around us swirled the never-ending stream of humanity going and coming, busy, screeching, quarreling, thieving, living.

"But I said—"

"And I thank you for it, Barty. But I truly think I will fare better on my own."

As you can see, I was very tender with this young man.

"Well. . ."

"So that is settled. You stay here and keep watch." With that I marched off through the bedlam at the gate without risking another word. For—what was he watching for?

If I did not reappear within a few burs what could he do? The soldiers and mercenaries would eventually venture into the Old City; but they would do so by mounting a proper battle-group. It was not that they were over-hated by the denizens of Drak's City or that they, in their turn, ever created wanton destruction. It was just that the law of Vondium did not run within the Old City and people preferred to let that lie, and not to disturb the sleeping leem.

The fly in this ointment was that Barty might take it into his head to go in after me if I did not return after a seemly interval.

The bedlam assumed a more bedlamish proportion within the Old City. People still jostled and pushed and shoved, yelling their wares, trying to thieve from the stalls and booths, trying to buy or sell at a profit. The stinks increased. People lived here jammed together. The ancient buildings tottered. Lathe and plaster and mouldering brick were far more in evidence than honest stone. The noise, the shoving, the stinks, all blended, as they so often do, into a picture that—seen and heard and smelled at a distance—presented a scene of great romantic attraction. This, one would think, was how a glittering barbaric city would carry on, heedless, drinking, wenching, laughing, uncaring, filled with cutpurses and daring cat-burglars and fences and shrill-voiced women and avaricious thief-takers on the prowl and grimy naked-limbed urchins learning all the tricks to take over when their elders went a-sailing down to the Ice Floes of Sicce.

Pushing through the throngs along the Kyro of Lost Souls, which extends within the Gate of Skulls, I kept myself out of mischief and out of trouble and headed for the tavern called The Ball and Chain.

If you wish to call the place a Thieves' Kitchen, I shall not prevent that description.

A straggle of ponshos wandered about, bunching, baaing, getting in everyone's way. Their fleeces were white. It is a fact that Vallians are a cleanly people, and even here in this run-down, brawling, odoriferous stewpot of a wen, and despite the spilled cabbages and rotting fruits and discarded skins, the place and people were surprisingly clean. There are towns on Kregen where even the aristocracy are clean, as there are towns where everyone is filthy. But Vallians take a pride in themselves and their country.

The Ball and Chain looked as though if the loafers moved away from the pillars of the front porch the whole lot would tumble down onto the heads of the throngs in the street.

I stopped under the awning of a man selling second-hand sandals and fingered a pair of curly-toed foofray slippers. They must have been stolen from some luxury-loving lord. The proprietor eyed me and prepared to sidle up to extol his wares. So, looking at the tavern, I became aware of two things.

A thin and incredibly dextrous hand was fingering delicately along my belt seeking the strings of the leather purse. And Barty heaved up, red faced, panting, shoving through, opening his mouth to yell over the hubbub.

First things first.

I took the thin and sinewy hand in my fist and pulled.

An urchin flew out before me, swinging around the elbow socket, starting to yell, rags and tatters of clothes fluttering. It was a young girl, scrawny, with a mass of brown hair, with grimy streaks down her cheeks. I eyed her with some severity.

"Diproo the Nimble-Fingered abandoned you, it seems, shishi."

"Let me go! Let me go!"

"Oh, aye. I'll let you go. And I will not even box your ears."

"Get away! Get away you hulu!" screeched the owner of the sandal stall.

I felt the second hand stealing around the leather purse strings, and I stepped back, dragging the girl, and took the lad—who was probably her younger brother—with my other hand.

I surveyed the pair of them, and shook my head.

Products of a city, living by thieving of any description, free and not slave, well—what were their futures to be? What the futures of a thousand or more like them in the Old City? A thousand—there must be thousand upon thousand of half-naked urchins like this running wild in Drak's City.

"Let us go," panted the girl, her brown hair falling across her thin face. She'd be about twelve or thirteen. "We'll be thrashed."

The lad tried to kick my shins.

Then Barty arrived, almost losing his brown blanket which

he was totally unaccustomed to wearing. He wanted to hand over the cutpurses to the authorities.

"The only authorities in Drak's City are the people who employ the fellow who employs these two," I told him.

He was a Vallian and so would know that; but it was not a fact easily digestible. The Laws of Hamal are notorious. The law runs differently, more quietly, in Vallia. Here in the Old City of Vondium the law ran as a mere trickle, the greater torrent passing outside the walls.

I managed to get the girl's raggedy collar jammed up under her ear, and with the lad picked up and stuffed under my other arm I had a hand free. I pulled out a silver sinver. Awkwardly, for the little devil was kicking and squawking—and no one was taking the blind bit of notice of all this—I gave the sinver to the girl. I released the collar of her tunic and let her go. I looked steadily into her face. She did not run away. Then I dumped the lad on his feet, and gave him another sinver. The two coins, here, were like spitting twice into the middle of a vast and burning desert—but it seemed to me there was little else in truth to be done. I had once fought a duel over seven copper obs.

"Now be off with you, you scamps, and next time Diproo may smile upon you."

The girl looked back at me. Her brown Vallian hair, her brown Vallian eyes—her gauntness could not conceal the beauty she would one day become.

"I give you thanks, dom. And would you be telling your name to any who inquire?"

"I am Jak Jakhan. It is not important."

Barty, wheezing alongside me, tried not to think. He eased closer and whispered. "Should we not ask them about The Ball and Chain—about Nath the Knife? They could give us useful information."

As I say, Barty was trying to think.

"I think not." I glared with great sorrow on the girl and her brother, doomed urchins of Drak's City. The silver had vanished from sight somewhere inside their raggedy clothes. "Be off. Get a decent meal. And may Opaz shine upon you."

The girl said: "My name is Ashti and my brother is Naghan and—and we give thanks. May Corg bring you fair winds."

They ran off and in a twinkling were lost among the crowds past the ponsho flock.

Barty was a Strom, which is, I suppose, as near an earthly

50

count as anything, and a noble and he felt like a stranded whale in these rumbustious surroundings. He gawked about at the spectacle and kept his right hand down inside his blanket coat. That particular gesture was so common as to be unremarked.

"Come on," I said. "You can't just stand around here. Half the urchins will be queuing up for their silver sinvers and the other half of the varmints will be out to pinch the lot."

We kept to the wall and walked along toward the tavern. Once we left the Kyro of Lost Souls the press became less thick. What to do about Barty puzzled me.

He said: "I wanted to ask what I was supposed to keep watch for, prince—"

"Jak Jakhan."

"What?"

I did not laugh. "You have not done this sort of thing before? Not even when you succeeded to your father's stromnate?"

"No, pri— Oh. No, Jak."

"It is sometimes necessary. It amuses me. At the least, it is vastly different from those popinjays at court."

"I do not believe there is any need to remind me of that."

A sway-backed cart stood outside the tavern. Cages of ducks were being unloaded. The racket squawked away and there was no need to inquire what the speciality of the house was going to be this day.

"Look," I said. "Do go into that tavern across the way and buy yourself some good ale and sit in a window seat. And, for the sweet sake of Opaz, don't get into trouble. Keep yourself to yourself. And if you are invited to dice—remember you will lose everything you stake."

"Everything?"

"They can make dice sit up and beg here, that's certain."

"You said you had never been into Drak's City before."

"No more I have. But these places have a character. There are many in the countries of Paz."

The tavern across the way was called The Yellow Rose. Barty took a hitch to his length of rope that held in his blanket coat and started across. He was almost run down by a Quoffa cart which lumbered along, lurching from side to side, scattering chickens every which way. A thin and pimply youth had a go at his purse as he reached the tavern porch but he must have felt the feather-touch, for he swung about, shouting, and pimple-face ran off. I let out a breath. I should never have brought him. But—he was here. I put that old im-

51

becilic look on my face, hunched over, let my body sag, and so went into The Ball and Chain.

There is a keen and, I suppose, a vindictive delight in me whenever I adopt that particular disguise. I can make myself look a right stupid cretin. There are those who say the task is not too difficult. With the old brown blanket coat clutched about me, the frayed rope threatening to burst at any moment, I shuffled across the sawdusted floor.

The room was low-ceiled, not over-filled with patrons as yet. Tables and benches stood about. A balcony ran around two sides, the doors opening off at regular intervals to the back premises. A few slave girls moved about replenishing the ale tankards. It was too early for wine. I sat near the door, with my back to the wall, and contrived to hitch myself about so the longsword at my side did not make itself too obtrusive.

Outside in the street rain started to drift down, a fine drizzle that quickly spread a shining patina across everything.

A girl brought across a jug of ale and filled a tankard for me. I gave her a copper ob. I stretched my feet out and prepared to relax and then jerked my boots back quickly. They were first-quality leather boots and someone would have them off me sharply, with or without my consent, if I advertised them so blatantly. I was a stranger. Therefore I was ripe game. I fretted about Barty. I should have run him back to the Gate of Skulls first.

This Nath the Knife, the chief assassin, had arranged to meet me here, so close to the walls of the Old City, clearly as a gesture of trust. His bolt-holes would all be deeper in Drak's City. He ventured within a stone's throw of the walls and this gate so as to show me he meant to talk. That, I understood. If they were going to try to assassinate me, they would not have requested this meeting.

My plan, a usual one in the circumstances, misfired.

Before I could get into conversation and so ease my way in and then seek a back entrance to the upper floor, the serving wench pattered across. Already, this early in the day, she looked tired.

"Koter Laygon the Strigicaw is waiting for you upstairs, master." She looked nervous. "The third door."

My imbecilic expression altered. I had put on a medium-sized beard. Now I stroked it and looked at her owlishly.

"Koter Laygon is waiting, master."

"Then he can wait until I have finished the tankard."

"He is—he will have your skin off, master—"

52

"You are sure it is me he is waiting for?"

"Oh, yes. He was sure."

"Who is he? What is he like? Tell me about him?"

I started to pull out a silver sinver. Her face went white. She drew back, trembling, terrified.

"No, no, master! No money! They are watching—they know what you are asking—"

She backed off, her hands wide, and then she ran away, her naked feet making soft shushing sounds on the sawdust. I glanced up under my eyebrows at the balcony. Up there any one of a hundred knot holes could hold a spying eyeball.

I shifted on the settle against the wall. A tiny sound, no more than the furtive sounds a woflo makes scratching in the wainscoting made me look down.

A small slot had opened in the wall. A pair of scissors on extending tongs probed from the slot. They moved gently sideways toward me. Had I not moved, the fellow operating the tongs would have snipped away to get at my purse. As I had now vanished from his gaze the tongs drew back, the scissors vanished and the slot closed. I waited, intrigued.

Presently another slot opened close to me. The scissors probed out again, silently, ready to snip most patiently.

I picked up the half-full ale tankard.

No doubt the cramph had a whole array of tools he could fix to the tongs. A curved knife would slice away leather clothing. With all the noise of the taproom that usually created such a massive sound barrier, he could probably even use a drill to get through armor, and not be heard.

With a smooth motion I swivelled and slung the ale clean through the slot.

A splash, a yell of surprise, a series of choked squishing gulpings gave me a more general feeling of well-being. Petty—of course. But it was all a part of the rich tapestry of life—or, as this was Kregen, of death.

I bent to the slot and said in that fierce old biting way: "Thank Opaz it was only ale and not a length of steel."

With that I stood up, hitched the blanket coat around me, and stalked off to the blackwood stairway.

Over my left shoulder I had arranged snugly a quiver of six terchicks. The terchick, the little throwing knife of the clansmen, is often called the Deldar, and a clansman can hurl them right or left-handed from the back of a galloping zorca and hit the chunkrah's eye. Of course, the women of the Great Plains of Segesthes use the terchick with unsurpassed skill.

The drinkers in the area below watched with some curiosity as I climbed up. This Ball and Chain might be situated close to the walls of the Old City and the Gate of Skulls; I fancied the Aleygyn of the Stikitches, Nath Trerhagen, had packed the place with his men. Deep rivalries no doubt split the people of Drak's City, as they do in most places, unfortunately, and Nath the Knife would have chosen the meeting place carefully. I went up and I was ready to leap aside, to draw and to go into action, or to fashion a smile and a Llahal and listen.

The third door opened onto a narrow corridor that led via a rainswept open walkway to the next-door building.

I had not envisioned this.

Barty could watch The Ball and Chain to no avail.

I pressed on. I remained firmly convinced that the stikitches did not mean to kill me. All this rigmarole would not then have been necessary—I had dealt with assassins before.

Two men in tatty finery met me at the far door and I was able to duck in out of the rain. They wore three purple feathers, all curved the same way, ostentatiously pinned to the breasts of their tunics. They carried their rapiers loose in the scabbards. Their faces, dark and lowering, with strips of dark chin beard, were entirely unprepossessing; but they greeted me cheerfully enough, evidently assigned merely as guides.

"Laygon the Strigicaw?" I said.

"He is waiting, dom. This way."

We went into the building and along dusty and unused passages to the far side. We descended a flight of stairs. The slope of the land here meant we were still one story above the street; but all the windows were covered with torn sacking.

Mineral oil lamps illuminated the dusty, half-wrecked room into which I was ushered. Houses were often left to fall down in the Old City, or knocked down. Rebuilding was on an entirely casual basis.

The air smelled musty. Dust hung in the beams of the lamps.

A table had been pulled across a corner and a tall-backed chair positioned before it. At the table sat three men and one woman. All wore steel masks. Their clothes were unremarkable, save for the badge of the three purple feathers.

My two guides indicated the chair and I sat down.

For a moment a silence ensued.

Then the woman said: "Llahal, Dray Prescot."

I said: "I do not like stikitches. You have asked me here. I

54

am to meet Nath the Knife. Is he here, hiding behind a mask?"

The man on the extreme left said in a voice like breaking iron: "I am here. But you will talk with Laygon the Strigicaw."

"Which one is he?"

The man on the right said: "Here." His voice sounded mellow, full of the rotundity of roast beef and old crusty port.

"Well, Laygon, speak up."

"You are the Prince Majister of Vallia. The writ of Vondium and Vallia does not run in Drak's City."

"I have never cared much for laws that cannot be enforced. Spit out what you want. I am due at the Temple of Opaz the Nantifer two burs after midday."

"We do not much go in for temples, here in the Old City," said the woman. Her voice gasped just a little, as though she had difficulty in breathing. Maybe it was just the stale air. "And you had best keep a seemly tongue in your mouth—"

"Tell me what you want, now, and stop this shilly-shallying."

Nath the Knife nodded his head, and the steel mask caught the lamplight. All the masks were perfectly plain, and covered the whole face. I looked at the other parts of the bodies of these four, studying their hands, the way they held themselves, the angles of their heads.

"Tell him, Koter Laygon."

"This position is, Dray Prescot, the bokkertu has been signed and sealed upon you. You are accredited a dead man and due for the Ice Floes of Sicce."

"I think twelve of you tried, and there were twelve holes in the canal. I, too, can write a fine bokkertu." The word bokkertu, as you know, can mean any number of legal arrangements.

Laygon plunged on, and if he grew warm, I, for one, felt pleasure.

"I have taken out the assignment upon you. You are my kitchew. But—" He paused.

The chill menace of the situation was inescapable.

These men were assassins, dangerous, feral as leems. They would unhesitatingly kill—but they liked to get paid for their work.

Now Layton the Strigicaw said heavily: "Half the money was paid to me. So far I have not completed the assignment." He paused again, as though expecting me to comment. Again

I remained silent. "The irregularity is that the person hiring us is dead. We will not be paid the balance of our fee."

I shifted back in my chair and leaned to the side a little, so I could get the exact position of the two guides fixed.

"That is nothing to me. Stikitches can be killed like anyone else."

He went on, and again I detected the note of suppressed anger. "The Aleygyn is not pleased with the situation. The Stikitches of Vondium possess the highest possible reputation. Our honor is in question."

"I will not ask you with whom this precious reputation is held in such great esteem." I waved a casual hand. "Probably the rasts of the dunghills."

They did not react. I give them credit for that, at least.

"You are a dead man, Prince Majister—"

I interrupted. "Ashti Melekhi is dead. Would you work for nothing?"

Nath the Knife, clearly a most important man here, letting Laygon do the talking because it was Laygon who had taken the contract but prepared to step in with all his authority, said harshly, bending the mask toward me: "We do not mention names."

"You may not. But the fact remains. You are working for nothing."

"Precisely. The offer is this: Pay us the balance of the fee and the contract is then closed. If you do not pay, we shall fulfill it ourselves."

The instant intemperate indignation that flooded me had to be squashed. I took a breath. I said: "You have not mentioned the amount."

"Ten thousand gold talens."

I didn't know whether to be impressed by the value put on my life or insulted.

"My life is worth more than ten thousand."

"We abide by the legal contract. Pay us five thousand in gold and the contract is fulfilled and you live. Otherwise—"

I shifted on the chair again. It seemed to have a spongy feel to the legs, as though it was not firmly anchored to the floor. Probably it was a trick chair, with a trapdoor below. I'd have to be quick.

"I am not in the habit of paying gold to cramphs to save my life."

"You can always start."

This Nath the Knife was an intriguing fellow. He spoke

evenly enough. He took no offense from my crude remarks. He wanted his money, or he would kill me.

"When do I pay?"

"At once."

"I am due at the Temple of Opaz the Nantifer, as I told you—"

"Then immediately your kow-towing is done."

With genuine curiosity, I said: "It is clear you know who I am, for your bowman delivered the message correctly. Yet I think perhaps you do not know me."

This trembled on the brink of boasting; but I am who I am, Zair forgive me, and I was intrigued.

"We know your reputation is very high in certain quarters," said the woman. She leaned forward and I caught the lamplight's sparkle from her eyes in the eye-slots of the mask. "But we have certain information that this great reputation is a sham, a boistered creation because you are the Prince Majister. Of course, the most puissant prince of Vallia must be a great warrior, a High Jikai, for anything less would demean the empire."

"It's a theory," I said.

"So you will pay five thousand gold talens and you may live. It is settled."

I pondered. It seemed clear they believed the story. They would never have taken out the contract to kill me if they did not. I have amassed a certain unsavory reputation, as you know, and there were places on Kregen where no one—not even a raving idiot—would even contemplate trying to kill me. But, here in Vondium, the capital of the Vallian Empire, I was not in one of those places.

The four people at the table believed this business was settled. They began to stir, ready to take their leave. The two guides shuffled their feet and stepped back. I put my feet under me, ready for the leap, and looked across the table.

"Settled? Why, you onkers, I wouldn't pay you a single clipped toc!"

The four figures stiffened as though I'd jammed a polearm up each one of them. These four formed the High Council of the Assassins of Vondium. Their powers were frighteningly great. For that single betraying heartbeat they could not believe they had heard aright.

The woman let out a gasp and leaned forward on her forearm and her hand splayed against me. Jewels flashed. Nath the Knife put a hand to her hand, and restrained her. Laygon the Strigicaw started to curse, his hand reaching to

57

his belt. The fourth man, who had not spoken, yet remained silent.

It struck me then that these assassins couldn't see the funny side of all this. They didn't think it was funny. To me, Dray Prescot, Lord of Strombor and Krozair of Zy, it was hilarious.

What my ferocious Djangs would say of it—their King of Djanduin solemnly being asked to pay someone for being kind enough not to kill him! They would bellow their mirth!

In the instant of the ensuing silence, when everyone in the musty room remained fixed, static, enwrapped with their own personal turmoil of emotions, the heavy beating of rain pelted against the closed windows.

The mineral oil lamps flickered.

Then, and only then, speaking in that iron voice, Nath the Knife said: "You will pay. You will pay—or you are dead."

"Not," I said, "a single clipped toc."

As the instant action followed I commented to myself that my rhetoric was entirely false. A toc is a tiny coin, one sixth of an ob, and who was going to bother to clip that?

Then the chair groaned and grated and flapped back into a black and cavernous hole and I spring-heeled up and onto the floor, and naked steel flashed in the lamplights.

This, then, was more like it. . . .

Chapter Five

I Drop in on a Great Lady

The trick chair vanished with an almighty crash into the black maw gaping in the floor like the mouth of a chank. The two guides, flustered by my non-disappearance, flicked out their rapiers. They were stikitches and therefore expert with weapons. They rushed on me, silently, determined to cut themselves a little of Laygon's fee.

My feet hit the wooden floor and dust puffed up. The whole floor groaned; the place was as rotten as the worm-eaten hull of the Swordship Gull-i-mo.

"Cut him down!" grated that iron voice. "'He refuses an accommodation in honor, now he must pay the penalty.'"

My own rapier ripped out—a nice blade but not a top-quality brand in its decorations, serviceable, well-used, the kind of rapier a fellow might wear in Drak's City—and the steel jangled and slid as the blades crossed.

The two assassins brought their four blades into play at once. I ducked and weaved and fended them off with the rapier alone. I did not draw the matching main gauche.

Before Barty and I had ventured in here I had insisted that he wear one of the superb mesh-steel shirts Delia and I owned. We kept them particularly well-cared for, on formers, well-oiled, safe in the armory of our Valkan villa in Vondium. One of those shirts cost more than even a relatively well-paid working man could earn in his entire lifetime.

The blades clashed and the lamplight glinted from the steel.

I vaulted back, slashed away, foined, and kept one eye on the four chief assassins at the table. They were the real danger.

One of the guides thought to play it clever and slid in below his fellow. His dark face glared up at me. He tried to hold his left-hand dagger up so as to parry any downward cut I might make, and thrust me through with his rapier. At the same time his companion pressed in strongly, seeking to pin me.

I leaped, thrust, landing a high hit along a shoulder above any armor they might be wearing under their drab tunics, brought a yell of agony, withdrew, and so kicked the clever one in the nose as I went by. His blade hissed past. He sprawled back, his nose a crimson flower, spraying blood.

I hit them both with the hilt—left and right, one two—and sprang away from the spot. A dagger whistled through the air where I had been standing.

The two guides sprawled on the floor. The woman still stood in the pose of throwing as I whirled to face the table in the corner.

One of the stikitches had gone. A door was just closing in the left-hand angle of the walls.

He was the silent one. Laygon and Nath had drawn their blades. They stood, clearly expecting the woman's dagger cast to finish me. Now I waggled my rapier at them admonishingly.

"I do not wish to kill any of you. Though, Opaz knows why not, for you are all ripe to die. But I am willing to spare you and so save future trouble."

I know. I know. That was weak. But I had work to do in

59

Vallia and I didn't want a pack of rascally stikitches on my neck, interfering. If they could be convinced they had no future trying to assassinate me, then I would have achieved a great deal.

That was the new Dray Prescot talking, of course. . . .

"You will die, here and now." The iron voice of Nath the Knife held not a single note of hesitation. Inflexible, he could not understand why what he wished had not already occurred.

A mocking thought occurred to me.

The two men, Nath and Laygon, rounded each end of the table to get at me. They were quite clearly hyr stikitches, top men, superb with weapons. Killing was their trade and they would have made of it an art.

"If I have to slay you, I will," I said. "But think. If you kill me, here and now, you will never have the chance of another client. No one else will offer you gold for my death."

As I say, I mocked them.

They did not reply but bore on.

The woman was the danger, now. She'd have another dagger or three stuffed down her bodice. I'd have to skip and leap and against these two my attention was likely to be fully engaged. Time for Remberee. . . .

The window, probably. . . .

It would be nonproductive to attempt to return across the rainswept walkway to The Ball and Chain. The door through which Silent Sam or Tongueless Tom had disappeared would open to a trick lock, and there wouldn't be time. So it would have to be the window.

The woman came back to life. Her hand raked out. Steel glinted.

My left hand flicked up to my neck, the fingers gripped, twisted, withdrew and the terchick flew.

Like a homing bee it buzzed clean into the woman's upper right arm. She let out a hoarse gasp, never a scream, and staggered. The dagger fell from her nerveless fingers.

"I would crave your pardon, lady," I said. "If you were not a stikitche. As you are, you may rot in a Herrelldrin Hell for my talens."

Then the two men were on me and I ripped out the left-hand dagger and we set to.

Even as the blades crossed a thought so shocking occurred to me that I faltered, and stamped back, and then back-pedalled most rapidly around the room aiming for the window.

What an onker I was!

These men believed I was a warrior of the imagination, a figment of the Vallian Empire's publicity machine. They had seen me enter the tavern, no doubt of that, and they took me at face value. The woman had been devastatingly contemptuous. And here I was, at last beginning to warm up, freed from talk and intrigue and into the business of bashing skulls, and taking that evil joy from it that sometimes overcomes me—to my shame. But—but! If they realized I could handle a sword that would make life far more hazardous in the future. And it was to the future that all my efforts had been directed.

All this talk, and inanity, and inaction—all had been designed to give me breathing space in Vallia. I did not wish to take on the work I had to do with a gang of cutthroat stikitches dogging my heels all the time.

If I slew all these, there would be more. . . .

The very correctness of my estimation of the situation was borne out as Nath and Laygon charged on.

"It is true!" bellowed Laygon in his rich voice. "We had a report from our spies. The twelve who were slain and of whom you boast, you rast, were killed by your friends. You did not even draw your blade."

That was true.

"Stand and die like a man," grated Nath the Knife, and started to work his way around to my back.

"I have had luck with the knife," I said. I ran backwards, casting a single quick look to see where I was going, aiming for the sacking-covered window. "But you are hyr stikitches—good at your foul work. But, you cramphs, you will not get my gold."

I was at the window.

I spun about, bracing myself.

"Nor my hide!"

And with a single leem-leap I went head-first through the window.

All this idle chatter as I fought—I was really lapsing into some fairy-tale layabout, all silks and graces, quite unlike the hard and vicious and totally practical fighting man I am. . . .

Rain lashed at me as I fell. I went head over heels. I had thought to land on my feet, and back, rolling, and so come up ready to fight.

Instead as I sailed from the window I turned over and fell splat into the back of an overfilled dung cart.

Muck pulsed up around me. The stink sizzled. I scrabbled around in heaving nausea, sloshing about in the odoriferous and sticky collections of a hundred cess-pits and stables. Shades of Seg and his dungy straw!

I flailed my arms and heard the squishings and squelchings.

The man on the cart yelled as the brown spray hit him.

I got a knee onto the rotten wood of the cart and heaved up.

Above my head three faces peered out of the shredded sacking. The woman's face was, like them all, hidden by the steel mask; but I fancied she was whiter than usual. I hoped so. The cart lurched and I managed to slide off the back.

Nath let out a yell.

"Seize him up! Tally ho! Stikitches! *Slay him!*"

The rain slicked across the cobbles. The smell rose despite the rain. The cart lumbered off. Men and women appeared in the shadowed doorways of the street. I was around the corner from the front entrance of The Ball and Chain, and if I went that way Barty would come prancing out of the door of The Yellow Rose ready to fight and ready to be chopped.

So I ran the other way and, by all the confounded imps of Sicce, here came Barty, red-faced, bellowing, running after me with his rapier naked in his fist. By Zim-Zair! I groaned. Now we're in for it!

"I am with you pri—Jak!"

"Well, stay with me!"

The three steel masks vanished from the window. A few men pushed out into the rain. In a few murs we'd be surrounded. Once the hue and cry was up we'd have all kinds of rascals out for a bit of fun and bashing running after us besides the assassins.

"This way, Barty. And put that damned sword away! Run!"

We pelted off through the rain heading away from the Gate of Skulls, along the side street parallel to the walls. The walls of the Old City of Vondium are mostly noticeable by their great age and their state of disrepair. But, for all that, they demarcate a very real line, a barrier between the Old and the New.

People stared after us. The rain was a blessing in one way, in that it had driven a considerable number of idlers into shelter and so we had a pretty clear run. But, in the other way, and a worse way, too, it meant there were far fewer crowds in which to become lost.

So—we ran.

I, Dray Prescot, ran.

I told myself that I ran because of Barty. I did not want him killed. I had never yet met my daughter Dayra to talk to her and I did not want our first meeting to be shadowed by the death of her fine young man who ran puffing and red-faced at my side. But Barty was young and tough and filled with ideas of chivalry and valor.

"Let us turn on them and rend them!" he panted out.

"Run."

We cut along the first cross street aiming to get back to the walls and find a loophole out. I had no real idea of the geography of Drak's City—I doubt if anyone had much idea of that crawling maze of streets and alleys and hidden courts as an entirety—and so could do no more than run and follow my nose.

It would be nice if Ashti and her brother Naghan turned up and out of gratitude for the silver sinvers guided us to safety. But, again, that was out of fairy books.

The reality came as a dozen men sprang from an alleyway and brandishing long-knives and cudgels and a sword or two came blustering down on us.

Very carefully I gave my palms a good wipe down the old blanket coat—on the inside. The muck fouled me abominably. But I needed fists that would not slip on hilts for the work that promised. As though Five-handed Eos-Bakchi decided it was time to smile—just a little—upon me, I spotted an abandoned orange-like fruit called a rosha lying in the water-streaming gutter. A single twist ripped it into half and I smeared the tacky juice over my palms and fingers. That would help to give a good grip.

It smelled a little better than I did, too.

"We cut through them in one go and keep running," I told Barty.

When they hit us I did just that. I used the hilt a good deal, for I had no wish to kill these fellows. One or two blades flickered around my ears; but with a bash and a whump or two I was through. I poised to run on. I was through—but not so Barty.

He pranced. He took up the stance. His rapier leaned into a perfect line. He foined. He was thoroughly enjoying himself. Like a student fresh from the salle he handled himself with all the perfection of a star pupil.

I sighed.

Many a time have I seen these fine young men fresh from sword-training go into rough and brutal action. If they live

63

they learn and then stand a better chance. But all the universities in two worlds don't teach what a man must know to keep a knife from his guts, a knee out of his groin, a flung chain from around his neck.

They'd have had Barty—had him for breakfast and spat out the pips.

Perfect in poise and lunge and parry, holding himself in the correct rapier-fighting position, he would have been easy meat for them. He was lucky—that I own—when a flung cudgel merely brushed past his brown hair. But he couldn't last.

So I went bashing back most evilly, with a knee here, and a clutch at a raggedy coat here and a jerk and a chunk of the hilt, and a bending-forward so that the attacker went sailing up over me, to be kicked heartily as he hit the ground.

No, if you want to stay alive on many spots of Kregen you do no good trying to fence by the book.

A stout-armed fellow with a kutcherer tried to stab the spiked back of the knife into my eye, and I weaved and kicked him between wind and water, and ducked a cudgel from his mate and elbowed his Adam's apple. My own rapier and main gauche flew this way and that parrying blows and thrusts. I jumped about a fair bit. I got up to Barty and put my foot into the rear end of the man who was going to slip a long knife into Barty's exposed back and kicked him end-over-end. I had to beat away another kutcherer, careful of that wicked tooth of metal.

Barty had allowed a ruffian to get inside his guard, and with his rapier pointing at the rain-filled skies was dancing around as though the two of them waltzed, neither able to step back to take a slash at the other.

"Barty," I said, in what I considered a most understanding voice. But Barty jumped, anyway. "Let us get on."

I stuck the main gauche back into my belt, ignoring the scabbard, took the fellow clasping Barty by the ear, ducked a cudgel blow from somewhere, and ran him across the street. He tried to emulate a swifter and rammed head-on into a moldy wall.

I grabbed Barty.

"And this time, young man, do not stop running!"

We took off. They followed for a bit; but I caught a hurtling cudgel out of the air and threw it back. The man who had flung it dropped as though poleaxed. After that the rest of them more or less gave up the pursuit.

But there were others, far more ruthless, who took it up as we reached the walls.

And, as I saw, two thin, furtive, weasel-like fellows remained dogging our footsteps as we ran up to the wall and looked about for the nearest way through or over or under.

The assassins had gathered their strength. Now the mob of men who flowed around a buttress meant to do for us finally.

I took a single look at them and hauled Barty off. We ran fleetly along the wall, dodging refuse, leaping covered stalls, almost treading on a family sheltering under an old tarpaulin. The rain washed away a deal of the muck and stinks; but enough remained for me with my odoriferous clothes to feel at home.

A splendidly orchestrated hullabaloo now racketed away at our heels. Barty kept on laughing. I own the situation amused me; but I am notorious for that kind of perverse behavior and I felt some surprise—pleased surprise, I hasten to add—that Dayra seemed to have found herself a young man of exceptional promise. So we ran along the wall and a gang of kids pelted us with rotten cabbages, green shredding bundles falling through the rain. We ducked into a house built into the wall and leaped over an old fellow who snored in a wicker hooded chair and so rollicked up the blackwood stairs. The upper rooms were filled with all kinds of trash and bric-a-brac indicating the storage places for the junk merchants who thrived on human stupidity and cupidity. Their ruffianly agents scoured around picking up antiques which were then sold at inflated prices to the wealthy of Vondium. Well, it takes all kinds to make a world.

We hared through the piles of old furniture and pictures and tatty curtains, past boxes and bales and bundles, heading for the windows. These were all barred. Barty put his foot against a wooden bar and the old wood puffed and shredded—I hardly care to describe that tired sagging away as a splintering of wood.

We bundled through and then tottered back, clutching each other, poised dizzyingly over nothing.

I grabbed the lintel. It held, thank Zair, and we hauled in.

We stood perhaps fifty feet up the sheer outside wall, in a window embrasured out over the cobbled road below. And at our backs the pursuit bayed up those dark blackwood stairs.

One window along a beam jutted out with a rope and pulley. The junk would be collected here and then hoisted out and lowered onto Quoffa carts below.

"Next window, Jak," said Barty, cheerfully.

"I had hoped there would be stairs—at the least a rope ladder." These drikingers of the Old City have their entrances and their exits. Drikingers—bandits of a particular bent—is not too strong a word to apply to some of the fellows in Drak's City. So we bashed along to the next window and kicked it open and seized the rope.

Loud footfalls echoed up from the room at our backs. Men fell over bundles, and a giant glass-fronted wardrobe toppled to smash to ruination.

"Time to go, Barty. Come on."

So, grasping the rope, we let ourselves down as the windlass held against the pawl. We were almost at street level when the first furious faces poked out of the window alongside the pulley-crowned beam.

"Jump!" I yelped. "They'll start reeling us in any mur!"

So we jumped, and hit the rain-slicked cobbles, and staggered and a flung knife caromed past my ear.

Barty staggered up and shook his fist. Men were sliding down the rope. I smiled. Oh, yes, this was a smiling situation.

"They mean to do for us, then. . . . More running is indicated."

"Why can't we stand and blatter them, Jak? By Opaz—I do not care much for all this running. I can't get my wind."

"They'll open up your body quick enough, my lad. Then you'll have wind and to spare. Run!"

Running off I was aware Barty was not with me and swung about ready to damn and blast him.

He was hopping about with his old blanket coat twisted around his legs, trying to disentangle himself, first on one foot then on the other. His face was a wonder to behold.

"By Vox!" he bellowed. "This confounded blanket is alive!"

"Not as alive as most of 'em in there." I dodged back and grabbed for the coat; but he kept toppling away and almost falling and staggering about. In the end I whipped a horizontal slash from the rapier at him and shredded the rope. The blanket coat fell away. He kicked it wrathfully.

"Opaz-forsaken garment! I nearly knocked my brains out on the cobbles."

"Run," I said. There was no need to draw any parallels between his outraged remarks and what would happen. So we ran.

Now we were outside Drak's City and, in theory, back where the writ of Vondium ran.

Whether Vondium's writ ran or not, we did.

66

I owe that the sheer zest of this running pleased me. The idea that I ran away from enemies had long since passed. The game now was to stay ahead. That became the object, the running was the thing, the escaping the prize. If we fought that would come as an anticlimax.

The stikitches pelting after us were still yelling. Near the Old Walls, some remnant of their own powers clung.

"By Jhalak!" one of them sang out. "Stand and meet your doom like men!"

"I'm all for standing," puffed Barty. He gave me a most reproachful look.

"Run," was all I said.

Pressing on we came into more respectable streets and Barty, with a comment to the effect that if I intended to run he had best run with me, and we'd best go *this* way and through *that* alley and so out onto *this* square, at last brought us into a part of the city I recognized. Although we were now in company with many other people all about their business, the assassins stayed with us. They kept a distance. But they dogged our footsteps.

I think most of them had removed their masks; but they all kept a fold of cloth over their faces, and this would be taken as a natural precaution against the rain. Their large floppy Vallian hats with the broad brims hanging down and shedding the water also afforded them a measure of concealment.

When the rain, after the Kregan fashion, started to ease up and the splendor of the suns began to shine through, I wondered how far the stikitches would press their pursuit.

Our mutual progress had now degenerated into a fast walk and we threaded our way between the people venturing out after the rain. No one took any notice of us. There were others running—slaves, mostly, about their masters' business—and our bedraggled appearance bespoke us for slaves or free men with unpleasant work to perform. We came to the broad arrow through either side of the building that is called the Lane of the Twins.

This leads to the broad kyro before the imperial palace.

Barty started up it at once and so I followed.

Although I say I recognized where we were this does not mean I was well aquainted with the area. Opening off the Lane of the Twins many side streets and roadways gave entrances to the streets and roads pent within two curving canals. A number of broad boulevards cross the Lane. We passed over canals bridged in a variety of the pleasing ways of Vondium. Just under the stalking feet of an aqueduct we were held up by a crowd who jostled and pushed along slowly, mingled with carts and chariots and carrying-chairs. And all these streets and alleys and canals and boulevards and aqueducts are blessed with names. . . . No—I knew only that if I went on along the Lane of the Twins eventually I'd reach the palace.

The crowds grew thicker and more solid. On the right-hand side a string of carts had come to a standstill. Each cart was piled with hay. They were filled to abundance with hay, and they were jammed tightly together, so that the pair of krahniks who pulled each cart were eagerly reaching forward to chew contentedly away at the hay dribbling from the tailgate of the cart in front. The carters sat slumped, hats over their eyes, phlegmatically waiting for whatever obstruction ahead was halting all progress to clear.

I looked back.

The two thin weasely fellows were padding on apace, and with them a dozen or so of the most determined stikitches.

For a moment we stood halfway between two side streets. The doors of the buildings flanking the Lane were closed.

"Now," said Barty, and he started to draw his rapier. "Now we cannot run any farther, thank Opaz. Now we can teach these rasts a lesson."

The backs of the crowd ahead appeared to be a solid wall; but we could worm our way through. I frowned. I did not relish the idea of Barty being chopped to pieces, and I knew he would unfailingly be chopped if those master craftsmen at murder caught up with him. I could not risk his life.

"Up, Barty," I said, and took his arm and fairly hurled him up onto the hay of the rearmost wagon.

He started to protest at once and took a mouthful of hay, and spluttered and then I was up on the high cart with him and urging him along. Reluctantly, he allowed me to help him over the somnolent form of the driver, with a couple of steps along the broad backs of the krahniks, to reach the next cart along. So, prancing like a couple of high-wire artists, we darted along the line of hay-filled wagons.

The massed crowds below showed little interest in our antics; a few people looked up, and laughed, and some cursed us; but most of them were content merely to push on in the wake of whatever was holding up progress.

The rain stopped and the twin suns shone with a growing warmth. The clouds fanned away, dissipating, letting that glorious blue sky of Kregen extend refulgently above.

We hopped along from wain to wain, leaping the drivers and the krahniks. The animals were hardly aware of the footsteps on their backs before we had leaped off and so on.

The assassins followed us.

Ahead the sense of a mass moving ponderously along the Lane turned out to be a large body of soldiery, all marching with a swing. The glint of their weapons showed they were ready for an emergency, which surprised me, although it should not have, seeing the troubles through which Vallia had just come—and was still going through, by Vox. Everybody followed the troops, either unable or unwilling to push past. A number of loaded and covered carts were visible within the ranks of the formed body, and there were palanquins there, too, with brightly colored awnings against the rain or the suns.

Barty missed his footing and I had to haul him up off the head of a sleepy driver, whose brown hand reached for his holstered whip, and whose hoarse voice blasted out, outraged, puzzled, alarmed at this visitation from heaven. I shouted.

"On with you, Barty. The rasts gain on us."

Ahead along the line of hay wains the purple shadow of an aqueduct cast a bar of blackness. That could cause us problems. We leaped the next two carts and Barty again slipped. He turned on me, then, thoroughly put out by my inexplicable insistence on running away. He held onto the high rail of a hay wain and spoke furiously.

"In my island they used to speak with hushed breath of the Strom of Valka—Strom Drak na Valka. But I have heard stories, rumors, that the great reputation is all a sham, a pretense, something to color the marriage with the Princess Majestrix. By Vox! I do not believe it—but your conduct strains my belief, prince, strains it damnably!"

The hay wains were lumbering forward again, slowly, rolling, and the purple shadows of the aqueduct fell about us.

"Believe what you will, Strom Barty. But you will go on to the next wagon and then jump down. You will mingle in the crowds. You will do this as you love my daughter Dayra."

"And? And what will you do?"

"I will go up." The aqueduct's brick walls presented many handholds. "They will follow me. That is certain. I will meet you—"

"I shall go up, also!"

I lowered my eyebrows at him. He put a hand to his mouth.

69

"You go on under the aqueduct and jump down, young Barty. Dernun?"

Yes, cracking out "dernun?" like that at him was not particularly polite. Dernun carries the connotation of punishment if you do not understand, meaning savvy, *capish*—but he took the intensity of my manner in good part, only going a little more red. He turned and jumped for the next cart without a word and vanished in those concealing purple shadows.

The bricks were old and here and there irregular patches of new brickwork had been inserted. The emperor liked to keep his aqueducts efficient. Even so, sprays of water spat in fine arcs out across the heads of passersby. I climbed up to the first row of brick arches and clung on and looked back. The assassins were almost up with the aqueduct, leaping like fleas over the backs of the haywains. I waved my arm at them and then made a most insulting gesture.

The slant of the brickwork ran the water channel out over the Lane at an angle. I climbed through the lower tier of arches into a dark cavernous space, lit by the semi-circles of brilliance in serried rows, feeling the looseness of old mortar and brick chipping below, the glimmer of random puddles showing up like unwinking eyes. Water splashed down from the leaded channel above my head. The stikitches clambered up after me.

The plan was to run diagonally along the first tier of arches all the way across the Lane and so free myself of the encumbrance of Barty. I had ideas on the mores and honor of the stikitches, and if Laygon the Strigicaw was among those pursuing me—as he must almost inevitably be—then I could finish this thing cleanly.

That time-consuming altercation with Barty had afforded the pursuers the chance to catch up. They ran fleetly across the strewn ground at me, spraying water from puddles, yelling, incensed, confident they had me now and uncaring of what noise they made in this arched space, knowing it would be lost in the greater noise from the procession which passed by below.

"*Kitchew!*" they bellowed, and closed in.

They were good. Well, of course, to be employed as an assassin on Kregen you have to be good. Quite apart from the fact that if you are not good you won't last, you will also starve.

The shadowy effect of the brick buttresses and the shafts of brilliant light through the arched openings lent a macabre air

70

of theatre to that fight. The blades rang and scraped and the first two went down. The others pressed in confidently enough and at the first pass with a large fellow wearing a ring in his ear, my rapier blade snapped.

Do not think it odd if I say I felt relief that the rapier snapped. Only eight of the rogues had clambered up the arches and followed me. So I was in a hurry, and with the rapier useless I could hurl the hilt in the face of the earring fellow, and then rip out the longsword.

"By Jhalak," one of the stikitches ground out. "That bar of iron will not serve you."

It served him through the guts, and the next fellow spun away with his steel mask shattered and blood spouting through. Two tried to run and two terchicks finished them. I was left facing the man who by his clothes and mannerisms I knew to be Laygon the Strigicaw. Time was running out. I had to be quick.

"When you are dead, Laygon," I said cheerfully, "no sti-kitche will pick up your contracts without payment. But Ashti Melekhi is dead, also. So that business will be settled, with full steel-bokkertu and in all honor."

He knew what I meant. Steel-bokkertu is a euphemism for rights gained by the sword and retrospectively legalized. So he leaped for me, snarling, and he died, like the others, and I ran to the edge of the arched space and looked down.

I might have guessed.

The procession was in an uproar.

The two weasely fellows had chosen to go after Barty be-cause they were not stikitches and fancied he, as a Koter of Vallia, would carry a goodly sum on his person. After the as-sassins had finished with me, the rasts calculated, there would be no pickings for them. The rest of the stikitches must have decided to chance the ranked soldiery. Barty had spitted one of them, clearing a space among the onlookers as the proces-sion passed, and was tinkering away with two more.

It was a long way down.

People broke away from the fight, screaming. In those first few moments of action when all was confusion, no one turned instantly to assist Barty. But he did look a sight, clad in his old clothes, bedraggled, red-faced, swearing away, thor-oughly worked up. One might almost be forgiven for believ-ing he was the murderer and the soberly-attired assassins his victims. They had removed their steel masks and now wore only the polite public half-mask often seen on Kregen, a use-ful adjunct to gracious living, as it is said with some irony.

71

Whatever might be said, in a mur or two he'd be dead.

The angle of the aqueduct had taken me out farther into the center of the Lane. Directly below passed a cart loaded with sharp-looking objects under a tarpaulin, the edges creased and unfriendly looking. To jump down on that would invite a punctured hide and a snapped backbone. Further along swayed the palanquins with their colored awnings. I eyed them savagely. The largest one—of course. It had to be the biggest and best to take the weight and the velocity of my fall.

I ran along the edge of the brickwork, ducked out of the archway right over the palanquin below, and launched myself into space. As I jumped I saw the soldiers at last break ranks and advance on Barty and the assassins. Just before I revolved in the air, falling, I glimpsed the assassins running off, and Barty twisting in the grip of a Deldar.

Then, rotating, I came down with an ear-splitting crash on the striped awning. It ripped. I went on through trailing tatters of cloth. The blue and green striped material had broken my fall and I landed with a thump on the wooden bed of the palanquin. I spat out a chunk of the blue and green banded cloth, and a strip of the white striping between the colors caught in my teeth. I ripped it out furiously and dived for the cloth-of-gold curtains.

The three women in the palanquin stared at me, petrified.

I took in their appearance at a glance—two handmaidens and a great lady. She was half-veiled, and she looked lushly beautiful, and dominating, and her color was rising and she was getting all set to spit out a mouthful of invective. You couldn't really blame her. Here she was, sitting quietly in her palanquin being taken along with all her people, and some hairy odoriferous blanket-coated oaf falls in from the sky.

I became aware of my obnoxious pong as the stink cut through the scents of the palanquin.

The Womoxes carrying the poles had yielded to the sudden extra weight; but one pole broke and the whole lot came to a shuddering crash, tip-tilted on a corner. The great lady was flung across the cloth-of-gold canopied space. She fell into my arms. I couldn't move. Her dark, intense face wrinkled up, the whiteness of the skin emphasized by the kohled eyes and the artful patch of color in the cheeks. Her flared nostrils widened. Her mouth, hidden by the veil but its outline visible as the silver gauze pressed back, curved down.

"You stink!"

"Get off, lady, I am in a hurry—"

"You dare—"

Somehow the longsword had not done any damage to the occupants of the palanquin—yet. I tried to twist it around to make it safe. She was screaming invective at me now and I half-turned to shove her off, so that she saw me. Only then I realized the medium-sized brown beard had been ripped off somewhere along the way.

She saw my face.

"Oh," she said.

"I am in a hurry, lady. Men are trying to kill me and I must—"

"Yes, you must run away. Well, let me sit up and you may run away—run to the Ice Floes of Sicce, and you will."

"Mayhap I will," I said.

She struggled to sit up against the slope of the palanquin. Her two handmaidens went on screaming. A soldier stuck his head in the opening of the cloth-of-gold curtains and saw me.

Instantly his rapier whipped in.

The longsword was still stuck somewhere down in among the cushions, the point jammed in the woodwork. I just hoped this great lady wouldn't sit back too heavily.

"Keep your damned rapier out of my face!" I yelled. The guard swept the curtains aside and started to reach for me.

"Do not kill him, Rogor!" snapped the lady.

"Yes—" began this guard Hikdar, and I twisted my foot around and kicked him in the guts through the curtains. I got the sword free. The lady stared at me with those fine dark eyes filled with a blaze of contempt.

"Run—go on, run! That is all you are good for!"

The Hikdar was whooping in great draughts of air. I stood up and hit my head on the awning post and cursed and started to climb out. The lady suddenly laughed. She trilled silver malicious laughter. She pointed.

"Is that what you run from?"

Her guards had caught one of the weasely fellows and they dragged him, all a-yelling and a-squawking, up to the canted palanquin. He was in a frightful state. He screamed as they twisted his arm up his back and the knife dropped with a clatter unheard in the din. His thin face contorted with his terror, and spittle slobbered. He looked thin and frail and ridiculous as a would-be murderer, all the weasely deviltry washed away in his fear.

"That was one of them," I said.

She laughed at me, hard, hating, hurtful laughter.

She did not hurt me, mind; but she would hurt Barty and wound him deeply, if he heard her.

"You carry a monstrous great sword and you run so hard you fall into my chair and ruin it—and *that* is what you run from, what so frightens you."

"If you like," I said. Barty? What had happened to him? I fretted, not giving this great lady much attention and, to be truthful, not much respect, either.

"Get out!" she screamed, suddenly letting her anger boil over. "You stink! You are an abomination! Get out! Get out!"

"I'm going as soon as I—" I started.

Then I saw Barty, bawling into the ears of a guard Hikdar and gesticulating, and so I knew he was safe. I own, I felt a great flood of relief, and let out a breath.

"Go on running," spat the great lady. "There are a lot more rasts like this one for you to run from. Take your stupid great sword and clear off. You are not a real man. You are just a fake, an apology for a jikai, a puffed up bag of vomit! *Run!*"

Chapter Six

The Black and Whites Make a Promise

The separate wing of the imperial palace in Vondium given over to the private apartments of the Prince and Princess, Majister and Majestrix, have been decorated with Delia's faultless taste, and yet, as she would exclaim, flinging up her hands in mock despair, you could never get any life ino the place. Still, this austere, frowning pile with all its fantastic traceries of balconies and colonnades, of spire and tower, of concealed grottoes and secret gardens, was where, for the moment, we were living. The villas belonging to the various estates in Vallia kept up in Vondium—those of Delphond and the Blue Mountains, and of Valka, Zamra and Veliadrin—were preferred by us. So I took a bath—a quick, scalding hot bath and not the Baths of the Nine—in the imperial bathroom and changed into the flummery of grand clothes demanded for the ceremony at the Temple of Opaz the Nantifer.

Truth to tell, I was heartily sick of all these endless ceremonies. Perhaps I have not stressed them enough in my narrative. Certainly, they bored me out of my skull. But I was the Prince Majister and the emperor my father-in-law still reigned and I was constrained to attend whenever I was in Vondium.

That seemed to me one perfectly good explanation for my frequent absences from the capital, quite apart from the periods spent in our estates.

"And she spat at you?"

"Well, my heart," I said as I struggled into the swathing bands of a ghastly pink robe. "Almost. She was uncouth, if that is the word. Crude in a gentlelady."

"And who was she?"

Delia smiled as one of her handmaids pulled up the long laypom-colored dress. We were never sticklers for the protocol that demanded a husband and wife dress in their own rooms miles apart. Mind you, I had always to keep my mind on my own clothes when Delia was thus engaged.

"Some great lady or other. She was not, I think, of Vallia, for she had violet eyes."

Delia gave me a quick duck of the head, a fast look and then that graceful turn as she looked away and said: "Not of Vallia, as you say, my heart."

Well, I imagine I know my Delia and so at the time I fancied she had more than an inkling who this bitchy great lady might be. Being Delia, and therefore a tease as well as the most gracious lady of two worlds, she forebore to tell me. And me, being me, I forebore to inquire.

"Hurry, my love," said Delia, hauling her jeweled belt tight around that slender waist and buckling up the gold clasp. "We shall be late in two flicks of a leem's tail."

"Grab that mazilla," I said to the palace servant loaned to us to take care of our garments. "The very largest, most ornate and ludicrous one in the whole wide world of Kregen, I do truly think."

Each rank of nobility of Vallia has its corresponding rank of mazilla it may wear; the tallest and widest and grandest by the emperor, the next size by any kings of Vallia who might happen to be living at the time, then the princes, the kovs, the vads and trylons, and so on through the stroms down to the ordinary haughty private koter. The koter—gentleman is only an approximation to the ramifications of meaning to koter—wears a neat curved mazilla, rather like a tall collar, of a dark color, usually a distinguished black, relieved only by braiding of his allegiance. The Koters of Vallia are proud of their neat trim mazillas. As I squirmed into the enormous magnificence of the monstrosity I had chosen to wear, I wondered if the game was worth the candle. Might the insult not better be conveyed by wearing a koter's mazilla in lustrous black velvet?

No time to worry over that now. We buckled on our weapons, slung our scarlet and golden cloaks on the zhantil-bosses, gave a last quick look in the mirrors, and then hared off down the marble staircases and along the rug-strewn corridors to the zorcas we would ride to the Temple of Opaz the Nantifer.

Shadow gave a curve of his head and a whinny to show he was pleased to see me. He was truly a magnificent animal and I was glad afresh each time I bestrode his back that I'd been able to bring him with me all the way from Ba-Domek.

Delia's zorca, a fine chestnut, had a somewhat small spiral horn in the center of her forehead; but she was a fine mare and Delia was fond of her Firerose.

The service of propitiation to Opaz, the spirit manifest in the Invisible Twins, passed. I will not dull your senses with a detailed description, for all that of the many religions and creeds of Kregen that of Opaz shines the truest. I swear allegiance to Zair, as you know, and to Djan; but these two lack something of the essential spiritual transcendence of Opaz; Zair and Djan—particulary Djan—are Warrior Gods. In Opaz lies a very great part of the future well-being of Kregen.

So I will pass on to the moment when Delia and I walked back to our zorcas where they had been tethered with many others and looked after by hostlers employed by the Temple. My usual traffic with the Racters was so minimal as to be nonexistent; public functions provided them with an opportunity to speak with me. I turned as Strom Luthien approached, very seemly to all outward appearances, his hat being in his hand and his head slightly inclined.

Yet I knew he, at least one Racter, would be only too ready to slip a blade between my ribs and then call for assistance too late. Luthien was one of those nobles without an estate, his stromnate being gambled away, probably, lost at the Jikaida board. Now he worked for the Racters as a messenger and agent.

He smiled at me under his moustache, a sleek, knowing, and yet faintly patronizing smile. My monstrosity of a brown beard bristled up, almost as though it had been grown by me instead of being hooked on my ears. I looked at him as he relayed his information. Those Racters with whom I had done business in Natyzha Famphreon's hothouse pleasure gardens wished to converse with me again.

"For, prince," said Strom Luthien, "much was agreed and yet little accomplished."

I did not make a scathing remark to the effect that I did not discuss details with errand boys. I said: "The Black Feathers were routed. Where?"

"The same place—"

"No. I remember the chavonths. And, and you will, convey my regards to Kov Nath Famphreon."

He kept his smile going famously. "Then where?"

"The Sea Barynth Hooked. There is an upper room. Hire it from the landlord. In five burs time."

I turned away almost before I'd finished speaking, and the springy feathers of the mazilla swished. What Strom Luthien made of my hauteur and my bad manners I didn't give a damn. I had to lay the foundations here for subsequent action. Delia, though, favored me with a look that was so old-fashioned as to be positively antediluvian.

We mounted up and shook the reins. Of course we drew disapproving glances from the nobles. The Prince and Princess of Vallia, riding alone, without a proper escort—it was shocking. It was also liberating.

"And what have those infamous Racters to talk to you about, husband?"

"More intrigues to kill your father, wife."

Her face—gorgeous, radiant—drew down, and I felt a pain at her look of sudden apprehension. She spoke quickly.

"You jest, my heart—but take care! There are spies everywhere—and the Racters are powerful. We all know they but bide their time. When they strike—"

"I firmly believe they will attempt to remain true to their own beliefs. They will obey the letter of the law when they chance their collective arms and try to oust your father. They will not order his assassination—not directly. What we have to fear is some lesser light—like Strom Luthien, for instance—taking the law into his own hands. We have come through great perils and your father still lives." I scratched my nose. "Anyway, where was he in the Temple? It is not

77

like him to miss a religious ceremony that brings political ac-
claim with it."

Delia shook back her hair and the lustrous brown ripples
flowed with those glorious chestnut tints glinting in the
mingled rays of the suns.

"His Grand Chamberlain excused him. An affair of state
that could not wait upon even this ceremony. You did not, I
may add, stand in very well for him."

"I would not have done so had he asked. Not when he is
in the city. By Zair! All this flummery is his job as the emperor."

She looked sidelong at me as the zorcas paced along the
stone-flagged way, past the fronts of other temples, and buildings housing the University of Vondium Ghat, with the passersby jostling along and some turning to stare at us. All the
time as we rode and talked I kept that old sailorman's
weather eye open. I fancied the Stikitches of Vondium would
accept as closed the contract Ashti Melekhi had put out on
me; but if they had not done so then I would have to convince them all over again.

During this time in Vondium the sense of great release that
had come with the return of the emperor to full health, and
the consequent liberation of bottled-up trade that followed,
warred with that ordained sense of impending doom. It was
as though one half of the citizens laughed and drank and
sang while the other half sharpened up their weapons and
bolted their doors and shutters.

I guessed what lay in Delia's mind.

"The moment I have settled up with these Opaz-forsaken
Racters, I shall ride for the Northeast. Dayra—"

"We shall ride."

I cocked an eye at her.

"And the Sisters of the Rose?"

She looked annoyed. "I have certain duties—that I would
tell you if I could—that may prevent an immediate start. But
do not think you can go galloping off alone, Dray Prescot,
and leave me out of it. Dayra has been going through a tumultuous period in her life. She worries me. And that is
sooth."

"She is our daughter. That worries me."

"I agree. She is your daughter, and that is what worries
me."

We both laughed, then, for laughing comes easily to me
when I am with Delia of Delphond. So we rode back to the

palace and to one of those slap-up superb Kregan meals that keeps a fellow and a girl going through the long day.

The Sea Barynth Hooked was situated down on the Kamist Quay—I say was, for it was burned down a few seasons later after a pot-house brawl—and catered for the skippers of the Vallian ships who frequented the Kamist wharves. It was a place where you might, if you wished, sup from superb eel pies. I usually stuck to roast vosk and momolams there. Sea food has never appealed to me.

The upper room was lit by four square windows. The long sturmwood table was covered by a decent yellow cloth and as I entered with a crash of polished boots, the people in the room stopped talking. They surveyed me with the alert interest of a man abruptly discovering a rattler under a rock.

"Let us proceed," I said. "Lahal one and all. I have little time for I have business that presses elsewhere."

Wearing simple Vallian buff, with a red and white favor, with the wide-brimmed Vallian hat in my hand, with a fresh rapier buckled on, with the left-hand dagger to match—the old one was being cleaned now with brick-dust and spittle in the palace armory—and with the longsword a-dangling at my left side, I suppose I looked to them my usual intemperate, boorish, hateful self. The false beards had gone. I was myself, and they knew me.

Strom Luthien motioned to the chair they had reserved for me. I sat down without hesitation. No trick chairs here.

Natyzha Famphreon sat like a parody created out of a nightmare, with her nutcracker old face, lined and shrewish and incredibly vicious with that sharp upthrust lower lip, and her pampered, beautiful, voluptuous body. She nodded to me. She had not forgotten the chavonths in her conservatory.

Her son, Nath na Falkerdrin, was not here.

Ered Imlien, just as boastful, just as bristling, short and squat, shook a fist at me wrathfully.

"Again my estates have been despoiled! And your daughter has been seen—"

He stopped himself. He was shaking. His face looked as red as a scarron. The last time he'd accused Dayra of raiding down onto his estates around Thengelsax from the northeast areas I'd half choked him, and scared him. Now he was harking back to the old sore, and so it was clear that more trouble had blown up—trouble of a serious kind—when I'd been away in Ba-Domek.

I said: "Look at that little fly, Ered Imlien, Trylon of Thengelsax."

79

The fly buzzed to a swooping landing along the windowsill. A long, slender, incredibly agile green tendril shot through the air and the suckered tip fastened upon the hapless fly. The flick-flick plant on the windowsill started to reel in his next meal. This object lesson, I thought, should not be lost on Imlien. Then an event occurred that always occasions amusement among Kregans—aye, and wagers, too—for a second flick-flick plant entered the struggle.

The flick-flick plant is found in most Kregan homes and it serves admirably to catch annoying flies. With its better than six-feet long tendrils it gobbles flies like luscious currants.

Irvil the Flagon, landlord of The Sea Barynth Hooked, had positioned the two flick-flick plants in their brightly colored ceramic pots too closely together. He'd been over-anxious to please his unexpected and distinguished guests. The two green tendrils writhed and fought over the fly.

Immediately Nalgre Sultant, an objectionable sort of fellow with whom I'd had trouble before, said: "I'll lay a gold talen piece on the left-hand plant."

Imlien did not answer, staring and licking his lips, and so Natyzha Famphreon said: "I'll take that, and make it two on the right hand flick-flick."

The trapped fly struggled weakly. The tendrils writhed and pulled. In the event they tore the fly in pieces and each suckered tip retreated, curving gracefully, ready to pop the pieces of the fly into the orange cone-shaped flowers.

"Mine, I think, Nalgre," snapped Old Natyzha, triumphantly.

"I think not, Kovneva. My plant took the larger portion."

They appealed to Ered Imlien, who shrugged and would not give a verdict. The evidence was now being digested within the orange flowers. So they looked at me.

"It matters not who wins. The fly was Vallia. The flick-flick plants were, one, you Racters and, two—"

"Two—this bitch queen!" flared Natyzha. She dismissed the matter of the wager with a wave of the hand. Thus important was the matter to her and the others, that a disputed wager which could be the subject of long and enjoyable wrangling should be summarily dismissed. "This Queen Lush of Lome. The emperor did not attend at the Temple of Opaz the Nantifer today, because he was meeting her. Once she gets her hooks into him—"

"He, then, is also the fly."

"Aye! And we will pull the stronger, if you will honor your promise and assist us."

80

"Do not think I forget your insolence, Trylon Ered." I said this just to keep him on his toes. He slapped his riding crop against his boots, and glowered; but had the sense to remain silent. "And, Kovneva, I made you no promises."

"We know you have been released from your banishment. But you and the emperor still hate each other. His death—"

"I will have none of that. I have told you. You seek to work in legal ways, or so I believe. But if you forget that and hire assassins to do away with the emperor, you will be brought to ruin. This I promise."

I do not make promises lightly, and this, I think, they knew. At the least, they were not to be sucked in by any pretense I might make at being an ineffective, a puffed-up jikai of the imagination, a publicity warrior. They knew better.

Again I found myself considering just what position and just how powerful these people were within the Racter Party of Vallia. Nath Ulverswan, Kov of The Singing Forests, was not here this day—not that you'd notice much for he seldom spoke in meetings. Natyzha was, indeed, a very powerful woman, the Dowager Kovneva of Falkerdrin. But the black and whites extended their tentacles of authority into every part of Vallia. They were owners of vast expenses of rich land, they were shipowners, they were slavemasters. I did not like them overmuch. But—were there people here just a front for the inner cabal of Racters, their High Council, their private Presidio?

One fact remained; through them I was dealing with the racters. I wanted to press on to the Northeast but thought I would try a little ploy with them here first.

"If the emperor marries this Queen Lush I, for one, will be heartily glad." I spoke harshly, emphasizing my words. "That will relieve me of an wanted burden."

Natyzha sneered at me, her lower lip upthrust like the beak of a swifter of The Eye of the World.

"And if they have brats? More Vallian princes and princesses? That will deprive you and your precious princess of the succession."

"As I say, it will be a relief."

"I do not believe you!" flared Ered Imlien, bluff, red-faced, and he bashed his riding crop down with a crack.

It would have been easy to have made some fierce declaration about men who spoke like that ending up with their guts hanging out; but I refrained. He was an onker who ran headlong on his own destruction. How he had lasted as long

81

as he had remained a mystery. And, truly, he was gnawed by fears for his estates.

"So you stand against the Queen of Lome?"

"Aye!"

"And, prince," pointed out Nalgre Sultant in his best offensive manner, "so should you be, too. We stood once before together against the Great Chyyan. I have no love for you. But enough though you are merely a wild clansman, you are now of Vallia. When Vallia is threatened we must all stand together."

And, of course, they believe this and it goes some way toward redeeming them, whatever their evil and however you may regard that devalued ideal of patriotism. They considered—no! They *knew* that they could rule Vallia better than anyone else. That being the case, anyone who opposed them stood against Vallia.

I stood up. "The deal we made still stands. I will assist you against the enemies of Vallia. I will make no move against the emperor and I will personally exterminate any of you who try to kill him or any of his family." With a small dismissive gesture I finished: "As for this Queen Lush—let her take her chances with the emperor. The old devil hasn't had much fun lately. And an alliance with a country of Pandahem is a good beginning—"

"That is traitorous talk!" burst out Imlien. "Pandahem, every country in the island, is our mortal enemy."

"You're a fool, Imlien. Hamal is our enemy. We must make allies of all the countries of Pandahem. And, one day, we will conclude a real treaty of friendship with Hamal, too."

They stared at me as though I had taken leave of my senses. What did they know of my greater plans for Paz? They would not understand, could not grasp the idea of all Paz as a single united grouping, standing against the savage Chanks from around the curve of the world. For these racters, Vallia must always stand supreme, ruling other countries, or warring with them.

Because Delia and I had bathed in the Sacred Pool of Baptism in far Aphrasöe, we were possessed of a thousand years of life, quite apart from being blessed with miraculous powers of self-healing. And the emperor had been bathed, also. He would outlive these schemers, he would remain emperor for a thousand years, he could afford to laugh at them and their plans.

All the same, he must take precautions. And knowledge of

those plans, information of the intrigues against him, would be essential.

I rubbed my chin, and turned back to face them, saying: "If you can speak plainly and without anger, Ered Imlien, tell me of the troubles you have around Thengelsax."

The gist of what he said, shorn of the expletives and the anger and the spluttering indignation, gave a picture of sudden and devastating raids by bands of riders from over the borders of the Northeast. This was crazy. All Vallia was part of the empire, ruled by the emperor, policed by his orders. But the movement for self-determination had flowered in the northeastern sections which were inhabited by peoples traditionally resentful of the authority imposed by the center and the south. That I could understand. What bothered me was the crass folly of people who wished to break the empire down into small units that could never, alone, stand against the hideous dangers of the future.

"Kovneva," I said, speaking in a deliberately thoughtful tone of voice. "In your opinion, does this threat from the Northeast constitute a real menace to the throne? Could they topple the emperor?"

She screwed up that clever, wizened, vicious old face.

"Yes and no. I do not think they could field an army that could break through to Vondium. But the troubles they cause can lead to such disorder that a strong and better-paced faction could seize the power. Up there they have great faith in their necromancers—"

"Necromancers? Of wizards and sorcerers, yes; but—"

"Necromancers I said, and devilish Opaz-forsaken corpse-revivers I mean!"

I digested that. Then: "And the strong and better-placed faction would be the racters?"

No one answered. The answer was writ plain on all their faces.

"Well, that is where we part company. I will stand against you for the emperor if needs must—"

"You fool! You destroy yourself! He hates you and will do nothing for you. Think again, Dray Prescot, Think of yourself and your family."

I did not answer that directly. I fancied it would too directly put a weapon into their hands.

"And the Panvals? The white and greens? Will they not strike for the power?"

They laughed their contempt. "The Panvals will fade away as salt dissolves in water when the racters strike."

83

"And the other factions? The Vondium Khanders? The Fegters who grow daily in strength? The Lornrod Caucus—"

"Them!" broke in Natyzha. "They are contemptible. Their only wish is to destroy everything, to pull down what has been painfully built over the centuries. No, we shall have no truck with them."

"As to the others," Nalgre Sultant amplified the kovneva's thoughts. "It is natural that accommodations and alliances will be formed. There are many small parties, formed for a particular reason, with whom we can work when the day to strike comes."

"And in that day you'll try to put your puppet on the throne of Vallia? You'll attempt to make some onker the emperor and then work him with your strings?"

They damn well knew I'd never be their puppet.

I was still smarting under the notion that I was the puppet of the Star Lords. I had been working on that, as you shall hear; but the idea aroused blind fury in me.

They did not say that since my interference they had lost a great deal of their power over the emperor and it rankled. They still held frightening powers; but these days the emperor could act with a greater freedom than ever he had before.

"If you directly oppose us, Dray Prescot, then you must take the consequences." Natyzha looked at me and then away, in that typical slanting look that so largely summed up the racter's way of influencing affairs of state. "You will probably find yourself dead and on the way to the Ice Floes of Sicce when we strike."

"But all legally, of course?"

"Oh, yes, prince. All legally."

So I bid them Remberee in an air of chilly hostility, tempered only by the understanding between us, and took myself off. I observed the fantamyrrh of The Sea Barynth Hooked as I went out, for the sake of Irvil the Flagon, the landlord. Then I went off to perform an errand and to uncover some more of the information I sought before leaving for the Northeast—and for an uncomfortable ride into the bargain.

Chapter Seven

News of Dayra

The place to which I took myself brought back vivid and happy memories, memories of a time that was, in truth, a happy one even though it was shot through with a deep anxiety for my Delia, and for others of my friends. Here we had roared out the old songs and planned what best to do about the dying emperor.

I went down to the Great Northern Cut and there, on the eastern bank, found that comfortable inn and posting house, The Rose of Valka. The landlord, the same Young Bargom, greeted me with genuine warmth and his delighted yells brought the household running. He wanted to know all the news and how we had fared in our voyage to save the emperor. Bargom, who was now grown a trifle grave with the years and his responsibilities, remained still the locus of feeling for exiled Valkans. Exiled no longer, of course; but Valkans who had business in the capital gravitated to The Rose of Valka like bees to honey.

If I dwell too long on my friends, and places that I am fond of, I think that natural. I'd far sooner think of and tell you of The Rose of Valka, and the good times we had there than speak of some of those places of horror into which I plunged on Kregen. But life being what it is, and Kregen being the splendid and terrible world it is, the dark and phantasmagoric times seem always to outweigh the lighter and carefree times. More's the pity.

They brought me through into that wide spacious room with the lights of Zim and Genodras flooding resplendently through the windows, where the flowers bloomed in their pots along the windowsill, and around me the happy sounds of a busy inn life tinkled merrily, and the superb smells of that divine Valkan cooking brought the saliva to my mouth. So I quaffed a few cups of unsurpassed Kregan tea and ate miscils and talked. No—I lie. I did not drink a few cups. I drank many cups.

At last, when my inquiries became more particular and

pressing, Bargom put his hands flat on his knees and stared directly at me. This subject had been glossed before. Now he pursed up his lips and looked judicial.

"Well, strom, it is like this, d'ye see. Yes, we have heard stories of the Princess Dayra. Nath ti Javvansmot, who runs The Speckled Gyp, told me what they did to his place. The fight they started smashed most of his windows, the best part of his crockery and a dozen amphorae, and the devils stove in two barrels of the best Gremivoh—begging your pardon, strom, but facts is facts."

"They started a fight and they laughed and left?"

"They laughed all right, strom. But they didn't leave until they'd had their bellyfull o' watching the fun. Fun!"

"Was Nath ti Javvansmot recompensed?"

"Oh, aye. Aye. The Princess Delia, may Opaz bless her and smile on her, paid up in full. Although——" And here Bargom scowled his heavy Valkan scowl. "Although 'twasn't entirely the Princess Dayra's doing, not her fault altogether, for she was egged on. I'm sure of that."

"And since then?"

"Nary a sight nor sound of her, strom. Nothing."

Well, no need for me to feel disappointment. If the reports were true, Dayra was up in the Northeast, somewhere to the north of Tarkwa-fash.

"And the name of the man she was with?"

Here Bargom looked at the floor, and twiddled the strings of his red and white apron, which bore the bright stains of wine here and there, and then he looked at the flick-flick plant on the windowsill which was just in the act of transferring a half-starved fly from one suckered and sticky tendril down its orange gullet. Flies found little dirt to feed on in The Rose of Valka.

"Come, Bargom. You and I are old comrades. Have no fear of offending me. I know Dayra is mixed up with a scoundrel."

"He's a scoundrel, well and true. And there is a gang of 'em—a dozen, at the least. But who is this scoundrel? Now there you may as well ask Poperlin the Wise! He calls himself any number of names, and not one of them his. Some say he's the illegitimate son of a high noble, others that he's a fisherman from the islands who stole a purse and bought himself an education beyond his real capacity. Others say he's a paktun, probably a hyr-paktun who may wear the pakzhan, who is living high on the vosk of his ill-gotten gains. Others—"

"Aye. Aye, I hear. You have not seen him? You can give me no description? No name, one name, at the least, with which I may begin inquiries?"

Bargon frowned and scratched his ear. "I did hear Nath say that his cronies called him Zankov*."

"Zankov. Now that is a strange name, indeed. Who are the other nine?"

"Why, strom! There aren't any, to be sure."

"Yes. It is only a use name. But it is a handle to begin with."

Now there was little time for more of the pleasant talk about the old days and of the beauty of Valka, and so I patted the heads of his smaller sons and daughters and gave them a gold talen each, and then I stood up and stretched and said: "I must be off, good Bargom. I thank you for your hospitality and your news. Zankov. I shall remember that."

They were disappointed that I would leave so soon; but the whole household waved and many were the shouted "Remberees!"

Bargom yelled after me: "And, strom, I wouldn't put too much store by Zankov. It's probably Naghan na Sicce by now!"

This was a great joke, if a standard one, as you who have followed my story will understand. Naghan is almost as common a name on Kregen as Nath, and Sicce; well, we all get shipped out to the Ice Floes of Sicce when our time is up on this mortal coil.

As my steps took me out of the gateway of the yard where a team had just been unhitched from a posting carriage and the passengers were alighting, ready to resume their journey on the Great Northern Cut, rejoicing that they would have a far easier passage on the canals, I reflected that Bargom had throughout called me strom. We had been in private. With other high nobles in attendance he would have sprinkled in at least a few princes and majisters. I would not call his attention to this, nor even think of venturing to correct him. Plenty of Valkans call me strom to this day. There is far more to it than simple forgetfulness. Often, I think—and thought then with greater cause—they were jealous that their strom was some prince of Vallia, as though that removed him a trifle from their loyal protection and special relationship.

A quick, a very quick, trip to speak to Nath ti Javvansmot at The Speckled Gyp yielded no new information save the

* Zan: Ten. Kov: Duke. Zankov: the Tenth Duke.

man who dubbed himself Zankov was a right slender spark, with dark hair, and merry eyes—"Brown Vallian eyes, prince. But, I swear, when he laughed, they went so dark as to be black. Odd." Thus Nath ti Javvansmot.

Thanking him, I mounted up again on Shadow and trotted smartly back to the palace. As ever, my weather eye rolled leeward and windward; but I fancied my dealings with the stikitches had borne fruit.

Although Kregans can tell the time to remarkable limits of accuracy by the positions of the suns or the moons, and many kinds of mensuration devices are known and used, truth to tell, I fancy, most Kregans tell the time by the state of their insides. Good square meals dominate the time-structure of Kregen. And, provided all get enough, who is to say this is not an admirable system? The trouble is, there are many who do not have enough, many who starve, many slaves who subsist miserably. These evils Delia and I had vowed to remove from the fair land of Paz, and, if the gods smiled, to eradicate entirely from all of Kregen.

But that objective—that dream—lay decades in the future.

Decades! Well, I was still, despite the length of time I had lived, still a comparatively young man then, and I was naive, hurtfully naive. . . .

So I knew the twin suns were telling me that my interior clock was true; I went roaring into the palace and toward the stairway that led to our private wing. The palace is enormous and convoluted, as I have said, and to save time I slid through a cross corridor that would chop off a whole section of the ornate courtyards. The Crimson Bowmen of Loh stood guard, where they were accustomed to stand, and of the Chulik mercenaries only a few were left. Their proud dark eyes looked alertly about, their sharp fox-like faces with the bristling whiskers reminding me that they were a race of diffs well-thought of as mercenaries. Their Hikdar was a paktun, the silver mortil head, the pakmort, looped on its silken cord over the shoulder of his corselet.

These were newly hired mercenaries. Kov Layco Jhansi, the emperor's Chief Pallan, had been busy.

A Crimson Bowman standing beside a tall balass door with silver chavonth heads adorning the bosses recognized me and stamped to rigid attention, his three-grained staff flashing into the salute. He was Log Logashtorio.

Seeing the old professional salute me, the Khibil paktun bellowed an "eyes right" and brought his sword into the salute.

I was hungry. But these niceties of military protocol are overlooked at one's peril. But it was no venal thought of that kind that made me return the salute with all punctilio.

I called out to the Hikdar as we passed: "A smart turnout, Hikdar. Congratulate your men for me, please. I welcome you to Vondium."

He was a waso-Hikdar, that is, he had climbed five rungs up the rank structure within the rank of Hikdar, which is, I suppose, nearly an equivalent to an Earthly captain, in that he commands a pastang, or company, usually of eighty or so men.

Going rapidly on I gave a half-turn to look back and saw the Hikdar speaking to Log Logashtorio. So he was finding out who I was. That was all a part of the duties he and his men must perform here. Being hired by the Emperor of Vallia to serve in the imperial palace was a plum job.

A parcel of slaves, all wearing the gray slave breechclout with red and yellow armbands, went past carrying an Azdon which they treated with all the care and frightened anxiety such a precious object always demanded. Past them I hurried, with a respectful salute from the Chulik matoc in charge of them. His tusks thrust up from the corner of his mouth, and he'd savage any poor damned slave who caused the slightest trouble.

A Relt stylor hurried past, his scrip bulging with ink and pens, his robe stained with blobs and spatters of ink. Everyone hurried in the palace. There was always a toing and a froing. I made my way along past the Chemzite doors and saw one of the emperor's Lesser Chamberlains scurrying toward me.

He looked puffed and immensely relieved, and he shook with the release of some pressing fear.

"Majister! The emperor has been calling for you these last two burs! He awaits you in the Sapphire Reception Room. Majister! We must hurry."

I try to be polite to these fussy, pompous little fellows; for they have been made as they are. His red and yellow robes with the silver embroidery fluttered as he waved his arms, his balass, silver-banded rod of office almost hitting me on the nose.

Having studied a deal of the palace architecture when I'd first taken up residence here, I had a fair idea where the Sapphire Reception Room was. I glowered at the little chamberlain whereat his knees knocked. It was in my mind to tell him to say he hadn't found me—him or his fellows who would be out looking—and bash on to my apartments, for I was sharp set. But that would only prolong whatever lay in store.

"I am hungry," I said. "Is there any food there?"

"Yes, Majister. A spread buffet—and the Princess Majestrix, upon whom Opaz shine the light of his countenance, also awaits you there, Majister."

That settled it.

So I followed the gaudily-clad Lesser Chamberlain to the Sapphire Reception Room, more interested in the spread food than in what my father-in-law wanted.

The Reception Room had been decorated out in colors that were predominantly green. Well, I have no need to elaborate my ambivalent attitude to that color. Long tables were spread with food. I barged in through the door. People stood about in groups, talking, eating and drinking, laughing. It was a proper reception. The air smelled sweet with perfumes and, best of all, with the appetizing aromas of exquisite food.

Four clowns in gaudy uniforms at the door slapped long silver trumpets to their mouths and blew blasts that nearly took my ears off. The major domo in his fantastical rig of red and yellow, silver and gold, burnished, awash with feathers and lace, bellowed in a voice that would have stood a trick on the quarterdeck of a seventy-four off Biscay.

"The Hyr Jikai, Dray Prescot, Prince Majister of Vallia."

He knew everyone and bellowed their styles as they came in. I gave him a dirty look, and rubbed my ear, and then headed straight for the food. Bargom's cook's tea and cakes had merely sharpened up my appetite.

This scene presented the refined, polite, society face of Kregen. Men and women in their early-evening attire stood about, daintily sipping and nibbling. The conversation was light and frivolous, and yet, here and there, serious talking went on as people disposed of Vallia's wealth and slaves and mines and ships. Politics was never a taboo subject here, either. A knot of people, somewhat larger than the others, contained the emperor. His leonine head towered, massive, purposeful, and he threw that powerful head back, laughing.

Well, let the old devil have a good time. He'd been at death's door until Delia had carried him into the Sacred Pool. He did not see me and, as I could not spot Delia, and the food beckoned, I strode across to the tables.

He must have heard the trumpets and the major domo's bellow. He must have thought I'd go straight up to him and be introduced. Well, maybe I would have done had I known the purpose of the reception.

There was no time for shilly-shallying around with a tiny plate and a few miscils, a few thin sandwiches, canapes, a spot of yasticum on the superb Kregan bread; I went for the real stuff. I piled the largest plate I could find with food. I stacked the biggest cup of tea available on the plate. Slaves hopped here and there trying to help people with silver trays of goodies; I brushed them away and got on with the job of loading the plate. Truth to tell; it was all light frothy stuff with not a solid mouthful all along the long table. The slaves wore white instead of slave gray, for they were privileged to wait on their masters here. I had to ignore them. The idea of slavery could always put me off my food, and I was sharp set. Come the day, I said to myself, and not the day which those damned racters dreamed, either. . . .

So, wearing still the buff suit in which I had traipsed over Vondium, my hat hanging by its string down my back, girded with weapons, a monstrous plate of food in my hand, and a cup—it was a basin, really—of tea to hand, I sauntered across.

The crowd around the emperor saw me and they eased back, moving away to let me through. The crowd was not so much congregated around the emperor as around the woman with whom he was having a delightful conversation, that kept making him roar with laughter and brought his color up brilliantly.

She saw me as I saw her.

Well.

The emperor half-turned to glare at me.

The woman started to laugh, a low malicious, velvety laugh that put my teeth on edge.

Delia was suddenly at my side.

The woman laughed her malicious laugh. "At least, you are not still running, prince. And the air smells quite sweet."

I said nothing, half choking on a piece of squish pie.

"You are late, son-in-law!" boomed the emperor. "You have been asked here to have the high honor of being introduced to the Hyr Serenity, Queen Lushfymi, the Queen of Lome."

I got the piece of pie down. I gulped.

I swung a fishy eye on Delia.

"You knew."

"I knew."

By Zim-Zair, but they breed princesses that are princesses in Vallia!

Chapter Eight

Queen Lushfymi of Lome

For my own part I would have liked to have taken myself off to our own apartments in the palace and indulged in a long wallow in the Baths of the Nine. Then I could do justice to a six or seven course meal—a light meal, that, by Kregan standards—and see about preparing for the coming journey.

But protocol demanded otherwise.

The scene hung sparks for a moment, as Delia's smile ravished me, and the violet-eyed woman, Queen Lushfymi—whom I would not call Queen Lush just for the moment—sipped daintily at her Yellow Unction and eyed me mockingly over the crystal rim of the goblet.

In some traditions it would be in order for me to say to you words after the fashion of: "And now I draw a veil over what followed," and then go on to tell you of what befell me on that Opaz-forsaken trip to the Northeast.

There are many events of my life upon Kregen I have not related, for one reason or another, many people I knew who have not figured in my narrative, and much, very much, of the customs and mores, the color and pageantry, the religions and the metaphysical aspects of that marvelous world I have omitted. But things were said here that proved of some importance later on.

The emperor wanted to know, by Vox, what the hell I meant by not being on time and why was I late.

I indicated my clothes and said that if he'd told me the Queen was to be met in this unoffical reception I would have been pleased to attend in proper style. For these kind of early evening functions, that are styled unofficial—as, indeed, in comparison with the stiff formality of public functions they truly are—people wear clothes that are relaxed and yet formal. Long gowns of bright dark hues, much gold lace, a modicum of decorated collar, the nikmazilla, and a dress sword or dagger complete a costume that is half-formal, half-lounging, relaxed and proper, really quite charming.

The emperor looked pointedly at my rapier and at the longsword.

"You are trusted by the guards now, and Kov Layco has vouched for you. I do not forget Ashti Melekhi."

A white-clad slave girl wearing a tall yellow and red mitred headdress—so she could easily be seen in a crowd—went past with a silver tray and I used my free hand to liberate a glass of Wenhart Purple, the emperor's favorite wine. I sipped. After I had taken just enough time to get the old devil in a mood, I said cheerfully: "The Melekhi is dead, slain by Kov Layco here." The Chief Pallan stood watchfully at the emperor's side, fingering his golden chain of office. "I leave you to remember how her friends died."

"All this talk of death," broke in Queen Lushfymi. She turned her violet eyes to the emperor in a long, languishing look. "Let us talk of happier things."

"Yet is death always with us," said Kolo York, the Vad of Larravur, a powerful, spare man with a lined wedge of a face. He wore a tastefully executed diamond brooch in the form of a krahnik. He was, so I understood, loyal to the emperor.

"The queen's commands are to be obeyed instantly!" exclaimed the emperor. He beamed. He was beside himself with pleasure in the company of this woman.

Well, I was forced to admit then, and see no reason to change that opinion, she was indeed splendid. Her full creamy throat, the brightness of her lips, her mass of dark hair and those great violet eyes, all were calculated to dizzy a man. Her deep-blue gown, relieved by green and white embroidery, stood out sharply in that Vallian gathering where blue is a rare color. She wore, I thought, rather too much jewelry. But she radiated charm and a dominating sense of womanliness, a mystery of perfectly controlled sexual allure. And, at the same time, I, for one, sensed in her a hidden and deviously repressed spirit, as though her outward form and the brilliance of her person and character concealed depths of feelings and emotions she would reveal reluctantly and at peril to those who inquired too diligently.

She took every opportunity to mock me with our first meeting, privately, between ourselves, malicious and bright and derisive.

She took pains not to stand too close to Delia.

She kept close to the emperor, laughing up at him, sipping her wine, nibbling miscils and daintily chewing palines. Why she did this was perfectly plain to me.

93

This Queen Lushfymi carried the reputation of being the most beautiful of women, mysterious, almost witchlike in the best sense, ruling her country and bringing fantastic wealth and prosperity. She was fabulously wealthy.

But beside my Delia she glowed as a candle glows in the radiance of the suns.

Delia wore one of her long laypom colored gowns, a pale yellow so delicate as almost to be platinum, and her brown hair with those rebellious chestnut tints shone magnificently. Her only jewelry, two small brooches, one in the form of a red rose and the other the spoked hubless wheel I had given her, eloquently destroyed the jeweled opulence of Queen Lush.

But, of course, Delia merely dressed naturally; it was through no fault of hers that other women faded into insignificance beside her. And, to be fair, Queen Lush was a beauty.

The talk wended on. There were even a few tentative feelers about the pact to be drawn up between Vallia and Lome. I spoke in favor. There was resistance to the idea from many of the nobles there. Of the racters I knew, only Nath Ulverswan, Kov of the Singing Forests, was present, and his black and white favor looked lonely and forlorn.

Queen Lush would get no real grasp of the true feelings in Vallia, then. . . .

I fancied she would have her spies busy, and was shrewd enough by all accounts to take the pulse of the empire.

Vad Kolo nal Larravur took the emperor's remark about the commands of the queen as a personal rebuke. He withdrew a little, his face shadowed. I kept the frown off my face. If the emperor could so thoughtlessly upset his own people, he would make himself even more isolated.

Vad Kolo's daughter took his arm and spoke quickly, softly, in his ear. He scowled a bit, and then edged himself back into the group around the queen, forcing a smile.

This daughter—she had some courtesy title, of course—was lithe, well-formed, glowing of face, open of countenance. She wore a dark yellow gown with silver lacing, and a long thin poniard of typical Vallian manufacture swung at her girdle. This was Leona nal Larravur. On the left shoulder of the gown she wore a brooch fashioned from ronil gems into the likeness of a purple bush, with a green emerald stem. By this device I knew Leona nal Larravur was a member of the Order of Sisters of Samphron.

One of the ronils was missing, the one on the extreme tip

94

of the bush-brooch. It was unlikely that the brooch for so meaningful a symbol was of Krasny work—inferior—nor was it likely that the stone would be knocked out by an ordinary accidental dropping of the brooch, even on the hardest of stone.

The gold mounting had been painted over purple.

A small vertical frown kept dinting in between Leona nal Larravur's eyebrows, then she would force a smile, and the skin would smooth out and those two worrying lines disappear.

The conversation became more animated as less tea was drunk and more wine flowed.

The emperor's huge bark of laughter crashed out with more and more frequency. Colors in cheeks heightened. Eyes grew warm. I looked across at Delia. It was time we departed.

Now, I did not then hear the words spoken, nor was I a witness to the entire scene. But voices around the queen were raised. The tones were still polite; but the venom was unmistakable. A hush fell over the rest of the Reception Room. Everyone looked and listened.

The queen's color was up. Her violet eyes were flying danger signals. The emperor was furious. His bulky body towered over the small, slight form of Foke Lyrsmin. Old Foke quivered, staring up, his elegant dark clothes shaking. A small, cheerful, wiry fellow, Foke Lyrsmin, the Kov of Vyborg. We had had a right old time of it at the uncompleted wedding ceremony he'd planned with Merle, the daughter of Trylon Jefan Werden.* The Lady of Vallia he had subsequently married was enchanting; she stood at his side, her face scarlet, her lips trembling. Their two strapping sons and two delightful daughters hesitated, as it were, on the edges of this ghastly scene.

". . . and I don't care what it is you meant to say, Kov Foke! You call yourself my friend." The emperor's voice boomed, rich and heavy, and everyone heard. "I do not account those as friends who insult Queen Lushfymi."

"Majister—I did not insult—"

"I heard, Lyrsmin! I am not deaf! Be thankful I do not order your head off this instant."

At this the Kovneva of Vyborg let out a little squeak of pure agony.

* See: *Wizard of Scorpio*.

95

Her two stalwart sons held her arms, supporting her. How Old Foke had managed to get them was a mystery.

"But, majister—"

"Begone, Foke Lyrsmin!"

"But—"

"*Shastum**! Not another word. Go! Leave my presence."

Poor Old Foke looked shattered. His thin body writhed in the elegant gown. He turned about, and his teeth chattered.

"And, Foke na Vyborg—I shall expect a written apology to be transmitted to the Queen of Lome, together with a gift of quality sufficient to show your sorrow and regrets and your wholehearted desire to make amends for your disgusting behavior."

Foke couldn't say another word. The emperor had commanded that. He trailed away. His delightful wife followed, helped out by the twin sons, and the twin daughters tripped along afterward, like naughty schoolchildren chastised and sent to bed. The colors of Vyborg, maroon and silver, looked pathetic as they left.

The Reception Room filled again with conversation as people started talking away. Scenes like this were no longer as common as they once had been. Delia caught my eye. I nodded sideways. We started to make for the doors.

If there can be said, at that time, to have been a party in a political sense around the emperor, then Foke was certainly a member. I suppose the people near him might be called the Imperial Party. They had nothing like the organization or the power of the racters. But they were men loyal to the throne.

"Poor Foke," said Delia.

"He looked shattered. Did you see what it was?"

"No. But Queen Lush was most put out."

"Oh no, my heart." We had reached the doors and the gaudily uniformed flunkeys were opening up again after the doors had been closed after the Vyborgs. "Oh, no. Old Foke was the one who was put out."

---

* Shastum! Silence.

Chapter Nine

Into Hawkwa Country

"Now," I said to Delia when all the preparations were complete. "This water bottle."

"I see it, my love."

We had gone up to our Valkan villa, which was still not fully brought back to habitability, despite the length of time that had elapsed since I'd acquired it by virtue of being made the Strom of Valka behind my back. But there were apartments enough beautifully furnished to make it a real home.

Nalgre the Staff was the current Chamberlain, a stout fellow and one I would trust. We kept no slaves. The villa was set somewhat back from the road, bowered in greenery, presenting an outward appearance of decay and neglect. I did not object to that. Further along on the Hill—the Valkan villa was situated on the Hill of Vel'alar—the villas of the nobles presented all the munificence of aspect expected of the rich and mighty of the empire.

"This water bottle." I hefted it. Plain leather, scuffed, worn, it was a scruffy-looking object. "We must keep it safely locked away in the stoutest iron chest."

Delia nodded understandingly. After I had mended my hurts in the Sacred Pool of Baptism I had filled this water bottle with the milky fluid that conferred life. My return from the island of Ba-Domek on which stands the Swinging City of Aphrasöe had been rushed with the help of my Djangs; but I had managed to bring back my weapons, that superb zorca Shadow, and this water bottle.

"It will be safe here." Delia placed the bottle in humespack, wrapping the cloth over it, and then wadding down household linen so that the iron chest almost overflowed. We closed the lid and sat companionably upon it and did up the locks. They can make fine chests in Vallia, for they have much gold and silver, jewels and precious objects to preserve.

The four keys and the master key were secreted away in a brick hole concealed within the wall of our bedroom. No picture covered that lenken paneling there; the wood had been carpentered to a close fit by men long since dead. I had found that small hiding place only by chance, and regretted it was not large enough to accommodate the water bottle itself.

As we went up to the landing platform I said to Delia: "We keep up five villas here besides the quarters in the palace. It might be a good idea to sell one or two."

She cocked her head at me. The night air breathed sweet about us. She of the Veils rode through a tracery of clouds. The landing platform was dusty, and dead leaves blew with brittle rustlings into the corners. We had slept enough to feel refreshed. I was sorry that Delia could not fly with me; but she was adamant. The Sisters of the Rose had to be attended to first.

"You may, my great grizzly graint. But I do not think I shall sell the Delphondian villa—"

"Of course not!" That was a superb, a delightful, a magical home.

"And the Blue Mountains—"

"No."

"So, as you have an affection for this place, that leaves the villas of Zamra and Veliadrin."

"Um," I said, throwing off the restraining chains on the flier I was using. "You are thinking of the children? They will need villas?"

"Perhaps."

I climbed in and Delia climbed in after. She looked at me gravely. The flier was a small two-place craft, trim, reasonably fast, and one I hoped would sustain me in the air. We must think about buying some more vollers for the villas we kept up at different places; one never knew when a fleet airboat would be required in a hurry. As you know, I had been in that kind of need before and was like to be again, Zair knows.

She kissed me good-bye. I said "Remberee" with a deal of anger; but this was a case of having to accept the needle.

When Delia stood once more on the dusty, refuse-blowing landing platform I looked down and waved, and shouted: "Remberee, my heart!" and took the voller up in a savage lunge of power.

The Twins broke through a carpet of clouds and the two second moons of Kregen, eternally orbiting each other, cast down their fuzzy pink light. She of the Veils, the fourth moon, rolled along before them.

So, once more, I, Dray Prescot, Lord of Strombor and

Krozair of Zy, raced through the nighted skies of Kregen, under the hurtling moons, driving headlong forward to action and adventure.

The thought of seeing Barty again cheered me up. He was to meet me in Thengelsax. Sax means fort, and many of the towns and cities along the arc of the old frontiers of central northeast Vallia grew up from the ancient fortifications raised against the barbarian reivers. There are plenty of other words for castle, fortress, fort, Kregish being a rich language; but one thing they all share in common: they refer to serious concerns, matters of building pride and cunning military fortification. The sprawling cities that festoon the old walls would give heart palpitations to those ancient builders. And this, as you will perceive, was the nub of the affair. For Vallia was a great and puissant empire. There should not be, under the law, conflict within the boundaries of the empire between province and province.

The emperor would be better advised seeking ways of settling these troubles instead of running after beautiful bitch-queens.

But then, he was a man. And Queen Lush was a woman—that was blatantly obvious. If she occupied his attention perhaps I could get on with my own affairs. At least, he had not made too particular inquiries about his grandchildren. I had to hoick Dayra out of the mess she was in and straighten her out before the emperor decided to take a hand.

And, again, that implied that I knew best for my daughter. That I was totally unsure must be obvious. But I thought, at the least, that smashing up taverns and raiding with a bunch of hairy reivers against innocent citizens of Vallia were not occupations she could in all honesty claim as morally defensible. Mind you, by Krun! She could easily have some explanation that would make me change my mind.

The Suns of Scorpio flooded down their mingled streaming lights of jade and ruby as I circled once over Thengelsax and slanted in for a landing outside the designated inn. The city presented the expected appearance of a well-ordered city of Vallia. Clean, neat, prosperous, situated where the River Emerade flows into the Great River, the city looked justly proud of itself.

As an interesting light upon the importance of those old fortifications, the Trylon took the name of Thengelsax, from the city, and not that of Thengel, from the trylonate.

Barty met me as the airboat touched down and the hostlers ran out to see to her. He looked excited and I felt a welling of hope that he had discovered some vital clue to the where-abouts of Dayra.

My hopes were dashed. As we went into the inn and post-ing house, The Hanged Leemshead, Barty started on cussing about the Strom of Vilandeul. He windmilled his arms and when we had pots of ale before us he sloshed suds about, scarlet-faced, almost incoherent, and yet, in the end, making lucid sense and betraying the very real depths of his affection for Dayra.

"That Nath Typhohan!" he raved. "I know him! I've wrestled him, and thrown him, and fenced with him and pinked him. Now he's the Strom of Vilandeul he has the ef-frontery to lay claim to the most beautiful land of my island! He wants the Shadow Forests of Calimbrev! I ask you!"

I nodded. "I had trouble with his father. Well—" I said, uncomfortably. "Not me. My son Drak and Tom Tomor. I was away at the time. The Strom of Vilandeul laid claim to parts of Veliadrin, west of the Varamin Mountains."

"The trouble is Nath's stromnate of Vilandeul is small and is penned in by powerful kovnates. He is land hungry."

"You can understand that."

"We must stick together, pri—Jak. If it comes to it, we'll have to hire mercenaries and go up against him. No damned Typhohan is going to steal my land from me, by Vox!"

Mildly, I said: "In Valka we have our own army. And I would heartily dislike having to fight Vallians. We threw the aragorn and the slavers out. Don't they trouble you?"

"A little. They take a few slaves from me. Nothing I can't live with."

My mildness vanished. "If you entertain any notions of marrying Dayra, I fancy you will have to manumit your slaves. The whole lot. And I will help you deal with the slav-ers."

He blinked.

Even so good-hearted a fellow as Barty could not really understand my attitude about slaves. Had not Opaz made slaves for other men to use? Of course he had. Therefore a good citizen of Vallia must employ what Opaz had put into his hands.

This must be pursued later. I said in my harsh old voice: "What have you discovered about Dayra?"

"I have spoken to the landlord. She was seen with a ras-cally gang of Hawkwas hiring zorcas and riding northeast."

Hawkwa was the contemptuous name given in hatred and fear by the civilized people of Vallia in the old days to the reivers from the Northeast, and in turn used by the barbarians in boastful pride and reciprocal contempt.

"Also, I have hired a guide."

Well, I could not complain. Barty had done well. In the time I had been making inquiries in Vondium and hobnobbing with the emperor he had been hard at work here. I warmed to him. He must cherish genuine feelings for my daughter, for he had not gone rushing back to his island to fend off the predatory demands of Nath Typhohan, the Strom of Vilandeul. Well, I would help him there, for his island lay close to Veliadrin. And the Elten of Avanar, Tom Tomor, had given the old Strom of Vilandeul a salutary lesson over land-grabbing.

"We will not ride," I said with a snap. "We will take your flier, seeing she has space for a dozen or more and the zorcas. My two-seat craft will be useless. The guide you have found—"

"Uthnior Chavonthjid. A hunter with a fine reputation. And expensive, by Vox."

"Well, this Uthnior will have to get used to airboats if he is not already familiar with them. We have no time to lose."

Transferring the gear I had brought to Barty's flier did not take long, despite the mountains of stuff Delia always insisted I take along with me on these expeditions. More often than not I lost most of it, and returned draggle-tailed and almost empty-handed. Weapons, food and—well, little else, really, on Kregen, apart from necessary clothing against the weather—are all that are required.

Of food we had wicker hampers piled up. Of weapons we took the usual Kregen arsenal.

Uthnior Chavonthjid turned out to be the picture of a leem hunter, lean, rangy, broad-shouldered, with that weather-beaten face that conveys an ample sense of experience and wide horizons.

His history contained nothing out of the usual, save for the incident that claimed for him the coveted jid appended to the animal he had slain bare-handed, or the danger he had overcome. The chavonth is a feral big cat, savage and tirelessly vindictive. Uthnior had met and bested one, breaking its back. The word jid is seldom used alone, which is why I always use bane—as, for instance, in the Bane of Grodno. I felt confident that Uthnior Chavonthjid would prove a fine, tough guide for us. As to his reliability, that remained to be weighed in the balance.

As we flew at the sedate speed of Barty's capacious flier

toward the Kwan Hills, in which rises the River Emerade, some forty dwaburs or so from Thengelsax, I was once more forcibly struck by the incongruity of having to hire a guide to any part of Vallia. But the truth remained—and, alas, still remains—that some parts of Vallia are barbaric and untamed still.

You may recall the Ochre Limits. There nature set the obstacles in the path. Here, the Kwan Hills, densely forested, alive with game, untracked and mysterious, were the haunts of the drikingers, the reivers, the hawkwas, who set the limits to strangers.

Uthnior, to my surprise, had refused to take zorcas.

"Koter Jakhan," he said in his grave manner. "Where we are going the totrix is the mount for us."

Only a half-mur's pondering convinced me I must heed the specialist knowledge of the man on the spot. Nath Dangorn, called Totrix, would have chuckled. But he along with the rest of the newly created Order of Kroveres of Iztar, was far away. This was a family matter, and Barty had his rights in it, also. So we took six totrixes in the rigged-up stalls in the rear of Barty's flier, and the awkward, stubborn, six-legged riding animals did not take kindly to being thus hurled helplessly through thin air.

We touched down at the edge of a wood well clear of the outskirts of the town of Tarkwa-fash. From here, with the blue haze of the Kwan Hills beckoning us on, we would ride. The voller was hidden in the trees with cut branches piled upon her. Uthnior eyed the mass of weapons and gear. Then he looked at Barty and me with a wary, reflective glance that was instantly appreciated by me, at least, although Barty soon understood.

Uthnior himself slung his personal gear on his baggage totrix. All six were provided with the riding saddle of this part of Kregen, a tall, broad, comfortable seat. Uthnior buckled on his crossbow with care, strapping the quivers of bolts alongside, checking the swing of the three swords and the variety of polearms he carried. His provision bags went the other side. Barty pulled his lower lip.

"You have brought a mighty fine array of weaponry, Jak. Tell me, Uthnior, what is it best for us to take?"

I did not fail to notice that the guide carried a short but powerful bow, a compound reflex weapon of considerable beauty and precision, over his shoulder. The quiverful of arrows to match were fletched with a neutral greeny-browny set of feathers. But the steel heads were all wide, keen, wedge-shaped flesh-cutters, with vicious barbs. This bow, it was clear, was his personal close-range missile weapon. The crossbow was for the fancy shooting.

Uthnior looked at my Lohvian longbow. The quiverful of arrows were fletched with the brilliant blue plumage of the crested korf of the Blue Mountains. As to the piles, they were my usual mix, different heads for different tasks. "That is a bow from Loh, I think," he said. "A longbow?"

"Aye. You have seen one before?"

His reply astonished me although it should not have.

"No. Never."

This showed yet again the sheer size of the island of Vallia. Away up here the hunters used crossbows or the reflex bow. The longbow was virtually unknown. And yet, the weird thing was, if I took a flier and flew due east for eighty or so dwaburs I would arrive in the island of Zamra. Most odd. Of course, the heartlands of the Northeast lay farther to the north, mainly around the Stackwamors, which was why the reivers had full rein down here.

"We must shoot a match, Chavonthjid, when opportunity offers."

"I would welcome that. Although I fancy this longbow of yours clumsy to handle."

Not prepared to get into an argument over that—what he said was true for one unskilled in the use of the supreme Lohvian longbow—I urged us to complete our preparations and to mount up and ride. We wanted to get into the foothills before nightfall.

In the end I stuck to my usual custom and took my accustomed arsenal. Barty hewed to the middle path and selected a mix of weapons that made Uthnior merely smile, rather than frown, and we set off. Uthnior, it turned out, had a grandmother from the Northeast. He was at home here. If I give the impression that for a Southern Vallian to venture into these parts was like trespassing into enemy territory, then I give a false impression. We were still in Vallia and the emperor's writ still ran here, albeit very often evaded or downright ignored. These people paid taxes to the Presidio and emperor in Vondium. They were Vallians and proud of it—if they could be Northeastern Vallians. It was the agitators who fomented unrest, hanging their banditry on the respectable peg of self-determination—or so I was led to believe. I thought them wrong. But, equally, I know that big does not equal best, and small can, indeed, be charmingly beautiful.

There is an old saying that has its echo on Kregen—A good big 'un will beat a good little 'un.

I looked always to the future, past the time when Vallia would have come to an arrangement with the countries of Pandahem, and achieved peace with Hamal—and I hoped without having to thrash them in a long and costly war—and brought in the whole fantastic continent of Havilfar. When the groupings of islands and continents called Paz were truly one—then we could deal with the Chanks.

We would have to deal with the devils from over the curve of the world before then, of course, dolefully so, as best we could.

We broke in among the foothills of the Kwan Range and we made camp in a secluded gulley with water and fodder to hand. We had seen not a soul. The game abounded, and regarded us rather in the light of trespassers, evidence of the infrequency of human intrusion.

In the course of a regular season Uthnior would guide just the one hunting party, and there were other hunters each with his own patch; he had been free to take employment with Barty because his hunting party had called it off over the recrudescence of the border troubles. He'd never married, seemingly preferring the open freedom of the hunter's life. His home was where he happened to be. He appeared to me a competent, grave, inwardly content man, with a deep understanding and love for the strange ways of nature upon Kregen.

As was becoming increasingly my habit these days when I met fresh acquaintances I studied this hunter with the Kroveres of Iztar in mind. Would he or would he not be found worthy to be admitted to the Order? Already I had been impressed by his manner. As for Barty, that young man for all his virtues had some way to go yet before the Order would consider him.

We pressed on again while the golden and pink moonlight gave us illumination, She of the Veils and the Twins lighting the way through the broken country. Ever upward we trended. The six-legged totrixes were an uncomfortable ride; but I am used to their waywardnesses and, deprived of a zorca, made the best of them.

We traveled for the rest of the night and as the last small hurtling moon vanished in the haze off to our left Uthnior indicated we should make camp again.

The fire we built was small, compact, shielded by a rocky overhang. When full daylight came we doused it and sat, resting, looking about as the light brightened. Barty could not rest for long.

"Can we not push on, Uthnior?"

The guide pulled a grass stem from the corner of his mouth.

"You hired me to guide you to the camp of the Hawkwas. I know the area they frequent—and avoid it. In general terms I can take you straight there. You will be observed closely over the last dwabur or so."

Listening quietly to him I made no comment; but I guessed accurately what he would say next.

"Complete directions can be given you. I will be happy to do that. But you must go on by yourselves at the end. I shall wait three days for you. No more."

Chapter Ten

Of the Pride of a Rapa Paktun

The mizzle of rain eased and a wan grayish daylight seeped through the massed clouds. Hillsides, woods, bushes, open swards dripped water. Barty swung off his hooded cape and the water sprayed. The totrixes ambled along in that skewed six-legged gait. Uthnior slid his cape off expertly and let the water drain off into the grass.

Gray clouds hung about the mountains. The pass ahead glinted with a waterfall's sudden silver.

"Five burs ride beyond the pass," said the guide, pointing. "Then I leave you to go on. There is a cave. Three days I shall wait. After that—"

"You needn't go on!" exclaimed Barty. "If we don't come back in three days we'll be dead. I know."

Uthnior had little experience of airboats, for his hunter clients liked to get into the saddle as soon as possible, and at the time I took at face value his assertion that fliers would be useless in the maze of valleys and gullies and hilly peaks around us. The Kwan Hills were no place to crash in, that was certain. Our six-legged mounts ambled along and the twin suns struggled to pierce the thick cloud layer above.

That pass ahead, with its thread of silver, the dark sodden

slopes on either hand, the cavernous bellies of the low-lying clouds above—my fingers began to twitch. *Fingerspitzengefuhl*. Yes, the Germans had the word for it, the twitch in the finger tips. The old breeze up the spine. I rolled my eyes about, looking up the slopes, seeing clumps of vegetation dripping with moisture, vague pale blurs of wan sunshine trying to strike glints from the drops and producing glimmering pearls.

"Here they come!" I bellowed and ripped out the longbow.

They bounded down the slopes screeching like demons, leaping from tussock to tussock, waving their weapons, ragged bands of men and women, their armor and harness dun-earth in color and wet, wet with the wet ground on which they had lain in ambush.

"Hawkwas!" yelled Uthnior, and his bow was in his hand.

Reflex compound bow and Lohvian longbow spat as one.

Barty's bow slapped out a little later, as the hunter and I loosed again.

In this kind of sudden fierce attack as fighting men and women roar at you, screeching, aiming to top you, you have to assume that, have to understand they are hostile and react to that, and not hang about wondering if this is merely a too-enthusiastic welcome. We shot to stop the attack. Men screamed with shafts feathered through them. They tumbled down the wet hill-slopes, tattered bundles, arms and legs flopping.

The arrows we loosed took their toll, and then it was hand-strokes.

All the old cliches about letting the mind divorce itself from the corporeal body, the sword being held and not held, the mysteries of the Disciplines, all these things chunked into place.

Because I was mounted and because I was in a hurry to get through these Hawkwas I used the Krozair longsword. The brand flamed in the weak sunlight. Hawkwas shrieked and fell away. Blood splattered. Barty was slashing about with the clanxer I had insisted he bring, the straight cut and thruster more use in this kind of work than a rapier. Uthnior struck mighty sweeping blows with a polearm, a scythe-like blade mounted on a staff, an overgrown version of the glaive my people of Valka know so well how to use. We urged our totrixes on, the baggage animals tethered to the saddles following willy-nilly, and we broke through the screeching mob. The Hawkwas fought us, for they saw we were but three and there were nineteen or twenty of them. But the deadly arrows had cut them down and the swords completed the task.

A last remnant, three men, turned to run back, casting aside their weapons. Uthnior slapped his polearm away and took out his bow. He shot cleanly into the back of the nearest fugitive.

He must have sensed my thoughts, for he bellowed savagely at me.

"They will bring their Opaz-forsaken friends, koter!"

As he dispatched the penultimate wretch, I, with some compunction and self-disgust, loosed at the last.

Practical matters despite all other concepts had to reign here. I valued my daughter Dayra above these bandits of the hills. It was horrible and messy; it was, as I took it, inevitable.

There was no point in gathering up the scattered weapons.

We rode from that accursed spot as quickly as we could move the totrixes along, after I had recovered my arrows.

And the rain came drifting back.

"You have, I think, fought before," observed Uthnior as we jogged along.

"Yes."

"Did you see that one—" began Barty.

"Not now, Barty," I said.

We drew our cape hoods up and slouched in the saddles and rode through the valley and past the feathery glinting waterfall and so came out to the saddle beyond, where the land lifted away from us, misty, clouded by rain veils, gray and wet.

Barty said, with an oath: "What I would give for a piping hot cup of tea—right now—vydra tea, for that is what I like best."

"I, too, am fond of vydra tea," said Uthnior.

I hauled out a wine bottle and passed it across. "You will have to make do with wine, Barty. For now."

"I suppose so."

When we reached the cave of which the guide had spoken we reined in. The rocky face of the cliff closed down, and the uneven track wound down toward thickly wooded and much cut up land beyond. The veils of rain blew across like vertical sweeps from gigantic sword blades.

Uthnior hesitated.

"To wait here, now, will not be advisable."

"Our tracks will be washed out," I said tentatively.

"Assuredly, koter. But the bodies of the Hawkwas will be

found. Their friends will search. It will not be difficult to find a lone man hiding in a cave."

"So you—" began Barty.

"Ride with us until you find a secure hide," I said.

Barty swung to face me, annoyed; but he saw my face and did not pursue the argument. We rode on.

The sense of desolation that depressed me here in these Kwan Hills lightened a little as the rain eased. I knew the atmospheric feelings were mine, that in other circumstances I would have joyed to explore here. Barty relapsed into a hurt silence, unable to comprehend why my companionship had so sadly fallen away. Uthnior led on, alert, sniffing the wind, his eyes forever scanning the distant prospects that opened up with each turn in our winding progress through the hills.

We had decided to approach the areas where the Hawkwas camped from a different direction. That, at least was all we could do to divorce ourselves from the fight. If we were connected to that massacre at a later date, that was in the lap of the gods. So the way took longer, and we spent the next day jogging across cross-grained country and feeling the spirits of the land invading our ibs. Barty was now most unhappy.

We fell in with a wandering man, wild of aspect, half mad, whose shrivelled face and white hair told eloquently that he suffered from that dread disease I have spoken of. A normal Kregan looks forward to better than two hundred years of happy, vigorous life. This disease, this chivrel, shortens a lifespan by a handful of years only, depriving people of that lovely golden autumn of life; but it destroys their strength and their appearance, aging them obscenely, shattering their powers.

Kregans hold in their hearts a deep horror of this particular disease; yet as far as anyone knows it is not transferable and people live in close contact with sufferers without ill effects. The disease strikes at random, it seems.

The camp we made beside a brook with crags above and trees massed about cheered me a little. Uthnior's desires I respected. Barty would come round once I got this black dog off my back. Dayra would be found. As for the wider problems of the empire, these weighed most deeply on my mind, fretting at me, worrying me in that I was traipsing about in some damned back hills instead of acting my part in Vondium and trying to thwart evil schemes against the emperor and keeping him safely on his throne.

Who knew what was going on in Vondium now?

A single dagger thrust can change the destiny of nations.

The old fellow waved his arms about, his lank white hair flying, his wrinkled face parchment brittle. His coarse sacking garment was hitched up by a rope girdle; but he carried beside the usual stout pipewood bamboo stick, a sword blade mounted into a pole, the steel broken and resharpened into a foot-long blade. He said his name was Yanpa the Fran—a suitable name given the pallor of that shrivelled face and the whiteness of his hair.

In answer to our questions he said he searched for the fabled Cher-ree. At this, Barty was all set to burst out laughing; but he caught my eye and subsided at my quick shake of the head. In this, Barty was prepared to accept my admonishment. After all, it was patent that Yanpa the Fran was makib, insane, and therefore entitled to pursue a will-o'-the-wisp search.

As my Djangs would say, Yanpa chased after Drig's Lanterns.

"But there are too many Junka-forsaken warriors bashing about the Hills," Yanpa complained. His hands shook. "They march everywhere, spoiling. They drive the spirits away."

"Warriors?"

"Aye! Hundreds—thousands. They gather to the war drums and the trumpets. The banners fly. A band chased me yesterday—"

"Hawkwas?" demanded Uthnior. His lean face jutted aggressively forward.

"Also. Many mercenaries, many warriors, many paktuns."

"Where is their camp?"

"Camp? Camp?" His withered old arms windmilled. "There are many camps. The leathers fill the valleys."

"The chief camp?"

His eyeballs rolled. If this moment of lucidity passed before he answered we would be no better off. But he licked his cracked lips, the spittle shining, and laughed and hugged himself. "They meet at Hockwafernes. I saw the temple. I saw and they did not know." He hugged himself in glee.

Uthnior pulled an earlobe. "Hockwafernes. I know it. Some would call it a place blessed and others a place damned. It is certain devils reside there."

"Devils!" tittered Yanpa the Fran. "Aye! Junka has taken them all up into his hand and some spilled through his fingers and scuttled away and hide and tremble in Hockwafernes."

"And others say, old man, that the devils wait there for the tombstones to be lifted, for the funeral pyres to suck in the smoke and flame, for the Ice Floes of Sicce to melt—"

"May Opaz the Light of Days protect us all!" exclaimed Barty, on a breath. He shivered, and looked across the fire into the enveloping trees.

A clatter of stones along the bank of the brook brought us about, instantly. Barty stared toward the source of the noise, hidden beyond a bend in the stream and a stand of trees. Uthnior looked about. I nodded, grim-faced, to the trees and we eased back into their cover. Yanpa came with us, casting a nervous glance back at his riding preysany and his pack calsany. The animals cropped grass alongside our totrixes.

The Rapa who trudged into view, walking sullenly along the river bank, was a fighting man, a warrior, clad in war harness and carrying a monstrous blanket-wrapped bundle on his shoulder. He muttered to himself as he walked, casting dark savage looks from side to side. The instant he saw the camp and the animals he threw the bundle down and the sword appeared in his fist in a twinkling glitter of light. He glared about, uncertain.

I called: "Llahal, dom. We mean you no mischief."

He was confident enough. Where he stood he commanded our approach and before we could get to him he could make the decision to fight or run. I caught the silver glint at his throat, above the armor, and guessed he would not run.

How he would withstand a cloth-yard shaft driven straight at him was another matter entirely.

I did not test him. I stepped out and held up my empty hand.

"Llahal, dom," he said in his surly way. People say all Rapas stink. This is not so. He turned his massively beaked face to regard me. He was of that family of Rapas with brilliant red feathers around the beak, and bands of red and black feathers running aft, and white feathers circling the eyes. His fierce vulturine face leered at me. I went forward.

After we made pappattu and learned he was Rojashin the Kaktu, a paktun, on his way to join Trylon Udo na Gelkwa who was raising an army and employing many mercenaries, Rojashin said with a surly curse: "And my confounded zorca fell and smashed two legs. I have walked two dwaburs like a common slave." His predatory eye fastened on our animals.

Uthnior's hand tightened on his sword hilt.

"You are mercenaries, also? I see you are not full paktuns."

He spoke with some contempt, this Rojashin the Rapa. The little silver mortilhead gleamed at his throat, the pakmort, proud symbol of mercenaries who have achieved the coveted

110

status of paktun. Of course, the word paktun is used loosely these days for almost any mercenary, and usage is changing. Kregen is a world that is not static, that is not stamped into an unchanging mold. Customs, habits, traditions evolve. It was becoming the fashion to call all high-quality mercenary warriors paktuns, and those with the pakmort consequently were called mortpaktuns. Hyr-paktuns, who wore the pakzhan, would then be dubbed zhanpaktuns. But it would be foolish to call a youngster newly left the farm and run off to be a mercenary a paktun. So new hands, green fighting-men, coys, tended to be called a variety of unflattering names, of which paktunik is perhaps the least offensive.

We were like to have trouble with this one. Rojashin went on grumbling, fleering derogatory remarks about a bunch of thieving masichieri masquerading as soldiers he had seen. He kept on looking at our animals, and fingering his sword, while he ate the food we gave him.

He answered our questions readily enough. Trylon Udo was gathering a great army in the Northeast. Men were coming from all over. Many traveled from across the seas. He, himself, had been lured by gold from North Segesthes. But for the mischance of the fallen zorca he would have been at Hockwafernes, having the directions written down safely. Then, he had been promised by the recruiting agent, the army would march south through Vallia and storm and take Vondium. The plunder would be enormous. The sack of the greatest city in this part of the world must yield fantastic wealth to anyone lucky enough to be alive after the assault.

"And, by the Ib Reiver himself, I am like to be cheated of the opportunity."

I decided I would offer this braggart Rojashin the Kaktu the use of my pack totrix and we would ride into Trylon Udo's camp together. That way I would discover at first hand the details of the threat to Vondium. Also, I had the shrewdest of suspicions that Dayra would be found there, too.

But fate has a nasty habit of knocking my schemes askew.

To call this Rapa a braggart may seem harsh; but I saw the newness of his pakmort, the sharpness of the silver edges, and guessed he was still in the grip of the elation that comes with the achievement. He stood up and drew out his sword with his right hand, wiping his left hand across that damned great beak.

"I will take a totrix now. If you resist, I shall slay you all."

I sighed.

He had summed up Uthnior as a guide, and us as his

111

clients, and he disregarded Yanpa the Fran as a diseased madman.

"You may ride with us—" I began.

The Rapa bellowed. "By Rhapaporgolam the Reiver of Souls! You cowardly rasts! I shall cut you all down and then take all."

With that he charged full tilt at Barty.

Barty had been sitting cross-legged munching on a handful of palines. As the Rapa bore down, the sword flaming lethally, Barty let out a yell and rolled sideways in a tangle, berries spurting up like pips from a squeezed fruit. Yanpa let out a pure screech of terror and dived for his preysany. Uthnior held back, glancing at me. I gave no sign.

Barty, all in a tangle, rolled desperately as the sword thwacked down. Uthnior let out a growl. His fist closed on his sword hilt and the blade slid halfway out.

Then, and only then, I said: "Shaft the cramph, if you have to, Uthnior. He will have only himself to blame."

Barty yelled again and flopped about like a stranded whale. He got a knee under him and shoved up, dragging his rapier out.

I sighed again. One day, I supposed, he would learn.

By my right side a usefully sized rock lay to hand. I picked it up, weighed it, tossed it up and down a couple of times, and then hurled it full at the Rapa's head.

The rock clanged off his neck guard. He staggered forward, arms flailing, tripped over Barty and sprawled onto the ground. His beak cut a swath through the mud.

But the helmet had prevented a knock-out blow. The Rapa was up on his feet, moving with ferocious speed, slashing the rapier away in a grating twinkle of steel. In the next second he would have had Barty's head off.

Uthnior loosed.

The shaft passed cleanly through the Rapa's wattled neck, bursting past the wrapped scarf, scything on to break free in a gouting smother of blood. Rojashin the Kaktu stood up, very tall. His fingers relaxed on the sword and it flew into the trees. He stood. Then he fell. His legs kicked. He lay still.

I felt most disgruntled.

"Why these idiots have to bulge their muscles and strut about like conquering heroes beats me," I said. "By Vox! He misjudged us, the onker. And a paktun, too."

"A very new paktun," observed Uthnior.

We went across and looked down on the body. The Rapa

112

did not die well. Barty stood up, untangling himself, and, looking most mean, said: "You cut that damned fine."

Gesturing to his rapier, I said: "Rapiers are city weapons, my lad. There is a different knack to using them out here."

"Yes, that may be true, but, well and all—"

"He could have had a free and pleasant ride to the camp. But no—he had to prove himself a great and mighty warrior." I noticed his smell, then, and turned away. Yet I have known Rapas with whom a great comradeship was possible. It takes all kinds to make a world.

Later on, when Barty's color had gone down and he had his breath back, I told them I would have to leave them at this point. They looked blankly at me.

"You," I said to Barty. "You will get back to Vondium as fast as the airboat will take you. Report on what we have learned. See Naghan Vanki. I expect Kov Layco Jhansi will be interested, also, and will arrange an interview with the emperor. The threat from the Northeast is more serious than they imagine."

"And you?"

I picked up the pieces of armor we had stripped from the Rapa. I would make them fit me. "Oh, I think I will join up with Trylon Udo's new army. Dayra is likely to be there—"

"Then I shall go with you!"

Uthnior wrinkled up those huntsman's eyes. "Yanpa the Fran has gone. I think my employment with you is terminated."

"Yes, and I give you thanks, Chavonthjid. Go with Opaz."

"And I," quoth Barty, "shall go with you, Jak, to the camp and—"

"And do you think you can carry off the part of a paktun?"

"We-ell—"

In the end I convinced him. It was not easy. But I bore down.

He would only be a hindrance. The life of a Strom at court and on his estates is far removed from the life of a mercenary. And that despite they may both meet on the field of battle.

We buried the Rapa, Rojashin the Kaktu, paktun, with decent observances, and then struck camp. I stood to watch Uthnior and Barty ride off, back-tracking, trusting they would get through safely to the secreted airboat. I gave them a cheerful Remberee, and then mounted up on the totrix and turned his head toward Hockwafernes and the rebel army of Trylon Udo na Gelkwa.

It was very good once more to be my own lone self, that old Dray Prescot who roared and bashed his way about the brutal and beautiful world of Kregen.

Chapter Eleven

Zankov

The valley was indeed, as Yanpa had said, filled with the leather tents of an army. The glitter of weapons and armor, the rustle of brilliant flags, the curvetting of saddle animals colored the scene and the sounds and scents of an army in camp brought back pungent memories as I rode down the trail.

A gang of masichieri—mercenaries who for one reason or another are not regarded as highly as really professional mercenaries, the paktuns, and who consequently are not paid as well, are not usually armed and accoutred as well, and thieve to make up the difference—had fallen in with me. A few cracked skulls and broken noses convinced them I was not to be trifled with, and we rode into the camp together.

This, although giving me good cover, also raised questions. No paktun would consort with masichieri on a social basis. They would stand in the line in battle together; that was as far as they would go.

Down at the far end of the valley where a river emptied into a lake, gleaming with silvery-green reflections in the lights of the suns, a township had been built. It surrounded with its wooden houses and stockade an edifice of considerable architectural splendor.

This was the Temple of Hockwafernes.

Truth to tell, I then paid the place scant attention. One glance convinced me the temple was of remarkable workmanship and outstanding beauty to be found tucked away here. Then I had to ease my way through the protocol demanded. Pappattu had to be made. The curvettings of social and military positions had to be observed. Rojashin the Kaktu had been traveling alone—to have donned his gear would not have been worth the trouble had he had companions—and I had to pick and choose most carefully among the various commanders recruiting their regiments.

The camp was large and was only one of many. Many races of diffs thronged the alleyways between the tents and crowded the open spaces. The usual camp followers plied their varying trades. I downed a long drink of parclear to ease the dust, for the rains had stopped and the twin suns shone clear, and looked about. The sheer size of all this could defeat my purpose.

Where, among this host, was my daughter Dayra to be found?

The hundreds of professional free lances were outnumbered by the thousands of irregulars. I was halted half a dozen times with offers of instant rank within this regiment or that, for the glitter of the pakmort at my throat attracted the regimental recruiting Deldars like flies.

It seemed a good idea to take the thing off. As you know I had been elected a paktun by a duly constituted court of honor, and was entitled to wear the pakmort. My own mortil-head lay somewhere in one of the drawers in the bedroom in Esser Rarioch in Valkanium in Valka. At that time I was not a hyr-paktun—at least, not officially so. I dodged behind a tent and unlooped the silver symbol and the silken cords. The name on the back read simply: KAKTU—presumably they had not felt there was room enough for Rojashin also. I stowed the pakmort away in my pouch. After that, clad in the Rapa's armor, let out around the shoulders, I was able to progress more easily, although still importuned to join up—though now as a simple swod.

The uproar and the noise and the rising clouds of dust and the stinks were all familiar. Fights broke out. Bets were shrieked. Some kind of drilling was going on, and a couple of parcels of totrix cavalry were attempting evolutions. Some of my first fears eased. This army was not ready for battle yet.

As to finding Dayra—well, if all I had heard was correct then it was not sheer stupid pride that led me to the commander's area. Dayra was running with the big boys of this outfit.

No one of this raffish mob being fashioned into an army was allowed through the gateways into the wooden-built town around the temple. The Hawkwas maintained their own integrity. I did not blame them. Chuliks stood guard. There were not a lot of them; but they had clearly been selected for the important positions as was sensible. I did not see many Pachaks, and for this was glad.

A Chulik ob-Deldar chased me away from the gateway where the men of his squad stood guard. I allowed myself to be chased off, not without a casually ripe insult or two. One had to maintain a camouflage in situations like these.

To occupy myself during the time until the suns went down I found stabling for the totrixes, paid good money to attempt to ensure some security for them and my gear, ate a huge meal, talked to the swods, sang a few ditties in the ale tents, and, in general, kept my eyes open and ears fully extended.

The talk was all of the plunder of Vondium and the south.

There were also darker rumors—and that shows just how murky they were—of a great enlightenment, a marvelous intervention of supernatural powers, that would be revealed before the army marched, giving the signal for the great adventure. The Trylon Udo had command of wonderful forces, and these would be summoned to aid the army.

The swods in the ale tent with whom I was drinking and singing were just finishing up that rollicking song well known under its euphemistic name of "Bear Up Your Arms" when the last cadences faltered and died, and the men broke out into cheers and jeers and lewd remarks. A company of women warriors swung past in the gathering shadows. They looked purposeful and businesslike, their spears all a-slanting in line, their helmets gleaming in the last light of the suns.

Intrigued, I threw down my reckoning and wandered out and so followed the martial ladies. Straight to the Chulik-guarded gate they marched. The Chuliks sprang back, at attention, and the Hikdar at their head led the Amazons through. I shook my head. No matter how matter-of-fact the custom is on Kregen, still I suffer from hidden phobias, deeply-driven ideas of womenkind, that make me view with unease the idea of girls taking their part in battle. That they do so—and have done for more years on this Earth than they have not, and will do so again in the future—has no power to move me. But I accept what is, as a fellow must. I was about to turn away with that dark feeling of unease strong upon me, when I saw the Chulik guard had been changed. I saw the Chulik who stood by the gateway, the fading light glistening on his tusks; I saw him clear.

There was little need for a flashing glimpse of the rapier swinging alongside the thraxter at his side to remind me. That

116

rapier hilt was fashioned ornately into the likeness of a mortil.

At once I knew him, and at once I turned away, forcing myself to move with the casual lecherous movements of a swod watching the women warriors. That Chulik was the one who had seen me over the side of the mysterious flier when I'd gone chasing from Vondium after Delia.

A blaze of speculation burst inside my old vosk skull of a head.

The man who commanded the flier had known me, so he had said. I moved into the shadows, smoothly, and breathed more easily when I was out of sight of the gateway and no alarm went up.

The fellow with the gratingly harsh voice commanding the flier had attempted to conceal the fact he was flying to Vondium. He had mischief planned there, and now he was here. At least, it was a fair assumption he was here. There were few fliers parked in this camp; I had heard the aerial wings of the army were quartered to the north, south of the Stackwamores.

In the eternal circle of vaol-paol all events may happen many times. In the tiny moment of darkness between the setting of the suns and the rising of She of the Veils I was up and over the wooden stockade and dropping lightly down inside the town.

I avoided the guards in preference to putting them to sleep, for many of the soldiers guarding the walls were these same warrior women I had watched marching so smartly in.

The wooden buildings surrounding the opulent temple revealed the types to be expected and I aimed for the largest, which must be the Kregan equivalent to the Town Hall. I will pass quickly over that episode, for although I wormed my way in and looked about I learned absolutely nothing. The trylon was away. Guards lounged about, and nothing was afoot. So I withdrew and waited in the shadows under the wooden eaves.

A great deal of noise spilled out with the yellow lamplight from a tavern across the dusty street; but I did not venture in. The troops in the city would be the trylon's own men, Hawkwas and well-trusted paktuns like the Chuliks who would be known. I would face instant exposure as an interloper.

Over there they were singing "King Harulf's Red Zorca" and then they started on "Sogandar the Upright and the Sylvie." A group of Chuliks staggered out, half drunk and dis-

117

gusted with all this decadent singing. The swods were bellowing out the refrain and killing themselves laughing as they warbled: "No idea at all, at all, no idea at all," when a fresh group of men emerged, their cloaks about their faces, and their swords drawn. Instantly I merged with the shadows and followed them.

There was little chance that the Star Lords or the Savanti sent the chance my way, even though Maspero, my tutor in Aphrasöe the Swinging City, had personally aided me recently. The credit was most probably due to Opaz, although I would not exclude Zair or Djan from the reckoning. Whoever it was guided me to those men, and I heard one of them whisper in a cutting voice: "If we are late because of your drinking and singing, Naghan the Neemu, Zankov is like to have your tripes out. You know what kind of maniac he is if crossed."

"Aye, Nundi, I know! You should have hauled me away before."

"Let us hurry, famblys," growled another. Wrapped in their cloaks, their swords bright in the rising moon, they bustled swiftly along the rutted street between the overhanging houses. I followed.

Zankov!

At last. At last I could feel myself closing with the heart of this mystery.

They led me to a shuttered house in darkness. The door opened and shafted yellow lamplight and then closed tightly again. I eyed the roof. To climb up was simple enough for an old sailorman and I gained the ridge and prised open a skylight. No matter how many times I stealthily clamber into a house to spy nefariously, it always sets the old blood a-thumping. Softly I padded down the blackwood stairs and so came to a tall curtain from which spilled the lamplight in a long beckoning finger from the central parting. Cautiously I applied my eye, saw what I needed, and then set my ear to the narrow opening.

The curtains covered a high window, a kind of mezzanine floor above the main hall. Below, a group of men and women sat around a table on which stood flagons of wine and dishes of fruit. To describe them all now would weary; suffice to say I recognized none of them. I could not see those directly below me. Had I done so—well, that is for later.

The man called Naghan the Neemu was being properly contrite and being cut to pieces by a slender, dapper sharp-faced fellow clad all in black leather. I looked at this one.

118

There was about his taut nervous manner, the sharp gestures of his narrow hands, the quick stutter of his voice, a sense of burning frustration, the smell of hidden fires, the idea of resentment spilling over and barely contained. He flayed Naghan the Neemu. And, as he spoke vicious, cutting words, I saw his eyes, and saw the Vallian brown change and darken and so remembered Nath ti Javvansmot's words at The Speckled Gyp.

For Zankov laughed as he verbally flayed Naghan the Neemu. He revelled in inflicting his own power on others, that was plain. He laughed hurtfully, and told Naghan what his punishment was to be, and his eyes darkened in that narrow feline face.

"Lucky it is for you, Naghan, our guest is delayed. Had he been constrained to wait for the likes of you—"

"I serve loyally!" spoke up Naghan. "I believe in the Cause. I care for the zorcas—"

"And you will personally sweep out the stalls! Personally! With bucket and broom. Our guest brooks no delays from your kind. Remember and do not forget. You are a mere tool and I shall use you as a tool—so keep to your zorcas and do not be late in future."

And Naghan the Neemu—and a man does not obtain that sobriquet upon Kregen lightly—meekly bowed his head.

The women gathered here looked as ruthless as the men. Probably they were far more vicious, I thought then. I had the macabre idea I would recognize Dayra. I had not recognized Velia. But I thought—then—that I must know my own daughter after the harrowing experiences through which I had gone with Velia, my Lady of the Stars.

She must be sitting directly below me, if she were here.

Gently I drew forth the longsword.

The longbow remained cased, for I had deemed it prudent to conceal that weapon in the camp. There was general talk among the swods about facing the Crimson Bowmen of the emperor, and tales that the bodyguard had been bought, which eased many an uneasy thought for the future in the army.

I would leap down among this unsavory little lot and hoick Dayra out of it and if anyone of them tried to prevent me he would feel what good Krozair steel might do.

These, of course, were the maundering and chauvinistic thoughts of a fond parent who failed to comprehend the working of his daughter's mind. But I would learn—bitterly.

Easing up ready to get a good purchase and so leap down

with a skirling yell to throw a startlement into them, I heard Zankov saying: "He is here now. You will all stand."

Amid a scraping of sturmwood chairs they all stood up. A door opened and a bulky figure appeared below me, going toward the table where Zankov stood, smiling, holding out his hand.

I saw the dark cloak of the newcomer, saw the low round helmet without feather or ornamentation. I saw a furtive flicker of steel and a whiplike tail bladed with a glittering dagger slice up in the long slit in the center of the cloak's back.

A Kataki.

And Zankov was saying: "You are heartily welcome. I bid you Lahal and Lahal, Ranjal Yasi, Stromich of Morcray."

Silently I resheathed the longsword and sank back into the shadows.

Chapter Twelve

Concerning the Throne of Vallia

They were all laughing and cheerful down there now, chattering away, handing out wine, quaffing, exchanging toasts, all very merry as nits in a ponsho fleece. I sat back in the shadows and glowered, my fists white on the hilts of my swords, my thoughts black as the cloak of Notor Zan.

"Your pass brought me safely through the gates, Zankov. But only, I think, because my men were on duty. There was a Deldar there also, a Khibil, most insulting. I would like him flogged tomorrow, flogged jikaider."

"It shall be done, Stromich."

"Are we all here?"

"All save for the Princess Dayra. She is expected the day after tomorrow."

At this I roused myself. My savage thoughts refused to come to order. So Dayra *was* mixed up with this evil bunch—and she was not here. The day after tomorrow. Almost, then, I withdrew. But the knowledge that with the arrival of this Kataki, the twin brother to the Kataki Strom, an old enemy, the stakes in the affair had been raised to an entirely new plane, I remained.

The Stromich Ranjal turned to shake the hands of those below me I could not see. But I could see his face.

Low-browed, the squat face of a Kataki, fringed with thick black hair, oiled and curled. Flaring nostrils and gape-jawed mouth with snaggly teeth has a Kataki. Wide set his eyes, brilliant and yet narrow and cold. Slavemasters, Katakis, aragorn, evil men to all they enslave. Their bladed whiptails curve arrogantly above their heads. Yes, Katakis are diffs who give to Kregen much of the evil in its brilliant reputation.

Many thoughts rushed through my head. Strom Rosil Yasi and I had clashed before. I had heard of his twin brother, this Stromich Ranjal who strutted below me now. The pair of them were prime candidates for the Ice Floes of Sicce. Down south in Hamal, the enemy of Vallia, these two Katakis held high office. They were here to injure Vallia. More—they were the tools of the Wizard of Loh, Phu-Si-Yantong. That devil had been balked in his attempt to control Vallia through the false creed of the Black Chyyan, and now, here he was again making a fresh attempt through these Katakis.

The man who had stood on the poop of the airboat upon which I had so incontinently landed, who had given his hoarse-voiced orders to throw my flier over and to spare me—that man was this same Stromich Ranjal na Morcray. There was no mistaking that voice, now I heard it again and had a face and form to put to it. I marked him. I marked him well.

Who had been giving Ranjal his orders in the flier?

Could that have been Yantong himself?

Could it?

I did not know; but somehow, even then, I doubted it. From what I knew of Phu-Si-Yantong, and that was precious little, I fancied he operated whenever he could at long distance through tools like these Katakis and like Vad Garnath ham Hestan. An old chapter of my life was being re-opened here. Yantong sought to employ me as a tool for his insane ambitions. That was why he had ordered that I should not be assassinated. I began to think again, around about then, and thought that just perhaps Yantong had grown weary of waiting, and with the Black Feathers of the Great Chyyan, and now this plot to arouse the Northeast of Vallia, he was committed to moving on an entirely new front in his aggression against Vallia.

As to myself, maybe I no longer figured in his computations.

As I listened to the conversation below some of the outlines came clearer.

"I look forward to meeting this Princess Dayra," Ranjal was saying in that hoarse croak. "My masters have great plans for her. You, Zankov, can answer for her?"

"Assuredly." All the nervous energy of Zankov showed in his nervous twitching, the spread of his hands, the wriggle of his shoulders, the fleer of nostrils. "She believes in the Cause. She is devoted. She has proved that."

"Good. When the army moves we shall strike swiftly. The Trylon Udo is a fool and will be put down. But he is a figurehead and lends color to the endeavor. But the throne and crown of Vallia will not go to him."

Everyone in the room—and I, aloft—knew who hungered for the throne.

Zankov fluttered his fingers against his ears, and cheeks, and then snapped his forefingers and thumbs together.

"No. Not to Udo. To him who deserves it—who will lay unqualified claim to the crown by virtue of marriage to the Princess Dayra."

Stromich Ranjal nodded matter-of-factly. "You will see to disposing of the rest of the family? There must be no other claimant."

"I shall joy in the task! I have a right to the throne—my ancestors demand it of me, in blood. But Stromich, your orders have been to spare the life of the Prince Majister. What—"

"Those orders stand, as of now. I think my masters will shortly issue new directives."

This was fascinating, listening to these schemers dispose of my life. I own I felt a little sorry for them. . . .

Now it is important to know that when a paktun is elected by those who thus become his peers, and receives the silver pakmort, he receives also a little silver ring by which the pakmort is attached to the silken cords. In the case of a hyrpaktun the ring is of gold. When a paktun slays another in battle or in the ritual of the jikordur—the strictly controlled duel to the death—he does not take among the consequent loot the dead man's pakmort. That goes to the stocks for reissuance with a new name, generally, although there are other uses to which it is put. But the victorious paktun claims the silver ring. This he strings upon a silken cord and wears about his person as a badge of prowess. If the slain paktun has a string of rings, the victor will take them all and string them with those he has.

These savage customs of Kregen echo down the long seasons and the ages reverberate with the clash of arms and glow with the brilliance of shed blood.

The dead Rapa, Rojashin the Kaktu, had owned a silken string of seven rings, one of them gold. These were attached to the left shoulder of his harness. This symbol, usually, is referred to as the pakai. The pakai I now wore hung down by my left shoulder.

"You will remember, Zankov, when you seat yourself upon the throne in the palace of Vondium, and are duly crowned and given the Jikai as emperor, to whom you owe all your fortune? You will remember to whom you owe your loyalty and to whom you will dedicate your service and your life?"

Zankov twitched his fingers and nodded. He was so suffused with anticipatory glory he could not speak—an unusual condition for him, I judged.

The door opened again—I could not see it; but it creaked upon a hinge—and a sharp hard voice said: "Jens! Koters! Koteras! Trylon Udo has returned unexpectedly and is calling for—"

The speaker got no further. At once the people at the meeting started to rise and to gather their cloaks and weapons and, at that moment, I shifted incautiously, and the pakai struck its string of rings against my armor.

The sound rang like a carillon.

No wonder, I said to myself fiercely, no wonder I abhor dangling adornments. Flying tassels and trailing scarves and whirling belts are no fit gear for a fighting man.

Zankov glared up at the curtained mezzanine window.

"Up there!" he shouted. "Quick, you cramphs! Someone spies on us!"

He was quick enough on the uptake, I'll give him that.

"Right, you nidge," I said under my breath. "By the Black Chunkrah! I'll sort you out and damned quick!"

I freed the longsword and prepared to leap down and slice them up a trifle. The thought of settling affairs with Zankov and with Stromich Ranjal pleased me mightily.

Then—and then, by Zair, I hesitated. I, Dray Prescot that wild leem of a fellow, took thought for events beyond the immediate prospect of a brisk bashing of skulls. My daughter Dayra was expected the day after tomorrow. Who knew what other villainy these fellows had planned? Far better to wait. Far better to be the calculating, cool, cunning Dray Prescot who took thought for the future and bided his time to strike.

So—as Zair is my witness—the Krozair longsword went snap back into the scabbard and I turned and ran back the way I had come so stealthily.

Even then it was nip and tuck. But I eluded them and I did not have to essay a single handstroke, which, I might add, displeased me at the time, for all my good resolutions.

Back over the town stockade I went and avoided all trouble. I found my billet, all paid for, and bedded down. One day I had to live through without trouble, and then I would see Dayra and bring her out of this rasts' nest.

The last thing I did before I slept was to rip off that damned jangling pakai and stuff it away in my gear. Confounded unwarrior-like trinket—it had nearly botched the whole affair.

Chapter Thirteen
The Battle Maidens Squabble

I sat next morning in the early radiance of the Suns of Scorpio polishing up the armor. I had bought a choice breakfast of vosk rashers and loloo's eggs, swilled down an inordinate amount of good Kregan tea, chewed a handful of palines, and now, stripped down to a breechclout—which was, incidentally, a normal sober yellow—sat companionably with a couple of other mercenaries hard at the task that would keep us alive on the day of battle.

We spoke in that rapid shorthand of warriors, at ease, knowing our own worth—or, at least, they did—and bending diligently to our tasks.

The Rapa paktun's armor had been fashioned from good quality iron with bronze fittings. The breast and back were molded, and so formed a quality kax, a corselet that covered the trunk and extended in a graceful curve below the belt and yet afforded free movement to the legs. I retained my own weapons. The longbow and longsword I kept covered; the other of my weapons excited no untoward comment, being a Vallian clanxer and a Valkan shortsword, and a rapier and main gauche. The Rapa's spear was not a quality weapon; but I kept it for the color it afforded.

Nalgre the Shebov worked on his armor on the other side of the blanket. He was the seventh son of his family and had taken up the mercenary life as a release from farm work. Now he carefully buckled up his armor, a kax tralkish—what on Earth is called a *lorica segmentata*—and whistled cheerfully as he worked.

Dolan the Sling methodically oiled his scaled kax, seeing that each bronze scale was firmly affixed to the leather. At his right side his sling lay ready to hand. With a leaden lozenge-shaped bullet Dolan fancied his luck against any archer. But then, as he said, he had not faced a Bowman of Loh.

"Although, Jak the Kaktu," he said, "we routed a bunch of Undurkers three, four seasons ago when we were working for the King of Sanderdrin. Quite a dust up, that was."

"We're likely to square up to Bowmen of Loh if they don't win over the emperor's guard," said Nalgre. "And damned quick."

"Undurkers," I said, rubbing the oiled rag methodically. "I had a dust-up with them a while back. Some Bowmen of Loh did for them, skewered 'em right through well beyond their range."

"Which side were you on?"

"Well, by Vox, I'm here, aren't I?"

"So you were on the right side."

They laughed. The paktuns of Kregen can see the humor in the situation, when from day to day they may be victors or slain. It gives them the old zest to life.

A whole day to get through. Forty-eight burs to the day. Fifty murs to the bur. And a Kregan bur is roughly equal to forty terrestrial minutes. A long time to keep out of mischief for a wild leem of a fellow.

Not that, recently, I'd felt much like a leem. Like a calsany, perhaps. And everyone knows what calsanys do when they get excited. Nalgre and Dolan talked on about the female warriors—Battle Maidens they called them, Jikai Vuvushis—and we sent a camp slave for a couple of bottles of parclear to ease our throats. The suns rolled across the heavens and everything was going splendidly, for these two like myself were tazll mercenaries, unemployed, determining to enlist with the trylon's regiments or none. I did not tell them Udo had returned overnight; the information had not yet percolated through. Even when the dust of a squabble

125

rose beyond the next row of tents I felt no inclination to become involved.

But when Nalgre and Dolan stood up and peered across and said: "That looks interesting," I realized I would have to go, for to do otherwise would be most odd in a paktun.

So we yelled at the camp slave—he was shared by the two comrades and for a fee I could join in the syndicate—to guard our gear. We strapped on a sword or two and ambled across to see the fun.

The dust billowed up from a cleared space and rose over the heads of the gathered swods. I call them swods, P.B.I. soldiers; in truth they were much more of a hastily gathered rabble, with a leavening of hardened professionals among them. No doubt, given time, Trylon Udo would smarten them up. By the time they'd marched all the long way to Vondium they'd either be an army or they'd be long since dispersed. We had little difficulty in shoving our way to the front of the ring. Bets were being wagered all around, and the excitement fizzed.

The sharp smell of the dust peppered nostrils and stung eyes. I was pleased Nalgre had thought to bring a bottle of parclear, that sherbet drink that so refreshes. The noise blattered skywards. The Suns of Scorpio shone down. On the morrow I would see my daughter Dayra. I knew the house. This time I would not wear a stupid dangling clanging object and the Krozair longsword would find business.

Two girls fought in the dust.

I grimaced my distaste.

So that was why the swods were so wrought up.

Inquiries elicited the fact they were not fighting over a man but over the ownership of a fine string of amber beads. So they remained girls despite their martial kit, and the daggers, and their spitting snarling invective. The blonde girl was having the worst of it, the redhead being altogether quicker and deadlier. I wondered, with a shiver of disgust, if they would fight to the death, for, as we quickly learned, this was not a jikordur but merely a common brawl.

A knot of Battle Maidens on the far side of the ring screamed advice and insults and encouragement. There were two sides here. The two girls fighting were not naked; but they might just as well have been. For an agonizing instant I wondered what Delia, if she were so unfortunate as to be here, would make of this spectacle. Then I brought myself up with a shock. Why should not girls fight and brawl in camp like men? Just because I viewed the scene with reservations

126

meant nothing. If girls could tend wounded men and see the ghastly sights of the battlefield at, as it were, second hand, and if they could don boots and armor and wield weapons, as they did, who was I to say they could not act completely as warriors? Did I not demean them by suggesting otherwise?

Each person must act out his own nature, as the scorpion said to the frog, always—and this proviso is one I hew to for it is so often overlooked and disregarded, always provided that the free-doer does not harm his or her fellows in the liberated exercise of his or her own psyche.

And by harm I do not mean the harm one of these girls was going to sustain in this free-for-all.

Blonde hair, damped with sweat and slicked with dust, bent to the ground. The redheaded girl, who was screamed at as Firn in wild excitement, had the upper hand. She had fought cleanly. All saw that. And now she was on the point of victory.

Already coins were jingling, changing hands as the bets were paid out. With a wild scream a third girl bounded into the informal arena. Clad in green leathers, she wielded a rapier and main gauche. Her dark hair flowed loosely. Her face was brilliant with malice and vicious determination.

She raced toward the two girls, the blonde submitting and Firn, the redhead, triumphant. With a shriek the girl in green leathers kicked the dagger from Firn's hand. The rapier twitched down. Its point hovered at the redhead's throat.

A hullabaloo broke out in red riot. Girls yelled, men cursed. Through it all no one took a single eye away from that central tableau as the dust fell.

"Firn! I challenge you! Prepare to die, here and now!"

"Karina the Quick!"

The noise lessened as we all struggled to hear.

Someone threw a rapier and dagger onto the settling dust.

A ferocious-looking apim at my side said: "Karina the Quick is notorious. Firn is as good as dead if she does not submit."

"Firn! Firn!" came the screeches and yells.

"Karina! Karina the Quick!" flew from the other group of Battle Maidens.

I felt the sorrow for redheaded Firn. To submit would bring life and to fight might bring death; but in these circumstances she had no choice.

Firn threw back her heavy head of red hair and picked up the weapons. She held them in a practiced grip. But at the first handstrokes those who knew about these things saw that

Firn faced a swordmaster—or, in this case, a swordmistress. Karina played with her, pinking that bright skin, bringing forth the ugly spottings of blood and all the time she taunted, foul-mouthing Firn, taunted her with torture and death.

This was a case for the Krozairs to decide. Could I, a man, step forward and stop the fight? No—this was not a case for the Krozairs, or for me. This was Savage Kregen, alive, vibrant, pulsing with blood—and ending with a life and a death.

If I attempted to intervene I'd probably be torn limb from limb by everyone present who could get a hand on me.

Now Firn's superb body was splashed with her own blood. Her scanty clothes hung in bloodied ribbons. Her hair swirled. The green leathers of Karina the Quick glimmered in the suns' light, unspotted, unfouled.

Very soon if Firn did not yield she would be dead.

The Battle Maidens had now clearly separated into two groups. If there was a preponderance of green about one group and of red about the other, I put that down to coincidence and my own views on those two sky colors. Looking across the swirling dust that billowed up as the girls stamped and retreated and stamped and advanced, I saw, abruptly, clearly, as though focused in a telescope the face of one of the Jikai Vuvushis. The face swam clear through all the confusion and tumult.

Open of countenance, glowing with the excitement of the moment, her brown Vallian eyes wide, Vad Kolo's daughter, Leona nal Larravur, stood and stared hungrily upon the fight.

She wore the green leathers, with a profusion of purple feathers. Now I understood why the topmost purple ronil gem had snapped away from her jeweled badge of the samphron bush. Rejecting the Sisterhood, she must have hurled the brooch from her in negation and disgust, and then, calculatingly, have picked it up to wear to the emperor's reception for Queen Lushfymi. The missing gem, not being found by her cowed slaves, perforce the missing socket had to be painted over. Yes, Leona nal Larravur was a real right scheming miss.

Dust puffed across as the struggling girls grappled and swung about. Firn was clearly weakening. Her blood glistered darkly upon her body, and dust patched her like camouflage.

The group of Jakai Vuvushis who wore russet leathers began to shout. "Ros the Claw," they called. "Ros the Claw."

In all the confusion others took up the yell. Money which

had changed hands twice now returned. The issue was, then, still in doubt. A girl in black leathers was thrust into the ring by the Battle Maidens, who chanted her name. Slowly, she walked to the center. Firn, panting, shrieked out: "She will slay you, Ros!"

The girl in the black leathers moved forward. The fighting girls staggered apart. Karina the Quick looked as lithe, as ferocious, as deadly as ever. She stood back, her blood-smeared rapier and dagger slanting up, smiling lopsidedly as Ros the Claw moved in. Firn collapsed, panting, dishevelled, done for.

"Do you challenge me, Ros the Claw?"

"If you will it. Either way—you cease and desist from tormenting Firn."

"Then you must make me."

"It is the Jikordur, then."

A gasp swept the assembly. The bets hovered, uncertain, for both girls possessed reputations. I knew the one in black leathers. I had seen her before, in those abominable caverns beneath Vondium where my Delia had been offered up on a basalt slab under the obscene idol of a giant toad to the fangs and claws of a real chyyan. I had seen her then, this Ros the Claw, as she released a mangled wight from a prison cell.

Two more girls in black leathers stepped forward. They looked grim. They were addressed as Zillah and Jodi, and they bore marks of authority. Ros flung out at them.

"This is overdue."

"Maybe. But we cannot allow the Jikordur. The Trylon has forbidden duels to the death."

"This began as a squabble over a bead necklace. What—"

"The Trylon Udo has commanded."

"To the Ice Floes of Sicce with Udo! This bitch leem has tortured enough. She must be—"

"You may be called a tiger-girl, Ros. You may stand high. But in this you cannot go against the orders of the trylon."

Now it was the turn of Karina the Quick to laugh.

The sightseers swayed this way and that to get a better view. All recognized this as a woman's affair; but with rapiers and daggers in play, a universal sympathy was involved.

I wondered what, if Dayra was here, she would do. She must have witnessed sights like this before. And that struck me as a most deucedly odd thought, I can tell you, I who had never to my knowledge seen my daughter. I wondered to which side she would hew. I did not think, with some assurance, that having a brother like Jaidur, Dayra could possibly have any truck with the green.

That, here in Vallia, was a stupid concept, where green was merely another heraldic color, where blue, if any, was the color of contempt. And that was a pity.

The streaming opaline radiance of the suns brought out the colors of the soldiers and the irregulars, glittered from armor and weapons, struck glinting metallic highlights in the hanging dust.

"Desist, Ros the Claw, or we will take you into custody."

This girl with her lithe feline form, the blood suffusing her cheeks, the sparkle in her eyes that told of venom and intelligence, hauled Firn to her feet. The redhead swayed.

"Look! Very well. As Dee-Sheon is my witness, not the Jikordur—a common brawl, then, a gutter fight."

At the words Dee-Sheon many of the women made tiny reflexive gestures with their fingers. Did they convey worship or did they ward off evil? Gods and goddesses and spirits throng the pantheons of Kregen. A New York City directory would contain not a half of them.

This was the moment I decided I could stand and watch no longer. I half turned to move away. The girls would not be constrained by the ritualistic trappings of the Jikordur and they would not fight to the death. This Ros had her way. But Karina laughed, derisively, showing her white teeth, her lips very red. Her body arched magnificently as she stretched, her rapier licking out in swift cunning passes. She vibrated confidence.

Slowly, Ros pulled from her waist pouch a thing of shining steel, an artifact shaped like an articulated metal glove, clawed with razor steel, sharp and cruel. She pulled it onto her left hand. The talons glinted. Metal splines extended up her wrist. She turned the tiger-talons this way and that. To call them tiger-talons is correct, for they shared much of the cruel curved beauty of a killer bird's claws.

The massed crowd fell silent.

The girls faced each other, Karina the Quick flicking her rapier and dagger about expertly; Ros the Claw poised with rapier ready and left hand glittering with clawed steel.

So, I, Dray Prescot, sentimental onker, turned away and pushed through the crowd. I had no wish to witness what might follow. But, if I had to lay down any bets, my money would be on Ros, every last copper ob.

I had gone barely a dozen paces when a bubbling scream

130

burst up into the bright air. I continued walking. I did not look back.

A vast sigh oozed from the crowd.

That was woman's business. They were welcome to it.

Chapter Fourteen

"You May Choose the Manner of Your Death."

"You are sure, Nalgre? Certain sure?" The seething anger and violence in me had to be held down. I could not show too much interest in the politics of Vallia here.

"Certain, Jak. I spoke to a flier pilot who returned with the trylon. The Lord Farris has been arrested and charged with treason. And others of like kidney, too."

"It will make our task easier," put in Dolan, idly swinging his sling around his legs. "Farris was loyal to the emperor."

"Yes," I said. "He was."

"And as Udo is back in camp we will go and enlist today."

"Very well," I said, to keep up my cover.

This news was bad. It indicated quite clearly that scheming people were burrowing from within. The Lord Farris was devoted to Delia and the emperor. How could he possibly be accused of so outrageous a crime? Accused, yes; that would be all too easy. But the accusation must be false. I was convinced of that.

Before we went to enlist the three of us ambled across to an ale tent, for the suns progressed across the sky, to spend some of Nalgre's winnings. Dolan had bet on Karina the Quick. And, as Nalgre said, with a guffaw: "That cat-girl cut her up a real treat."

I was not interested. The day passed too slowly for me. On the morrow Dayra would arrive and I knew I would have to be quick to fetch her out of it before Zankov moved. I'd summed up that villain, as I thought, and how I kept moving and speaking and acting normally I do not know.

The problem of this acting as a paktun and hiring out to Trylon Udo also worried me. If I gave my sworn oath to serve, as any mercenary would do, I would not wish lightly to break my word. That the whole thing was a sham, a facade, would not count. My word would have been given, and here, in the camp of Hockwafernes, I *was* Jak the Kaktu, paktun.

Well, it is the same with problems as with plans. Men sow for Zair to sickle.

Coming out of the ale tent after a goodly interval—a goodly interval—Nalgre wiped his lips and belched.

"By Beng Dikkane," he said, comfortably. "I am in the mood now."

A pang for old days and for Nath and Zolta swept me. We turned along the line of booths and tents where the trafficking went on all the live-long day. A party of warrior women marched along, all in step, all spears ranked, their helmets gleaming.

Dolan nodded.

"I warrant they'd not be so regimented when the moons are in the sky, eh?"

"They wouldn't give you a calsany's offering," quoth Nalgre, and he laughed.

The Jikai Vuvushis marched with a swing. There were equal numbers of those in green leathers under their armor as those in russets. On duty animosities were forgotten. At the head marched Zillah and Jodi, and Ros the Claw was there, with Firn. They approached and we three together with other swods casually sauntering nearby moved out of the way.

Leona nal Larravur pointed at me.

"There he is!" she shouted. Her voice rose, cracking with strain and excitement. "There he is! The Prince Majister! Seize him!"

It was damned quick.

I was ringed by spear points. My comrades fell back, gaping. Many of the irregulars ran off in terror. Zillah, tall, buxom, high of color, fronted me. Her rapier glittered at my throat.

"You are the Prince Majister of Vallia?"

I stared about the hostile ring. Damned quick, by Krun!

To go drinking in camp we had merely donned rapier and dagger. My fighting equipment lay buckled up in its leather coverings along with the gear of the others, guarded by the camp slave. Even then I could have broken free, skewered a few of the guards, slashed a few more, and so broken to liberty.

But I hesitated.

These were women. Mind you, they were women dressed

132

up as warriors, carrying arms, armored. All the same, they remained girls. At that time I couldn't bring myself to stick a length of sharp steel into any one of those delightful forms. It was a weakness.

"No!" I bellowed, for everyone to hear. "You are mistaken! For the sweet sake of Opaz—take that rapier out of my Adam's apple."

"You are the Prince—"

"No! No—do I look like a prince! I am Jak the Kaktu. A paktun, ready to right for you—you make a mistake—"

Some of the girls believed me. But this Zillah and this Jodi, and this Ros the Claw and Firn did not. And, with her fine frank face glowing with passion, this tricky Leona nal Larravur knew absolutely I lied.

"Take him to the trylon!" she brayed, swirling her rapier. "I shall soon convince him. Oh, what a prize we have here."

"Yes," spat Ros. "A contemptible rast of a man! A cramph ready to be unmanned and chopped and flung down unmourned to the Ice Floes of Sicce."

I shook my head. "You are mistaken—"

"March him off!" shouted Zillah. Her nostrils widened. "How the sight of him offends me."

Amid a scathing torrent of abuse they led me off. I went. A few sharp spear points up my stern convinced me they hadn't heard Phu-Si-Yantong's orders not to kill me. Anyway, maybe that schemer had changed his mind. I'd soon find out.

Trylon Udo na Gelkwa turned out to be a square-set man with a sharp brown beard and thin harsh lips, with eyes that were darker than the normal Vallian brown. This is common in the Northeast of Vallia. He did not rise as I was prodded into his room in the town hall. The place was bare and sparsely furnished, with furs hanging on the walls and a large table smothered with maps and lists. He looked up narrowly.

"So you are the Prince Majister."

"No—"

The girls at my back all took their chances of giving me a crafty prod or two with their spears. I jumped. They'd taken my rapier and dagger away. I had let them. Every time I tried to speak I was poked by a spear.

"Larravur says you are. She frequents the court of the imperial buffoon and decadent drunkard in Vondium. She is our eyes. You are the Prince Majister. You will receive scant courtesy from anyone here in the Northeast. But, one boon I will grant." Here Udo leaned back in his chair and pulled his bear. He smiled. "You may choose the manner of your death."

I opened my mouth and Udo lifted a ringed hand.

"Let him speak, Zillah."

The girls glowered at me. Even Karina the Quick had come in to see the fun. Not a one of them showed a single spark of mercy; now all believed I was that miserable rast I was accused of being. Karina sported a large bandage over the right side of her face. But she had not lost an eye. She did not stand near Ros. Jodi and Firn separated them. The animosity I felt from these girls puzzled me. It seemed to me overdone, abnormal, almost unreal and certainly damned unhealthy.

Leona pointed a rigid forefinger at me.

"He does not speak. He admits his guilt. His terror contaminates us all. Thrust a sword through him and have done."

Ros whipped out her steel claw. "Let me take him apart!"

The others voiced their own highly unpleasant ideas on the way I should go.

The whole episode smacked of a dream sequence. It was not even a nightmare. It just seemed unreal. Had I been hemmed in by foul-mouthed guardsmen then a flick of a leem's tail would have seen a few of them down, spitting blood, and a sword in my fist, and a corpse-strewn trail of blood to the door, if one of them did not try to shaft me as I went. But these were girls. As I say, I was weak in these matters in those days.

By Makki-Grodno's disgusting diseased dripping left eyeball, I can tell you! I felt the hugest of huge idiots, a nurdling onker, a get onker—a ripe charley, the complete fool. And yet—and yet, at that stage in my development on Kregen, what else could I have done?

A stir at the back of the room and a swaying aside of the Jikai Vuvushis heralded the intemperate arrival of Zankov. He stood twitching before Udo, shaking, controlling himself with an effort of will I found amusing. He wore a fancy uniform which included a gilt cuirass all carved and engraved into the likeness of a writhing devil face, fangs and staring eyeballs and wild hair—I think it was intended to be one of the devils of Cottmer's Caverns—and he kept running a finger around the collar and hitching himself about. I judged he was not much used to wearing armor.

"This man is not to be harmed, trylon," he said without as much as a Lahal.

134

"Oh?" shouted Udo. "And who says so?"

At this Zankov checked. He managed to get his finger from the cuirass to spread his arms and shrug. "It would be unwise. He is a bargaining counter, a hostage—"

"I run things here, Zankov—or whatever your name is. Remember that. But—" And here Udo pulled his beard again. "It is so simple as to be moronic. But it might be useful."

Ros pushed forward. "He deserves to die, here and now." The claw glittered ominously.

"Oh, aye, he deserves to die."

"Well, let me scratch him a little."

During all this I stood silently, watching the byplay, wondering just how much of his gloating feelings of superiority Zankov could not stop from showing through. He was making a good job of appearing the zealous subordinate to the trylon. They argy-bargyed, discussing my life like a rotten sack of moldy gregarines. Finally Udo waved his hands and gave his judgment.

"Take him away and bind him and set a watch over him. If he dies or if he lives is my decision. I will take it myself. You will be told when necessary."

A couple of girls grabbed my arms to drag me off.

I remained where I was, with the girls tugging away. I stared hard at Leona. She tossed her head back, her eyes bright.

"If I was this confounded prince, girl—why would you hate me so?"

"You are, and you know."

"Take the rast away!" bellowed Trylon Udo.

The two girls were joined by two more who tugged at me. I remained firm. "Hold on a mur," I said. "I want to know what this fellow, this Prince Majister, has done to you to arouse such heated emotions."

"Get him out of here!" The words slashed from Zankov.

Ros pushed forward. She was breathing heavily, and patches of color mantled her cheeks. The claw looked highly unpleasant, for she had donned it over her left hand and wrist. "I should rip your eyes out, here and now! You betrayer! You deceiver! You lecher! You heartless wretch! You—you—"

"Now easy on," I said, for she broke down from the violence of her emotions. Firn took a swipe at me with her rapier and I had to sway aside. This was getting out of hand. Leona kept on shrieking at me. Zillah and Jodi, who were

135

clearly in command of the Jikai Vuvushis, added their yells and orders. I shook the girls free and took a step toward Trylon Udo. Instantly a shortsword flicked up into his hand.

"All right, all right, trylon," I told him. "I'm not going to hurt you."

"Get him out! Drag him by the heels!" foamed Zankov.

One, two, three strides took me to Zankov. He tried to rip his rapier out and I took him by the throat and lifted him up off his heels. He dangled in the air, choking, his face turning that old interesting purply-green rotten gregarine color.

"Hear me!" I bellowed.

The walls of the room did not shake to that foretop-hailing voice; but a silence dropped.

I shook Zankov, who was bubbling like a punctured boiler.

"Just suppose I were this Prince Majister—" Here I swung my left arm across and swept away a flung spear. Another was caught and reversed in a twinkling. I looked at the girl who had hurled, and smiled, and shook my head. Her face went as white as the underside of a chank.

"Can't you hulus tell me what is going on?"

Strangely, no one wished to speak. I glanced up at Zankov and, regretfully, plunked him down on his feet. I let him go. He fell to pitch forward into Karina's arms. She glared at me venomously; but a flicker in her eyes, a swift betraying gleam of sympathy? I was not sure.

But she said: "Zankov may overrate himself. But he is one of us. You are a southerner—a clansman—prince."

"If I were. And is that all? That the Prince Majister is a stranger?"

"Aye!" said Firn, looking at me with scathing contempt. Her red hair looked marvelous. She breathed deeply and unsteadily. "A stranger. A stranger to Vallia for all of the time. A no-good calsany, a rast who betrays those who love him."

The bewilderment would not leave me. I looked around them, at those lovely faces, all flushed and bright-eyed, all staring accusingly at me. Contempt, hatred, disgust—all were written clear on those fair faces ringing me.

I shook my head.

Zankov held his throat, croaking, trying to speak and unable to force out a sound. The marks of my fingers glowed in livid weals.

"I'll go," I said. "And I will go peacefully. By Vox! But if I really were this Prince Majister then I truly think I'd begin to feel a little sorry for myself."

I did not. But I wanted to test still further the way the wind blew. But no one responded.

Trylon Udo had summoned male guards. He did not know it; but that was a mistake. Had he done so before, I might be away from here now, cleaning up a blood-splattered sword. As it was, I had said I would go peacefully, and so I went. Spear points ringed me as I started off. It was left to Udo to have the last word.

"The reports are true; and yet I harbor a doubt." He was speaking to Zillah and Jodi. "Prescot is a Hyr Jikai only through the proclamations; he is a puffed-up image, we all know that. And yet—"

"He took the spear smartly, enough, Udo."

"Yes, well, that is a common trick. Guard him well. You have a great prize there, for the Princess Majestrix will pay an emperor's ransom for him. That is well known."

I heard a gasp at my back, and I turned. The girls tautened up instantly; but I raised a hand to calm them. I decided not to let the trylon have the last word, afer all.

"It is well known, Udo. Do you know also that she will have your head and your tripes into the bargain?"

And with that I, Dray Prescot, Prince Majister of Vallia, did my best to stalk out.

Chapter Fifteen
Of San Guiskwain the Witherer

They tied me up as they would tie up any common criminal and chucked me into a narrow wooden stockade by the town wall. Captive—I was a captive once more. Well, by Zair, I've been captive before on Kregen and plenty of times since that occasion in Hockwafernes. Being a Captive of Kregen is an occupational hazard to a wild leem of a fellow like me. Or so I am led to believe.

The guards were prattling on about the great news the trylon had brought and how on the morrow the tremendous ceremony would be performed and all the promised and looked-for supernatural powers would come to the assistance of the Hawkwas.

Male and female guards took turn and turn about to stand watch outside the wooden cell.

The thongs broke free after a bur or so. I stretched and felt the blood tingling. They didn't know me, then. . . .

So far I have spared you the innumerable aphorisms widely current upon Kregen attributed to San Blarnoi. He was either a real person of wide learning or a consortium of misty figures of the dim past. Either way, many sayings are attributed to San Blarnoi. He is a fount of wisdom, both superficial and of deeper significance, and among the many maxims are to be found one or two to fit almost any situation.

Some are merely of the order of: "San Blarnoi he say. . . ." Others are Christmas Cracker mottoes in scope. Some give a little comfort or insight.

It was Filbarrka na Filbarrka who first told me of the saying that I used now. Filbarrka, as you know, is that wide and marvelous area south and east of the Blue Mountains that is zorca country supreme. I think there are few finer zorcas bred on Kregen anywhere else. Filbarrka ran the area. He was not a Blue Mountain boy. His name and that of the land were as one.

Anyway, in his bluff, red-faced, cheerful way he'd once cautioned me: "As San Blarnoi says, waiting is shortened by preparation."

I had the remainder of the day to wait through. It was clearly useful to be able to spend that waiting time in this prison cell as a captive, out of mischief. If this sounds paradoxical, it is; but it was nonetheless for that true.

So, unwilling to break out at once, I perforce followed San Blarnoi's dictum and prepared myself in the only way left. I thought. I pondered the problem.

Dayra would arrive on the morrow. And on the morrow the trylon would produce his miracle that would make his army invincible. He was well known in the occult areas, and had a wizard in his employ, not a Wizard of Loh, who was one of these renowned Northeast Vallian sorcerers, a Hawkwa necromancer.

Natyzha Famphreon had spoken of them, calling the ghastly practitioners Opaz-forsaken corpse-revivers.

Brooding in my cell it occurred to me I might wisely pay a visit to the ceremony on the morrow. Dayra must come first. But from the guards' conversation I learned further disquieting information as the day wore on. The rumor of the arrest of the Lord Farris on treason charges was confirmed. And, with him, other men I would have sworn loyal to the emperor had been imprisoned. I had distinguished company as I languished in prison. Also, an army had landed in the south, west of Ovvend, and was marching on Vondium. This news caused me grave concern. That the army had come from Pandahem seemed reliable information. The emperor had marched out to destroy them. Everyone awaited the outcome. There had been only a slight panic in Vondium. I chafed. But, this close, I had set my thoughts and desires on Dayra, and I was not prepared to change my direction now.

My careful preparation of hard thinking led me to the unpalatable conclusion that this Opaz-forsaken ceremony might include me as a sacrifice. It would be in keeping with all those dark and horrific forces of the occult side of Kregen. If that were so, I'd best be about my business a little ahead of the time I had set myself.

The time to make the break came, I felt, when the guards were a mix of Fristles, Rapas, Khibils and apims. No women stood outside my cell door. The guards talked among themselves in desultory fashion. But they'd be alert enough.

A Rapa was saying in his vicious hissing way: "And the rast knows nothing of all this?"

The voice of the apim talking, which had been a mere mumble before, strengthened and grew clearer as he approached. He laughed.

"Know? He is a fambly, that one. I know it to be so."

"His fearsome reputation is all a make-believe—yes, that is known. He is no true Hyr-Jikai. But, this other—?"

"I had it from my second cousin twice removed. He was in Vondium at the time. Oh, yes, this precious Delia, Princess Majestrix, is notorious. Her lovers are legion."

I listened, flexing my muscles, waiting until they positioned themselves just so.

"Before she took up with this Turko fellow it was a Bowman of Loh—a Jiktar, I believe. And there was a visiting diplomat from Tolindrin—and where that is Vox knows."

"In Balintol. And?"

The apim started asking about Tolindrin; but the Rapa, who was joined by a Fristle, although they were stiffly polite one with the other, wanted to know more about the amatory exploits of the Princess Majestrix. This gossip was all over Vallia.

"She has a secret room furnished erotically in all her villas. She spends money like water. Her lovers—mind you, dom, they don't last."

139

"No?"

"No. It is a sack and a leaden weight and the Great River for them."

"Bitch."

"Aye. Leave well alone there, if ever her eye falls on you."

"I am a Rapa." The surprise was genuine.

"It makes no difference to her. You're a man, aren't you?"

The Rapa courts of women are notorious. I had once gone chasing madly through Zenicce at the mere threat. The guards changed their positions casually, leaning on their spears. I watched them through the wooden bars. The Khibil was likely to be the most dangerous. When he moved in, half-interested in what was being said about the amatory adventures of the Princess of Vallia, his alert fox-like face bright with all the intelligence of his race, I fancied my time had come.

With a surging shoulder charge I burst through the wooden bars, shattering three of them in a welter of flying splinters. The hands and arms they thought so securely bound whipped up from behind my back and two throats clamped into my grasp. Two savage shakes, and then two clouting blows, and the four guards lay stretched senseless upon the packed-dirt floor. The Rapa, the Fristle, the Khibil and the apim slumbered. I had killed not a one of them.

The cramphs had not fed me, and I found a crust and an onion in a scrip and wolfed them down. I took a clanxer, a dagger and a spear, and set off.

The dawn would soon be here in a washing radiance of jade and ruby light—and with the dawn, Dayra.

Pretty soon the hunt was up. But I sat tight in a space under the roof of the house where the conspirators met, and I, Dray Prescot, chuckled as they searched for me in vain.

Again it was a question of waiting. But to this house they would come to plan the final schemes, and to this house would come my daughter Dayra, to be duped and betrayed by them.

I was wrong.

Wrong—completely wrong.

The day wore on. The heat began to build up in that tiny cramped space under the roof. And the house below me remained ominously still and silent. Outside, the sounds of many people moving convinced me the time for the ceremony grew near.

What form that ceremony would take I had no idea. This dark wizard of the trylon's, this San Uzhiro, would officiate.

After all the mumbo jumbo, the poor swods of the army and the irregulars would believe they were invincible. This is a trick that has been tried on armies before, and, oftimes, it boomerangs. So I sweated and waited and then, as the murs ran away through the glass eye of time, I jerked up as though in that confined stinking sweaty-hot place someone had flung a bucket of ice water over me.

Fool!

Of course—the house was empty. Dayra was flying in to attend the ceremony. That was where I would find her—not here.

Chagrined at my own stupidity—more than chagrined—raging with a vicious intemperate self-scorn, I swung down from the roof and dropped into the street. The town was practically deserted. Everyone had gone to mass in the wide space surrounding the temple. In that temple, that blasphemous Temple of Hockwafernes, that was where I should be.

A passing Och halted as I called to him. His six limbs trembled under the weight of a sack, and he wore the gray breechclout.

"What time does the ceremony begin, slave?"

"Master—a bur after mid—"

I jerked a thumb and he staggered off. My face must have scared him clean through.

Time, then, for an errand. . . .

That errand took me over the town wall contemptuous of the guards. One saw me and shouted, and I bellowed back a rigmarole about a message for Jiktar Haslam, and blast your eyes, you rast, and so ran fleetly across the dirt toward the leather tents. The quietness everywhere lay a strangeness over the camp. Not all the army by any means had been invited to attend the ceremony, even to stand outside the temple, for that would have been an impossibility given the numbers; but enough had gone to leave the rest feeling lacklustre and out of it. They would partake of the good news to be bought by occult means, and so did not complain more than soldiers ordinarily do. Which is to say they grumbled and cursed most fearsomely.

Nalgre and Dolan were not at their tent. The camp slave cringed back as I ripped out my gear. It was all there. I strapped on my weapons. I did not have a rapier and main gauche; all the rest I had and intended to use if need be. Then I hared off back to the town, having to dodge down a

141

side avenue of tents as a search party ran past, no doubt alert-
ed by the sentry on the walls I had shouted at.

Gigantic gong notes began to reverberate from the temple.
I had to hurry.

The cape I swathed about myself attracted no attention,
being similar to a thousand worn by the swods, and the cased
bowstave easily passed for a spear. The crowds outside the
temple moved like a cornfield in the breeze. The suns shone.
A wind blew the dust. The noise susurrated like waves on
pebbles. I pushed through, gently, gradually working my way
toward the front. If this Opaz-forsaken temple was like most
there would be a side way in. It would be guarded, of course.

There was a small side door, and there was a guard.

The door opened easily enough after the guard lay scattered about, and the door slammed harshly in the faces of the
shocked men who had witnessed the fury of sudden destruction that had fallen on the guard detail.

As I sprang four at a time up the spiral tower steps it occurred to me, wryly, that all my careful planning might as
well have never taken place. So much for the good San Blarnoi.

The stairs led onto a balcony and I peered between carved
stones onto the scene below. This was not planned at all.

The vibrant gong strokes rang still in the air. But the gong
hung silent. Men moved below on the dais, men in garish
costumes. I checked them all, swiftly, judging them to be
priests or sorcerers engaged about their diabolical pastime,
and raked my eyes over the gathered mass of people.

Where was Dayra?

Then, the destructive thought hit me, would I, could I,
recognize her? A girl I'd never seen? Born when I was four
hundred light years away from Kregen? I cursed the Star
Lords then, and went on looking intently at the gathered
people.

The temple was, truly, a marvel of architecture. The
people filled it tightly, so that not a speck of floor was visible.
The dais stood high at the center, and incense rose, stinking.
Grotesque carvings entwined obscene forms. A crystal ovoid
lifted at the center of the dais, draped in black and purple
hangings, with golden tassels. Bells were ringing now, bells
twirling and clanging in the hands of girls, half naked, dancing and twirling around the catafalque.

Like Bacchantes, with swirling hair and naked rosy limbs
they danced and pranced, gyrating, ringing their bells,
arousing everyone to a feverish anticipation.

142

Trylon Udo stepped forward. His costume was a sumptuous blaze of jewels. He lifted his arms high into the air and the bells ceased their clanging and the nymphs ceased their gyrations, although as they stood they swayed rhythmically like fronds of seaweed.

He began to speak in a high chanting voice.

Someone would be doing something about the guard detail now; the locked door would be forced, more guards would pile up the spiral stairs. Other guards would block all the exits. I moved around the high balcony, and found half a dozen more sentries who died quickly and cleanly. Now I could see down onto the catafalque more clearly. Beside the trylon stood the Hawkwa necromancer, San Uzhiro. Clad all in purple with golden tassels, he presented a grave, chilling picture of absolute dedication to the occult forces beyond the bounds of normal human knowledge.

Udo's words formed merely the prelude, in which he promised much and, chiefly, that his army would be invincible.

Then San Uzhiro stepped forward upon the dais below the catafalque.

With shocked gasps of surprise from the congregation, abrupt and brilliant bursts of flame and colored smoke shot up from the crystal ovoid. It glowed with an uncanny inner light, like torches seen through rain-spattered windows.

"Behold!" thundered Uzhiro. Every word rang and vaulted in echoing clarity around the wide temple. "Behold the corpse of San Guiskwain! San Guiskwain the Witherer, San Guiskwain na Stackwamore. Behold and marvel. Behold and tremble."

The people trembled in all truth. This Guiskwain, a most highly remarked sorcerer of Vallia, had lived and died no man knew how long ago, but it was certainly more than two and a half thousand seasons. And here he was, perfectly preserved in his crystal ovoid, his form and features showing clear and clearer as the lights spurted up. Here was sorcery at its most dire.

For Uzhiro waved his arms, sweating, chanting cadences of power, sprinkling dust, sending ripples of fear through the throng. We all knew what he was doing. The guards chasing me would have left off doing that; they would be transfixed by the awful powers being unleashed in this place. Everyone craned to see, barely breathing, as Uzhiro chanted on and the corpse within the crystal coffin upon the catafalque grew in

143

clarity and all might see the thunderous expression on that lowering face.

That was a mystery, how plainly the face was visible, even to me, high on the balcony. At that distance the other people's faces were mere blurs. But the ancient sorcerer's face glowed with supernatural tyranny.

The foul stench of the incense puffed high into the interior of the temple. The dome opened, it seemed, onto infinity itself, although common sense said that the myriad specks of light were merely painted spots of mineral-glittering pigments. The long low moaning chants of the acolytes, the rooted swaying rhythms of the temple maidens, the cloying stinks of incense, all were calculated to tear away the senses from the brain, to impose false images, to induce a phantasmagoria of hallucinations.

Did San Guiskwain the Witherer *really* open his eyes? *Did* he reach out a skeletal hand? Did a man dead two thousand five hundred seasons really return to life?

San Uzhiro chanted and he had no doubts. His commands imposed themselves on the multitude, so that they saw with his eyes and heard with his ears.

Guiskwain, dead yet alive, sat up in the crystal coffin and looked about, that skeletal arm raised admonishingly.

No one fainted, no one passed out. All were transfixed, held scarcely breathing by the sheer occult power. And a sense of darkness gathered and coalesced under the dome. A brooding sense of power beyond the grave, of a stubborn life that two and half millennia could not quench, of perverse defiance of the natural order of life and death pervaded the temple and puffed upward in the rotting miasma of swamps and the fetid air of tombs sealed against the light.

"He lives!" screamed Uzhiro. "San Guiskwain lives!"

The cry was taken up in a tumultuous swelling cacaphony of voices raised in rapture.

"He lives!"

Here was the miracle. Here the proof of the necromancer's power.

"Through Guiskwain the Witherer shall the army become invincible!" screeched Uzhiro, flailing his arms. "Through the greatest sorcerer dead yet living shall the Hawkwas gain all! Guiskwain lives!"

The long moment of triumph hung fire. The darkest pits of a Kregan hell had been opened. Now all, everyone present, turned to gaze with rapt adoration upon the lowering, vindictive, ashen face of Guiskwain the Witherer.

Transcendental, sublime, blasphemous—call it what you will. It was certain sure that all gathered here and held in this hallucinated trance believed with all their hearts.

But—was this hallucination? Was this trickery? Or was a long-dead necromancer really revived, brought back to life, dragged once again into the light so as to destroy all I cared for in Vallia? Could the trick be no trick at all?

Did Guiskwain the Witherer, dead two and a half millennia, live?

Chapter Sixteen

The Fight Below the Voller

Whether he lived or was dead made no real difference.

Whether he still moldered away in his crystal coffin or whether he had been blasphemously raised by necromantic power into a semblance of full-booded life did not matter.

What mattered was the belief, the impression, the effect.

These people believed.

The long low moaning shudder passed over them like a rashoon of the Eye of the World. They bowed. In a giant sighing rustle and the jangle of weapons and accoutrements they bowed their heads, crouched, extending their arms in swath after swath of ranked submission.

Was my daughter down there now, one of that hypnotized host? Did Dayra bow her head and tremble with all the others at the sight and stink of a long-dead wizard raised from the grave?

How in the name of Makki-Grodno's disgusting diseased tripes could I know?

I was shaking. Sweat ran down my forehead and stung into my eyes. I blinked, swallowed, cursed—all the actions of an idiot without a thought in his thick vosk skull of a head.

A girl in the russets and armor of a Battle Maiden ran lightly up past the half-naked temple girls. She spoke rapidly to Udo. His head went up; he gestured to Uzhiro. They conferred. Then Uzhiro swung back and called for everyone to rise and stare upon the sublime face and form of Guiskwain.

Trylon Udo stepped forward. He held up a hand. He spoke with tremendous emotion, forcefully, jolting these people.

"Now are we invincible in battle. Now the potent force of San Guiskwain the Witherer is with us. He will waste away our enemies. Long and long have the Hawkwas waited for this time. And now it is here." His lifted hand gripped into a fist. "There is more. The army from Hamal landed in the south of Vallia has gained a great victory. The hosts of the emperor are withered away, his warriors strew the ground in windrows, their blood waters the dirt. This is a further sign! Guiskwain is with us and nothing can stand in our path."

I had to stand peering through the stone bars of the balcony and listen, grinding down my nature that sought to burst out in bestial ferocity.

So the cramphs had come from Hamal, the bitter foe of Vallia, and not from Pandahem. An armada of skyships had brought them; that was a safe conclusion. And the emperor, Delia's father, had been worsted. Had his bodyguard, the Crimson Bowmen, bought and paid for in red gold, betrayed him?

What of the men loyal to the emperor? What of the Blue Mountains, of Delphond, of my own Archers of Valka who had been sent for from Evir? What had happened down south?

And Delia?

Dayra. . . . Dayra. . . .

I had selfishly sought out my daughter here, and in that space of time I had been away from Vondium the empire might have fallen. Udo was shouting again, flushed, triumphant, overweening.

"Our own fleet of airboats will fly us south. We will join with our friends from Hamal. We will march upon Vondium and take that great city and utterly destroy all who stand in our path. All hail to San Guiskwain! All hail to the Hawkwas!"

Here once again was the hand of Phu-Si-Yantong. I was convinced of that. He had extended the tentacles of his authority through Hamal, manipulating the pallans around the Empress Thyllis. He had provided the money and the weapons and now a fleet of vollers for Trylon Udo to take and sack Vondium. And, when the time was ripe, Phu-Si-Yantong's tools, in the guise of Stromich Ranjal and Zankov, would strike down Udo and take all for the greatest puissance of Phu-Si-Yantong.

It must be so.

"Sink me!" I burst out. "If you are alive, you necromantic kleesh, you'll soon be dead again!"

The bowstave hissed from the cover, it seemed to string itself of its own will. The blue-fletched arrow nocked and the bow bent in a long sinuous flow of motion. The steel pile glittered. I loosed. The shaft flew sweetly. Clear across that wide space under the dome the arrow sped, piercing through the winding veils of incense smoke, drove hard and savagely full into San Guiskwain's breast.

I saw it. I saw the arrow curve upward. It ricocheted up with a high singing note of steel against crystal. It curved to fall away and be lost among the gathered host.

And San Guiskwain remained upright, unmoved, unharmed.

"By Krun!" I shouted. "Sorcery and more sorcery. I'll have you yet, you cramph."

Twice more I loosed and twice the sharp steel-tipped shafts caromed with that high crystal ringing from the unholy form of the dead wizard who yet lived.

Guards boiled along the balcony toward me. They were men. If I had to fight I had to fight. But, for the last time, and even as I loosed knowing the gesture was futile and useless, I cast a last shaft at the blasphemous form of Guiskwain.

Had I used the few brains I boast I should have shot at Uzhiro. Trylon Udo was a mere pawn. But my incensed fury was all directed at that towering, impregnable, loweringly obscene form of a living dead man.

Then, after a handful of shafts into the first of the charging guards it was handstrokes along the high balcony.

The shortsword, built by Naghan the Gnat to specifications drawn up from careful measurement of the deadly shortsword of my Clansmen of Segesthes, chunked in gleaming silver and ripped out gleaming red. I put my shoulder down and bashed into the guards, anxious to carve a way through them and reach the outside air. The notion of finding Dayra in all this hullabaloo had still not left me, although I was having to face the fact that with all my plans gone wrong I was hardly likely to find her now.

Four Rapas tried to work as a team and do for me. No doubt they were accustomed to quick victory utilizing their intricate teamwork on the battlefield or in camp brawls. But a fighting man must tailor his work to circumstances. The balcony was narrow. Even as the first Rapa prepared to open the gambit and feint away I slashed his beak off, burst past

147

him, sank the blade into the next one—just far enough—ducked a wild clanxer swipe and so chunked left, right, and felled the other two.

They couldn't know, of course—but anyone who did would understand why the shortsword gleamed in my fist and the deadly Krozair longsword snugged still in its scabbard.

The guards expected me to go one way, and so I went the other. A narrow slot opened in the wall, one of the many runnels all these huge old buildings possess, crevices between facing walls, cavities under domes, tunnels left for the maintenance that must unceasingly go on to stop the whole fabric from toppling to destruction. With a last flicker of the shortsword I ducked down the slot.

The first fall was some ten feet and I hit with a thump. On my feet in an instant I padded between rough brick courses, a thread of light wanly illuminating the patches of damp and the mold. The way led via wooden ladders and dusty passages downward. The sounds of pursuit followed me. I stepped past a skeleton—it had been a plump wallpitix, poisoned by the temple caretakers and crept away here to die—and pushed on boldly. Wherever the way led I was sure to meet guards.

Brittle bones crunched underfoot. A whole nest of wallpitixes, those furry, bright-eyed household scavengers, had died here. Beyond them and around a harsh masonry corner where the dirt had been cobbled over, a lenken door, banded with bronze, barred the way. I gave the door a look and put my shoulder to it.

With a creak like some poor soul being crushed between millstones it grated open. Red and green light flooded in. Cautiously, I poked my head out, the blade raised, ready to defend myself. Around me stretched the ranked arcades of stone coffins. Some had toppled over and a detritus of bones and skulls littered the stone-flagged floor. I had penetrated below the temple and entered the crypt. That seemed apt at the time. Thoughtfully, I closed the door and shot the massive iron bolts, turning the heads over with a succession of sharp and satisfactory snaps. That took care of the bloodthirsty soldiers at my back. Now for the no-less bloodthirsty warriors in front.

The light streamed from tinted fireglass crystals set in niches along the coves. I guessed San Uzhiro had been down here earlier, needing light, to fetch out the crystal coffin of Guiskwain the Witherer. There were telltale marks in the dust. A skull rolled away as I marched across the flags.

The eerie effects of witnessing a corpse brought back to life began to wear off. I found I was thinking again.

I have always said that if you can't join them, beat them. As a principle of life on Kregen, I think that well-exemplified in the account of what befell Dray Prescot there. But, now, it would be convenient to join them for a space.

The fusty smell in the crypt led by way of the almost imperceptible wash of fresher air to the outer door. By its configuration I judged it stood at the bottom of a flight of steps cut into the earth leading up to ground level. Carefully, easing the door open a whisker at at time, I peered out.

No matter how many times I tangle with guards, I am forced to fight sentries, hide from or dispatch watchmen, I can never think of them as mere lay figures. Guards on duty face a thankless task. At times it seems they are there merely to be slain by the princes and captains who seek to go where they should not. But a guard is a man, doing a rotten job, and glad when his duty is over and he can traipse off to the guardroom and take off at least a little of his equipment and put his feet up for a time, until he is due to roust out again.

Guards stand in gaudy uniforms with ornate spears and are ripe targets. No—I do not devalue guards, no matter that I have been forced to deal harshly with them in my time.

The guards at the top of the steps were Chuliks. This complicated matters from the point of view of joining them, and made the physical exertion of dealing with them that much more hazardous. Chuliks are not apims. They are diffs. They are powerful, ferocious warriors, trained from the earliest age in the manipulation of weapons, lacking in the lighter side of humanity, abhorred except as mercenary warriors. This, at the time and, I admit, to my shame, made the moral side of the problem that much easier of resolution.

I could not join this little lot—so I was forced to beat them.

The fight boiled up along the steps and out onto a grassy sward between upflung buttresses. The courtyard closed in with gray stone walls. It formed one of the many surrounding enclosures penned by the cyclopean walls that uplifted and supported the bulk of the temple. Roughly wiped, the shortsword slapped back into its scabbard.

The Krozair longsword twinkled out, and flamed silver for only a heartbeat, and then turned into the bloody brand of destruction that shears through all opposition.

"Cut the cramph down!" And: "By Likshu he Treacher-

149

ous! The man is a devil!" And: "In the name of Father Chalkush of the Iron Brand do not let him pass."

Blades clashed and slithered, blood flew, we leaped and contorted across the grass, Chuliks spun away, pierced, slashed, degutted, the longsword flamed a circle of savage destruction. The very size of those towering walls deadened sound. We trampled across the grass and I had to skip and jump right smartly, for Chuliks are rightly renowned as superb fighting men. But for the dead Rapa paktun's armor I would have been nicked a couple of times. But, in the end, I had them all, and so could plunk the dripping point of the Krozair brand into the turf and spell a moment or two, breathing deeply, gulping the air which stank now with the tang of freshly spilled blood.

The Chuliks wore the colors of Gelkwa. The colors were green, silver, black and yellow, arranged in the Hawkwa fashion as a regular pattern of circles, silver, black and yellow, upon their green sleeves. Finding a tunic that was not too bloody I stripped my own tunic off—or, rather, the tunic that had been Rojashin's—and donned the garment of Gelkwa. All the same, the kax that had served me well went back on. The letting out of the shoulder straps and pauldrons had not affected the harness's efficacy. The longbow could be unstrung and slid back into its sleeve. How long that would pass as a spear remained to be seen; it had deceived before. Settling a fresh helmet on my head—gaudy with colors, heavy with feathers—and curling the long cape about me I surveyed the scene.

A grassy sward filled with dead Chuliks. Blood. Stink. Flies. And me, Dray Prescot, helplessly and hopelessly looking for a wayward daughter, and all Vallia in flames.

Through the far gateway I came out onto the temple precincts and was able to mingle casually with the departing throngs. The talk centered on one subject only. I walked with bowed head, as though profoundly affected by the awesome occurrences within the Temple of Hockwafernes.

I felt that all Vallia was alight. Once the emperor was seen to falter, once a blow was struck against his authority, many people would stand forth from the shadows and openly challenge him. You know of many of the parties and factions; there were more, people determined to have their own way with the Empire of Vallia and to the Ice Floes of Sicce with anyone who opposed them. There had been a battle and the emperor had been defeated. I wondered if he had been there in person or had sent a general to deal with the invasion. I wondered if the old devil was still alive.

My course was now clear cut. Despite all my ineffective attempts to see Dayra and to rescue her, I had achieved nothing. Even this corpse revived to blasphemous life lived and I had been unable to send him decently back to the grave. Between Dayra and Delia I was being forced to choose, and the alternatives were odious, agonizing. But—Delia. Yes I must assure myself she was safe first. If her father went down in ruin, Delia would become the prey of the leems prowling and scenting blood.

Somehow, I sensed that Dayra had survived with the wild bunch with whom she ran because she knew how to handle both herself and them. She would not be suddenly in dire peril now, just because I had not seen her. Why should my arrival make any difference to her? After all, I had not affected her life up until now. She had lived and grown to womanhood without me. So, feeling the deep hurtful wounds pressing in on my spirit, I set off to see about stealing a flier.

The careful watch of the guards lay all at my rear now. The temple was still the focal point. How long I would have before that dreadful courtyard was discovered I did not know. But a flier I needed and a flier I would have.

At the least, I have some skill in stealing vollers.

The Chulik guard had included a Hikdar among their number and I assumed he had been checking up on his posts. That was the last item of military procedure he would ever perform. A Hikdar—nearly enough to an Earthly captain in that he commands a pastang, a company of around eighty men—is the first of the more important ranks, and it is possible for wealthy young men, well-connected and with military aptitude, to enter the army directly as ob-Hikdars. What the Deldars say about that may be imagined. So I had hung the Hikdar's rank insigne on my harness and was prepared to be somewhat blunt to any swod who offered to halt me.

Everywhere a transformation had swept over Trylon Udo's army. Where they had been a collection of irregulars, leavened with a few professionals, and aware of that and apprehensive of their own capacities and of the emperor's Crimson Bowmen, now they were a united force, filled with a surging confidence that would carry them on despite casualties to ultimate victory.

With sufficient spear carriers to hurl forward, and with the hard-core elite troops to follow swiftly on, even well-disci-

151

plined enemies may be overcome. It is all zeal, morale, burning conviction, the sense of invulnerability through belief.

And the emperor had already been once defeated in the field.

My duty, clearly, lay in Vondium and the rapid creation of forces to withstand the two-pronged attack Phu-Si-Yantong had thrown against Vallia.

As I walked steadily on, avoiding the areas near the leather tent of Nalgre and Dolan, fliers cruised into view, high, then circling and descending. The transports were gathering. I watched, counting, estimating, storing away information. To amass an aerial fleet of this size, and with vollers of this capacity, was a task beyond the resources of a trylon of the Northeastern part of Vallia. Once again the hand of the Wizard of Loh showed itself.

One of the tragedies of the situation was that Udo desired self-determination for the Northeast and his Hawkwas. Yantong's ambitions ranged further, for through his tools he would rule Vallia himself. Udo was expendable, and where men and women are concerned that is a concept that always fills me with disgust. And yet—and yet it is a tactic used more than once. But, always I think, with volunteers. Not a pleasant business. . . .

The fliers were parked neatly and I strolled along marking out the small flier I would take, judging from her lines she was a swift craft. She would have to serve me well and not break down. And then I smiled—just a little. If Yantong had provided these vollers from the arsenals of Hamal then they would be first-class, they would function, they would not break down. Capital!

Now I have indicated that very many folk of Vallia believed their Prince Majister was a blown-up paper tiger, a fake Hyr-Jikai, holding a reputation he had not earned and did not deserve. This belief had been fostered by my long absence. And my enemies had no doubt put these rumors about. Phu-Si-Yantong would know differently, Rosil Yasi, the Kataki Strom, knew differently from personal experience. His twin brother, the Stromich Ranjal, would therefore presumably know better, too.

I overlooked that fact and as a consequence prepared to stroll up to the little voller and send her racing into the sky without any fuss.

There were guards about, as was natural, and volmen working on the craft preparing them for the triumphant expedition south. These people I ignored and walked steadily toward my flier.

A group of guards and volmen and Jikai Vuvushis stood gaping upward as a large flier circled preparatory to landing. Others looked aloft. This was my time. I advanced toward the craft I had selected more rapidly. Unfortunately she was not at the end of a row; half a dozen other craft surrounded her.

The Fristles jumped me when I had but a score of paces to go.

Scimitars upraised, their cat-faces distorted, shrilling spitting war cries they flung themselves at me.

"The rast! The Prince Majister!" They screeched their rage and triumph. "He is here! Ho! Guards! The Prince Majister!"

In an instant I was surrounded by a glittering hedge of steel.

This was inopportune. The longsword flamed out, striking away scimitars, slashing cat-faces, carving a path toward the voller. More guards were running up. The whole place came astir like an ants' nest. I started running and slashing in real earnest. So near the voller I was not going to be denied.

That particular pack of Fristles went down. I reached the voller. Before putting a hand to the coaming and leaping aboard I swung about. The old Krozair Disciplines snapped into place. Four Undurker archers were lifting their laminated bows, were letting fly. The Krozair longsword swatted this way and that and the short brightly-tufted arrows slapped away harmlessly.

Heading the group coming up from the side ran Zankov. I wouldn't mind spitting him; but beside him raced the dark and sinister form of Stromich Ranjal. That wicked tailblade lifted high. The Battle Maidens were there also—I saw Leona nal Larravur, and Ros, and Firn, and Karina the Quick, the bandage awry, pelting along. I had no wish to slay them.

This group fouled the range for the Undurkers. Those diffs with their supercilious canine-faces ran up, trying to spot me and shaft me properly this time.

Zankov was yelling: "He is a coward A no-account! A nulsh. Take him alive."

"I'll stick him through!" screeched Leona.

"I'll take his eyes out first!" screeched Ros. The left-hand claw glittered menacingly.

I leaped up into the voller and slammed the levers over to full forward and full lift.

The airboat lifted two feet and then halted with a shuddering surge, a violent constriction of effort, hung swinging. I stuck my head over the side.

"By Vox!" I yelled, baffled.

The cramphs had affixed thick chains to the keel and locked them firmly into stakes driven deeply into the ground.

I was anchored fast.

Then they were on me.

Even as Zankov hurled himself forward, his rapier a glinting bar of light, Ranjal yelled: "Beware, Zankov! He is a warrior—"

"A bag of vomit!" shouted Zankov and slashed wildly at me.

I slid the blow and put my left fist into his face. He fell backward from the voller with a scream.

Ranjal flicked his tail at me and then hauled it back just in time. The longsword hissed through air.

"Let me get at him!" Ros was screeching.

"Let me!" screamed Leona. She knew how to use a rapier and the thin blade snickered past my ribs. Mind you, that was a waste, for the rapier would never puncture through the kax.

I clouted her over the head—very gently.

An Undurker arrow whistled at my head and I ducked and flicked its fellow away with the longsword. A Rapa tried to climb onboard and I cleft his head down. There was nothing else for it. I would have to go overboard and release the chains.

With a wild whoop—a deliberately theatrical war cry which was not, in those circumstances, an entire waste of breath—I jumped from the flier.

A short and violent scuffle ensued in which various guards staggered away holding bloody fingers to various portions of their anatomy, or who slumped to the blood-soaked grass, and then I was familiar with the chains hooked into the stakes. One came free and the longsword bit around in a flailing slash that left a grotesque wake of lopped limbs. This was not fancy any more, this was sheer savagery in the attempt to remain alive. Zankov came at me again—he had courage, that one—and I hit him again with the hilt and the blade shocked on to skewer through the neck of a Rapa following him. Zankov dropped and I put a foot on his wrist, grinding fist and sword hilt into the dirt.

Firn tried to spit me and I had to knock her away.

In the next split second I had my hand on the last remaining chain.

A blow thunked down on my helmet and I whirled, the longsword slicing, and a Chulik—who should have known better—staggered away looking surprised. He collapsed. And then—somehow, somehow—with devastating speed, the lithe feline form of Ros appeared before me. She disdained her rapier. Her left hand whipped for my face.

My own left hand leaped from the longsword hilt and caught her wrist. I felt the harsh steel splines. Her face—that glorious, glowing, superbly beautiful face—bore down on me with hateful virulence.

Under my foot Zankov thrust himself wildly sideways. He squirmed. With a vicious grinding twist I tramped down on his arm and he screamed.

And then—and then I felt a spiteful cutting agony pierce through the fingers of my left hand. With an oath I let Ros go. Along the metal splines sharp teeth stood out, and gleamed wetly with my blood.

I could have thrust her through then with the longsword.

I did not.

I staggered as Zankov writhed around, yelling.

The cruel curved talons slashed toward me. I warded them off and Ros whipped her hand back in a cunning backhand blow that revolved at the last minute and so brought the claw in a long razoring slash down my face. The slicing blow stung.

A Chulik tried to degut me from the side and the longsword twitched and he fell away a dying man.

"You devil!" gasped Ros.

Zankov was screaming now, screaming all the bile and viciousness out, screeching words—impossible words.

"Kill the rast! Slash his eyes out!"

Again the claw razored toward my face.

"Kill him!" screamed Zankov. "Dayra! Kill him. Slay him for good and all, Dayra! *Dayra!*"

Chapter Seventeen
The Gathering of Shadows

I looked down into lustrous brown Vallian eyes. I saw that glowing face. I saw and I could not understand.

Almost, almost, then, I was a dead man.

But the longsword of itself sliced and slashed and the two Chuliks screamed and spun away, bloody wrecks.

The blood dripped down my face from the razor slashings of the steel claw.

"Dayra?"

Zankov screamed again: "Now is your chance, Dayra! Slay the rast and have done."

I stepped back, out of the lethal swing of the claw and kicked Zankov in the side of the head. He slumped. My left hand reached for the last hooked chain.

"So mother was right, after all, and these fools wrong," she said, this girl, this Ros the Claw who was my little daughter Dayra. "For no other man could do what you have done and lived." She lifted the steel tiger talons on which my blood glimmered darkly. "You are a Hyr-Jikai."

"Only a fool would do what I have done," I said.

"That is sooth."

"You have fallen among evil company—Dayra. Come with me. I must go and see if Delia your mother is safe."

"She will be. I have given orders—"

I broke in, exasperated, still dizzy with the shock. "Don't you know what kind of villain this rast is? He means to kill all of us—all the family—"

She shook her head. "Not true."

"If only I had known. . . . They said you were arriving today."

"How do you know that? I do as I please. I take orders from no one—from no man—least of all from a father I have never known."

This could be resolved later, for now soldiers pressed on and time was on a short fuse. I gripped the harsh steel hook ready to slip it over the ring. "Come with me, Dayra. Your mother—"

"You are not fit to speak her name! Leave her out of it."

An arrow pitched into the blood-soaked ground. Another punched through the fabric of the airboat by my head.

"You must hurry, Dayra, or they will shaft you, too."

"Go, go away! Run! You have been running all your life so go on running. You betrayed us all and you will continue to betray us, no matter what you say. Go before I slash your eyes out."

But since she had understood that I, at last, knew who she was, she had made not a single move to attack me as she had been so savagely doing before.

A quick glimpse of booted feet and the glint of a bladed tail past the keel of the flier warned me I could dally no longer. If this wayward sprite of mine would not come home with me, she would not. And if I tarried here arguing I would be dead. I gripped the hooked chain fiercely in my left hand and flicked the longsword about and so deflected an Undurker arrow.

"Then I bid you Remberee, Dayra. I shall tell your mother I have seen you." The metal hook lifted. Around me now the guards were closing in, confident I was at last done for. There were very many of them. I could not slay them all. But not a one of them showed anxiety to be first.

With the incongruity of the situation strong upon me, I said: "Take care of yourself—daughter."

She spat at me, and slashed the claw and I wondered as I lifted the hook if she would, finally, have tried to do for me at last.

The flier jerked away as the last chain came free. Gripping the hook I was wrenched aloft, dangling and swinging under the keel of the voller, hurtling away and up into the air.

A few arrows winged after me; but the voller leaped away so fast and gained height so rapidly the arrows fell away uselessly. Like a parcel of laundry at the end of a rope I was whisked up. Climbing the chain proved tricky; but without sheathing the longsword I managed that maneuver and tumbled over the leather-wrapped coaming. Presently I took the flier under command and set the controls for full speed for Vondium. Udo and Ranjal and Zankov—if his headache improved—would send the pursuit after me; but I had chosen exceeding well and the voller outran all pursuit.

When I considered what I had just discovered I was aghast. I was beset by confusion, unable to believe it had really hap-

"Gripping the hook, I was wrenched aloft, dangling."

pened, and yet knowing that what Dayra said was true, true, damn the black Star Lords to hell and beyond.

The only sane course for me to follow was to do what I could for Vallia. I could not put out of my mind that terrible experience—how her claws had slashed—but I could attempt to comfort myself with the reflection that she had lived this long without me and so could live a while longer until I managed to persuade her I was not entirely the rogue, the cheat, the liar, the deceiver she dubbed me. I was those things; but not in the way she meant.

That was a dark and dismal flight back to Vondium.

The claw cuts in my face could be cleaned up and in time they would heal without a scar; but the real scars on me they would leave might never heal. My own daughter! But—at the end, she had stood back. She had made no further effort to stop me. She had bid me go.

Better, I suppose, to be thrown out than to be killed, to a pragmatic kind of fellow, although the more sensitive might well dramatically prefer death. To me, they are the fools, for although one can see their artistic point of view, they do rather show their contempt of the gift of life, which is not to be taken lightly. Perhaps a taste of the Heavenly Mines would cure them. . . .

So I forced myself to look at this unnatural situation with Dayra's eyes. She was perfectly entitled to her view of me. I fancied the company she kept could be revealed to her as the bunch of villains they were and their dark purposes destroy her belief in them. That was one area in which she could be straightened out. That was general. In the private and family quarrel she had with me—that was something else again.

Even then, in those bleak moments of near despair, I once again forced myself to consider the concept that Dayra's companions were honorable people, working for what they truly believed in, and seeing Delia and the emperor and me and the family as villains overripe for the chopping. It was difficult. But, as Zair is my witness, I tried.

And, by Vox, it was not too difficult where the emperor was concerned, either. . . .

All these worries must for the moment be pushed aside.

However difficult that might be, I had to realize that all Vallia could be drenched in blood. I had to do what I could to prevent that. Also, it would not hurt to remind myself I had two other daughters, not to mention three sons, to worry over. . . .

All the same, the story of how Dayra had spurned the Sis-

159

ters of the Rose and taken the name of Ros and learned the trick of using the Claw and become involved with Zankov and that gang would make a fascinating task to unravel and learn. Like me, she used aliases as it suited her. In that, at the least, the very littlest least, she was like me.

It was damn small comfort.

Vondium hove into view and the place was burning in many areas, the fierce orange flames reflecting in the canals, the proud buildings on their hills and islands burning and collapsing. I stared, shocked back to present crises.

The long straggling black fingers of fugitives clogged roads leading away from the capital, the canals lay deserted with all the narrow boats gone, and not a flier sped through the sky apart from my own sole voller I had stolen from Udo.

The palace was not burning and a Pachak guard ringed it to prevent looting. The devoted loyalty of the Pachaks through their honor system of nikobi was never better demonstrated.

I landed in the great kyro before the palace. A guard checked me quickly and efficiently—those guards again, men, just men, doing a job, and faithful, not mere lay figures to be spitted and chopped and cast down all bloody and forgotten—and I was led off to their Chuktar.

A few quick glances told me that all the Pachaks hired by the emperor for duties in various wings of the palace had been collected together. Even the Pachaks from the wing given over to the use of Delia and myself, for with the Chuktar stood our Pachak paktun Jiktar, Laka Pa-Re. He greeted me warmly. The Chuktar, the highest of the military ranks apart from princes and kovs and generals and kings and their like, was Pola Je-Du. He looked more haggard than I liked.

"Lahal, prince. The situation, as you see, is ripe."

"Lahal, Pola Je-Du. Your orders?"

"To guard the palace. Since the defeats the emperor—"

"Defeats? I had heard of one."

"The Hamalese fought well, so I am told. The Vallian army was defeated in detail. The Crimson Bowmen fought brilliantly, those that marched. The others—"

I looked at Laka Pa-Re, remembering how he had warned me that the guards were being bribed. Laka nodded. "The guards who took bribes were weeded out. Naghan Vanki saw to that. But the damage had been done."

"And the various elements disaffected in the capital and the provinces took the chance to rise. There has been much mischief, prince." The Pachak Chuktar pulled his moustache.

Smoke billowed up from a dome across the kyro and the distant sounds of shouting and the crashings of masonry reached us, thin and attenuated. "The emperor marched out with all that was left to him. For us, we guard the palace."

Not for the first time I wondered how the emperor had ever remained emperor for so long. With these Pachaks a great deal might be done—and then I reconsidered. There were perhaps five hundred of them. Against the Hamalese army, against the mobs and the irregulars and the mercenaries of the factions, would they have made all that much difference? The Pachaks would fight in their superb fashion when the first looters arrived with whichever army reached Vondium first. As a reserve, as a hard core, they would serve. Maybe the emperor was still the crafty old devil I thought him.

"And the Princess Majestrix?"

The question was followed by a general shaking of heads in the small, round, unadorned Pachak helmets. No one had any news of the Princess Majestrix.

More information was given me—of the arrests of men hitherto considered loyal to the emperor, of the way Queen Lushfymi more and more obsessed him to the exclusion of all else, of the riots, the burnings and lootings and killings, of the exodus from the capital as the various hostile armies closed in, Hamalese, rebels, insurgents. And I knew a fresh and powerful host inspired by a revived corpse could now be added to that number. . . .

It seemed to me that Phu-Si-Yantong was drawing ever closer to his insane dream. But he could not control all the foes of Vallia advancing on Vondium. In that, paradoxically, lay a slender hope.

In that wide and grandiose kyro with its surrounding colonnades and superb architecture the slender line of Pachaks ringing the palace and the small knot of officers all looked fragile, alone, gray chalk marks against the brilliance. In the radiance of the suns a chill wind blew dust across the flagstones.

A confused noise drew our attention to the far side of the square. The sound of a multitude, the ragged tramp of feet, the jingle of weapons, the creaking of carts, made the officers walk along the ranks, tautening up their men. The Pachaks moved with the quiet, well-ordered air of men waiting for business. They were ready. They would earn their hire.

Calmly the Chuktar gave a last few orders. I said: "I will stand and fight with you, Chuktar Pola Je-Du, if you will."

161

"I will it so, prince, and deem it an honor."

No victorious army of irregulars, no raging army of mercenaries broke into the square. A beaten army debouched and began to straggle across the stones. They were wounded, and dusty, wrapped in bloody bandages, exhausted. At their head mounted on a drooping-headed zorca rode the emperor.

This was an army shattered and near-destroyed.

Krahnik-drawn carts brought in the seriously wounded. A few flags drooped here and there, ripped and bloodied standards. A couple of squadrons of totrix cavalry retained their guidons. But for all else these men formed a mere mob.

The emperor rode slowly toward the group of high ranking Pachak officers. At his side, mounted on a pure white zorca, rode Queen Lushfymi. She wore armor. Somehow, it did not look absurd; gilded breastplate, flaunting helmet crowned with the red and yellow of Vallia, a jingling assortment of weapons buckled about her and her mount. I stood, grim-faced, prepared to be exceedingly nasty.

Chapter Eighteen
The Hand of Phu-Si-Yantong

In the emperor's private inner sanctum he placed his goblet of wine on the polished table and banged a fist down on his knee.

"I'm not finished yet, son-in-law, so don't take that tone with me. Queen Lushfymi thinks we have as good a chance as any of defeating these rasts from Hamal."

Only a few of us had gathered here after the shattered remnants of the army had been attended to as best we could. The Pachaks still stood guard. Now Queen Lush, half a dozen of the pallans who remained, Chuktar Wang-Nalgre-Bartong and myself conferred with the emperor. The news was as bad as it could be without being total disaster. In detail all the forces arrayed against the foes of the emperor had been defeated.

"Kov Layco Jhansi will yet bring in a victory, son-in-law. Once he disposes of these scheming rasts of Falinur the rest will see they had better toe the line."

"Falinur?" I forced myself to remain calm.

"Aye! The kovnate you made me give to your so-called friend Seg Segutorio. They have risen like flies and march to war—and where is this precious Seg Segutorio, Kov of Falinur? Skulked off as you do—or does he lead his host against me?"

The emperor's hand curled in a claw about the stem of the goblet. I couldn't tell him that Seg had been hurled back to his home in Erthyrdrin after his baptism in the Sacred Pool—banished like all my friends to their homes. So, instead, I said: "And what of Vomanus? His Kovnate of Vindelka marches with Falinur. They quarrel over Vinnur's Garden, so—"

"Vomanus? That great rascal. Where is he you may well ask."

I judged that many a wight had taken himself off from the capital in these troublesome times; but I felt disappointment with Vomanus. He was a careless fellow, true; but he was half-brother to Delia. . . .

All the time we spoke and argued and planned meaningless plans in the face of the catastrophe, Queen Lush sat upright, toying with her wine, looking at the emperor fixedly. When he glanced fondly at her she would smile. She wore a simple robe of a deep yellow, and not a scrap of jewelry. She looked different from the easy, casual, bitchy minx I had left here.

"Layco Jhansi will subdue the central provinces. The southwest awaits events. The southeast—" Here the emperor looked pointedly at Lykon Crimahan, the Kov of Forli. Him you have met before. Now he was the Pallan of the Treasury, the new pallan, for Pallan Rodway had long ago passed away and the last incumbent suffered from a cleavage where his neck should be.

Forli, often called the Blessed Forli, lies up an eastern tributary of the Great River and extends to the east coast opposite northern Veliadrin. Lykon Crimahan had no love for me. Yet, I believed he hewed to his own faith with the emperor, evil though he might be, and had the welfare of Vallia at heart, even though he had tried to obstruct my plans to build a great aerial fleet. So I waited for Crimahan to speak, ready with bitter, mocking words of my own.

"I can vouch for Forli, majister. As for the rest—they attack my lands. I would be there to fight for them; but—"

"Your duty is here, at the emperor's side," said Queen Lush.

Her face was bright, her eyes alive with passion. I looked

163

away from her. Her influence, I felt sure, along with many other fighting men, had weakened the emperor, and yet the old devil was full of fight, firm in his resolve to go on with the struggle.

"And, Lykon Crimahan," I said, "where is the great fleet of skyships I wanted to build? Are your friends in Hamal pleased at your handiwork?"

He would have drawn his rapier and rushed on me; but the emperor put up a hand and bellowed, and protocol saved the fool.

"I am loyal to the emperor and Vallia, prince majister! I sit still under no insults—"

"Still, Kov Lykon. Remember the skyships we do not have when those from Hamal cast down their firepots upon the city."

"Our varters will shoot them down," said the emperor. He believed it, and he had taken part in the Battle of Jholaix.

"The Northeast is solidly against you—" I began.

"That I know."

"They fly an army here." I told them what I had learned. Barty had not reached Vondium. Probably his flier had broken down. In these last dark hours that witnessed the death of an empire Barty Vessler must take his own chances. Maybe he had gone home. I did not speak of my daughter Dayra who was called Ros the Claw.

"Trylon Udo. Very well. I have a high tree ready for him. As for this Zankov, he can be dealt with when they get here. I am the emperor, and I understand these foolish plots. By Vox! My emissaries are already hiring thousands of paktuns for me from overseas."

"By the time they arrive all will be over," said Chuktar Wang-Nalgre-Bartong. He licked his lips. He was a Bowman of Loh and he did not like to say what he had to say. "My men are loyal. They have been selected—"

"Aye," put in a pallan, fierce and intolerant and with a wounded arm in a sling. "The rest of the rasts took bribes."

The Chuktar was the last in a line of commanders of the Crimson Bowmen. He had been vouched for by Naghan Vanki, the emperor's spymaster. Now he roused himself again to say: "We fought. We fought as Bowmen of Loh can fight. But we were ambushed in detail—do not ask me how for it is a mystery. Our plans were divined. We had no chance. So, I repeat and with sorrow, I see no other course for us than honorable capitulation."

The Vallians glared at him. He was a mercenary, a hyr-paktun with the pakzhan glittering golden at his throat.

Softly, the emperor said: "And Chuktar, when you capitulate in all honor and take service with our foes, what becomes of us?"

"That is the way of the fall of empires," said Chuktar Bartong. Again he licked his lips. "It is all one in vaol-paol."

The wrangling went on. These men were like children whistling in the dark to keep their courage up. All except the emperor. There was about him a spirit I had not expected. He was far from cowed, disdaining defeat, eager to resume the struggle. A calm and supreme confidence radiated from him.

In those burs in his private sanctum as we planned against catastrophe I understood how he could be the father of Delia.

The Chuktar of the Crimson Bowmen would from time to time shake his head and repeat: "We had no chance. All our movements were known in advance. No chance at all."

"And the northwest?" demanded the emperor briskly.

"Racter country," said a pallan with the exhausted and yet vicious air of a rast trapped in a spring cage. "The last reports remain unmodified. The Black Mountains and the Blue Mountains are bathed in blood. What will happen no one knows."

I felt the pang of that. The Black Mountains was Inch's kovnate, and the Blue Mountains—I forced myself to ask for details. All that was known was the northwest had tried to raise a host and the Blue Mountain Boys and the Black Mountain Men had barred the advance. After that, silence.

So the schemes of the Racters had not gone as they planned, then. . . . The black and whites were waiting quietly in other areas, waiting to step in and take up the pieces after the holocaust. Well, the onkers, they did not know that Phu-Si-Yantong was there to forestall them.

For, make no mistake, I felt, I sensed—I almost *knew*—that Phu-Si-Yantong was this minute employing other agents to wreak his will in Vallia quite apart from the duped tools of his I had so far encountered.

So far there had seemed no good purpose in telling the emperor the truth of this Wizard of Loh. He would be best employed fighting each threat on the ground uncluttered by an overall fear. And, anyway, it was most likely he would not believe me.

"All known Racters have left the city," said Lykon Crimahan. His jaws rat-trapped shut, and his thin fuzz of dark beard below his chin, the prominent cheekbones, the mali-

165

cious intelligence of his dark eyes all conveyed the seething frustration and despair in him. At times of troubles before he had contrived to be away on his estates. This time he was here, in the capital, Pallan of the Treasury; and this time the trouble was likely to be the biggest of the lot and final. That, at the least, was good for a laugh.

Now he opened that rat-trap mouth again to say with some evil satisfaction: "The Fegters rose to loot and burn and many of them were killed." He looked at me. "Your trip to the northeast was fortuitous, prince majister."

"Had I been here," I began. And then stopped. To boast would be criminal and foolish—and also useless; Kov Lykon saw my hesitation, and misconstrued it. I had been about to say something entirely different from what he expected.

But I wouldn't tell this bright malicious rast that concern over my daughter Dayra might have cost an empire. It might have. And, again, it might not have; for could I have done any differently from what the emperor and his advisers and the Presidio had done? The forces arrayed against us were too strong.

As I suspected had been the case with all the war councils the emperor had been holding, we broke up with nothing decided.

Only one thing remained clear. We would go on fighting for as long as we could. But that time was short and was growing shorter with every bur that passed.

Just before we rose to leave, with the emperor already turning to Queen Lush and smiling at her, holding out his hand, I said: "I'd like you to consider certain—speculations—I shall lay before you." I'd been about to say facts; but that would put their backs up too firmly. I stared around the gathering as they paused, some half-risen, some in the act of finishing their wine, others gathering their cloaks and weapons.

"Consider the plight of Vallia. A puissant empire and a strong emperor who yet must manipulate the factions within the empire. Consider the ambition of another, someone of equal or greater stature, someone with—extraordinary powers. Someone who can extend his tentacles of power over vast distances and subvert the good and use the evil for his own ends. Someone who will take Vallia and rule it through his puppets."

"How can there be any such man?" demanded Crimahan.

I went on doggedly, wondering, to tell the truth, just how much to reveal, and knowing they would hardly believe.

166

"All these risings are connected. There is a master plan. Where, emperor, is your personal Wizard of Loh, Deb-sa-Chiu?"

Queen Lush gasped.

The emperor smiled at her, patting her hand, and turned to me.

"He was ill. He craved leave to return home."

"And you let him go?"

"One does not easily ignore the reasonable requests of a Wizard of Loh. Their powers are—are strange."

"Quite."

I'd bet a first-class zorca against a broken-down calsany that Deb-sa-Chiu, who had sought out Delia for me, had been made ill by the conjurations of Phu-Si-Yantong. It was one more carefully arranged part of his plan. Even though no other Wizard of Loh might be as powerful as Yantong—with the possible and hoped for exception of Khe-Hi-Bjanching—that devil would take no chances and had got rid of Deb-sa-Chiu.

"What has a Wizard of Loh to do with—" started Crimahan in his spiteful way.

But the emperor was not Delia's father for nothing. His smile for Queen Lush altered, subtly, as he said: "And, Dray, you think—?"

"Aye. And not think. Know."

Queen Lush put a hand to her breast. She was very pale.

"Rest easy, my queen," said the emperor, and I noted the form of address. "Here, a glass of wine. This news, if true, is very dreadful. But you have been a comfort and a support to me. I could not have gone on without you at my side. Do not fail me now."

"I shall stand with you. I swear it!" She looked distraught and this was no wonderful thing, for the idea of having a Wizard of Loh pitted against you is unnerving, to say the least.

The others in the room looked shaken. Even if, later, they would pooh-pooh what I had said, at the moment they were a badly rattled bunch.

Well, I had told them some of it. Maybe that was a mistake and I certainly would tell them no more. But the black pall over Vallia needed men and women now who would fight to the end even when they knew the end would be evil and filled with sorrow, people who would rend that black pall even though the end was doom-laden horror.

A somberness held them all as they departed to go about

the petty business of supply and reorganization we had decided. Not a one knew a whisper of the whereabouts of Delia. As for my inquiries about the islands of Vallia, they were out of it. Nothing from Rahartdrin, Ava, Womox, all the others, not a sound or sign from Veliadrin or Zamra or Valka.

Deciding to make myself useful I took a tour of the sentry posts and found all quiet. There was time for a yarn and to chew a handful of palines with the Pachaks. Then I crawled off to our wing of the palace hoping to get in at least a few burs sleep before the alarums and excursions of the morrow.

Queen Lushfymi waited for me in my bedchamber.

Of slaves there were none here, they had all run off. Even the emperor's apartments were served only by a few slaves left to him. I gaped at her. Magnificent, she looked. Sheerly clad all in white that threw the ebon glory of her hair and the long passionate violet eyes into startling contrast, she sat up on the bed and clasped her hands together over her breast.

"The emperor—?" I said.

"He sleeps. I must talk to you."

"You make that plain."

If I expected another wearisome scene after the fashion of those I had endured at the hands of willful, passionate, lovely women in the past, I was swiftly disabused of the notion. She was no new candidate to be spurned after the style of Queen Lilah, and Queen Fahia, and all the others.

"The Bowmen of Loh were most wroth at their defeat."

I poured her wine and took some myself—in chased silver goblets—and sat beside her on the bed. Her perfume scented with a mysterious power I ignored. She appeared to radiate a light and a warmth in the dim chamber.

"They would be, seeing they are proud fighting men."

She was nerving herself to say something. It hovered on those full voluptuous lips, and would not come forth. So, to ease the situation, I sipped my wine and offered palines, and tried not to be too much amused by the ludicrous affair.

Then, seeing she was having this difficulty, I said: "You and the emperor are very friendly. You have got on like a house on fire—"

"I love him."

She said this simply, unaffectedly. I sipped wine. She was a cunning, devious queen. She had brought her country of Lome to a position of immense wealth and power in Pandahem. She was possessed of witch-like powers—or so it was said. Why did she tell me this? Was it even true?

"It is true, Dray Prescot."

168

I sat up.

"No, I cannot read your mind. But I can divine much that is in a man's heart. So I would not attempt to seduce you, for I know of your passion for Delia, the Princess Majestrix."

I said nothing.

Then, out of deviltry, I said: "And if that were not so and if you loved the emperor as you claim, would you try to seduce me?"

Frankly, her violet eyes bearing down on me, she said: "Yes. I would. If by doing so I could help the emperor. Believe me."

I rubbed my chin. I needed a shave. I said: "When we met—when I fell through your palanquin awning, you did not much like me and, I confess, I did not much care for you. Why do you seek me out to tell me this?" Then, thinking I understood, I added: "I shall not stand in your way. I should be glad if the emperor wed again and brought forth a whole regiment of princes and princesses—"

"It is not that."

"Perhaps, Queen Lush, you had better tell it all to me."

I used the name without thinking—and she amazed me by smiling. "From you, Dray Prescot, that comes as a declaration of intent."

"There is nothing wrong with the name Queen Lush. Anyway, it suits you. Names are more important on Kregen than most folk care to admit—"

"Yes. Oh, yes!"

That surprised me. So, ignoring a sudden wash of unease, I told her to spit it out and have done.

"It is not easy. Promise me you will remember that I truly love the emperor?"

"If you like."

"I know you, Dray Prescot, know far more of you than you can possibly dream—so that answer will suffice. I know of you—" She held up her hand to stop me asking her how she thought she knew so damn much about me, and she rushed on now, in full spate, getting it all out. "The Crimson Bowmen. Their defeat was horrible. How do you think their enemy from Hamal knew the plans, knew what the Vallian army would do? How was it that the Hamalese lay in wait and slew and slew?" She nodded and I reached over and gripped her wrist. Her flesh was like ice. "Yes, Dray Prescot, yes! I told them. I, the Queen of Lome, through my occult arts, I told the Hamalese all the secrets of the emperor's

169

plans, and the army was destroyed and the blood flowed, and—"

I slapped her face.

When she calmed down—but only a little, for the situation was fraught and she was in a sprung-steel state of nervous excitement and remorse, I told her to tell me the rest.

"The Hamalese conquered Pandahem as you know and Queen Thyllis slew my father. But at the Battle of Jholaix the Vallians conquered and Pandahem once more threw off the yoke of Hamal. But new enemies arose. Far more powerful." She wrenched away and stood up. Her long white gown glimmered in the dim, tapestry-hung room. She began to walk up and down, jerkily, her hands now clasped together, now raised to heaven, her lovely face passionate with remembered terror, a drugged horror that turned her violet eyes into shadowed deeps. "I must tell you, for you are the man to support the emperor now and the southwest will rally to him, and the islands, and we can still win, still win against—" She faltered, and that lissom body drooped.

"Who made you betray the Vallian army?"

"I think—I think, Dray Prescot, you know."

She turned away, half-fainting with her emotions; but I made no move to assist her. A shadow moved in the doorway at my side and I held up my hand to the emperor, a commanding gesture that would ordinarily have sent him flying into a rage; but he looked long at Queen Lush and listened to her, and the old devil remained silent, a shadow among shadows of the bedchamber.

Speaking in as soothing a voice as I could manage, I said: "Lome has become rich and splendid since you took the throne. Is this also the work of he who now owns you?"

Her shoulders trembled. "Yes." The whisper barely reached.

"In return for all he has done for Lome, with you as queen, he demanded you come to Vallia, seduce the emperor, gain his confidence—and then betray him?"

"Yes."

The emperor moved and I reached out my hand and grasped his forearm, and gripped enough so that he understood. Truly, the times had wrought on him. He stood, a bleak dark statue, in the shadows of the bed at my side, and, together, we listened as Queen Lushfymi of Lome choked out her confession.

Phu-Si-Yantong.

She had never met him. But his agents and his own lupal

170

projection had convinced her. The terrors she felt were reflected palely in her stammering voice. Yantong had moved into Pandahem in the wake of the dissolution of the Hamalese armies and in his own surreptitious, cunning, devious ways had exerted his own authority. His puppets now occupied the thrones of the kingdoms of Pandahem.

A fleeting twinge of guilt at thought of Tilda and Pando passed across my mind; but that was of and for another time. Here and now the dark and treacherous scheme to destroy Vallia was being revealed to us.

"See!" cried Queen Lush, her laugh too close to hysteria for my liking. She drew from her sleeve a black feather. "See! I was prepared to make the emperor a convert to the Great Chyyan; but you, Dray Prescot, destroyed that scheme. Now my master sends warriors to do his work." She blew the black feather from her. It gyrated and was lost in the shadows. She laughed again, the hysteria hideously near, so near as to be madness. Her glimmering form moved in the shaded lamplight of the bedchamber. Silently, the emperor stood at my side, watching and listening.

Queen Lush drew from the bosom of her dress a dagger, sheathed, ornate, crusted with gems, the style of weapon a queen might carry. She waved it wildly. "Look upon the death of the Emperor of Vallia, the man I love, the man I was forced to betray, the man for whom I would give my life—the man for whom I *will* give my life!"

The stiletto flashed clear of the scabbard. Twin deeply cut grooves marked the shining blade.

"This blade is poisoned. One nick and the emperor is dead. I am to stab him, when my task is done—but I cannot, I cannot."

Moving with a purposeful slowness I reached out across the bedclothes and hooked my hard old fist around the hilt of the rapier that hung by the bedpost, angled so as to be drawn in a twinkling. I had vaulted ahead in my thoughts. Khe-Hi-Bjanching had shown me what gladiomancy could do and although I did not know if a Wizard of Loh could manipulate a sword or dagger over immense distances, I wouldn't put it past that Wizard of Loh who had contrived our downfall.

I said sharply: "And will the death of the emperor make so much difference to the schemes of Phu-Si-Yantong?"

"He must die. The master has said so and must be obeyed."

171

"This evil man is no longer your master, Queen Lush. Do not think of him as your master ever again."

She turned her head, slowly, tilting, peering at me with her head on one side, half over her shoulder. She looked quite mad. "No. He is my master—"

"He is not your master. He is a real right bastard and a kleesh—a damned Wizard of Loh. But he owns you no longer."

The poisoned dagger looked mightily unpleasant.

Now the emperor was an emperor and anyone who forgot that deserved to have their heads off; but, far more important, he was the father of my Delia. That was the fact that gave him character in my eyes, and now he proved himself.

Without faltering, he moved past the bed, stood upright in a patch of light thrown by the shaded lamp. He stared at Queen Lush, who regarded him with a bright, avid look that made my hand jump on the rapier hilt.

"Queen!" declared the emperor. "You say you love me as I love you. We have meant much, one to the other, in these dark times. Will you stab me? Can you slay me? I am here—see, I lift my arms. Stab, Queen Lush—if you can."

As they stood, facing each other, frozen, I wondered if the old devil realized how he had called his queen.

She took a tottering step. Another. The dagger lifted. I eased the rapier out and stood up.

With a shriek of virulent fury or of hysterical triumph—a shriek of such violence that the emperor jumped—Queen Lush hurled the dagger to the floor. It thwacked into the floorboards through a priceless carpet of Walfarg weave, thrummed with the gems glittering in its hilt, the poisoned slots dark and sinister along the blade.

"No, my emperor—" Then they collapsed into each other's arms.

A sharp and chilling tang struck through the close air of the bedchamber. Queen Lush screamed. The emperor, still holding her, swung about. We all stared at the far wall.

In a ghostly swirl of color and shadow, a mist of madness, a shape formed in thin air against the wall. Hunched, that dire form, hunched and malicious, malefic with power as the two dark eye sockets abruptly glittered with twin spots of light. The ghostly form thickened and solidified and yet remained insubstantial, unreal, a projection of the mind.

"Master—" croaked the queen. She would have fallen but for the emperor's arms.

The lupal projection of Phu-Si-Yantong writhed in my bedchamber. What forces he was employing to overcome or by-pass the sealings placed there by Khe-Hi-Bjanching I could not know; but the lupal projection wavered as sand wavers on a stream bed, as the mirages dance in the burning deserts.

An arm lifted. Clawed finger pointed. The queen screamed as though tormented with red-hot pincers.

The emperor shouted, an agonized bark of pure horror.

I saw the tableau hold for a heartbeat; then the sorcerous image of the wizard shimmered and faded and I thought I heard the distant sound of golden bells, tingling and tinkling in a dream, fading, dying, gone.

"Dray!" gasped the emperor.

His face looked gray in the patch of lamplight, gray and filled with a horror so great he could barely stand.

The woman slumped in his arms, the white dress strangely loose.

He turned her so I could see her face.

Queen Lushfymi—so glorious, so darkly glittering, so regal with beauty and voluptuousness—hung slackly on the emperor's arm. Phu-Si-Yantong had smitten her with chivrel. Her white hair straggled in brittle strands, her shrunken face bore a spiderweb of cracks, the wrinkles destroying all the purity of that face. Spittle slobbered from brown and leathery lips.

Hideous, a hag, Queen Lush whimpered feebly and clung with skeleton arms to the Emperor of Vallia.

The decaying smell of her stank in our nostrils.

Chapter Nineteen

Vondium Burns

The moment of doom for Vondium the Proud could no longer be delayed.

The day dawned with a particularly brilliant flood of jade and ruby lights, pouring in commingled beauty from the Suns of Scorpio. But this day would see the end of the empire, the death of hundreds, perhaps thousands, of people, the enslavement of hosts, the shedding of blood to stink rawly into the shining benign sky.

We did what we could for Queen Lush. An aged crone, trembling, shaking, her white hair brittle as dried leaves, she gasped with the effort of breathing, her eyes filmed, her mouth slack and drooling. The devil-cast chivrel had not much longer to run for her. Old before her time she was doomed as the Empire of Vallia was doomed.

The emperor was stricken.

"My strong right arm," he said, clasping his head, his strong handsome face ashen. "Stricken down—torn from me when I needed her most."

I was torn, also, at sight of this great and puissant emperor in these straits. I had little cause to care for him save only that through him I had been blessed with Delia. He had ordered my head off—had banished me—I do not to this day know whether he hated me or merely tolerated me. Certainly from time to time, when he recollected, he showed he appreciated a little the services I had rendered him. But now all that was mere tawdry tinsel. The empire was doomed, Vallia was rent asunder and Vondium burned.

The manner of the burning was strange, for we could see the boiling black smoke clouds from one section or another of the city rising into the bright air, and then they would dwindle away and die. Fresh smoke would rise elsewhere and we would hear the distant clamor of mobs, and then the smoke would die away. Chuktar Wang-Nalgre-Bartong had the explanation.

"The mobs burn and loot, led by the Lornroddorn, and someone else is putting out the fires to preserve the city. And, I think, seeing we have had no sight of the Hamalian skyships, it must be the Hamalian army."

That made sweet sense. Phu-Si-Yantong had no wish to preside through his puppets over a destroyed city. He was methodically taking control. His men were putting their new house in order. Only the imperial palace and the great kyro and the webwork of surrounding canals remained to be taken. It seemed the Hamalese high command was in no hurry.

Two probing attacks were made and were flung back with ease but not without loss to us. We had the remnants of the Crimson Bowmen, a handful of Chuliks and Khibils, a few Rapas and Fristles, mercenaries all, and the Pachaks. Of artillery we were woefully short, having but five pieces, two catapults and three varters. Of cavalry we had the two squadrons of totrixes and they were in sorry case. At the first

174

real attack despite our determination to fight we would be overwhelmed.

Kov Lykon Crimahan told the emperor: "You must flee the city, majister. There is no other way to preserve your life."

"And where should I flee?"

A babble of voices answered this, all proffering different destinations. I felt the ugliness in me. In these circumstances I would not care to chance any of the provinces on the main island and even, dare I say it, even Valka might not offer any sanctuary from the avenging hosts determined to do away with the emperor.

"If only," said that great man now so shrunken, "if only the queen could advise as she used to do."

I turned away in disgust. To go to Lome now would be to go to certain destruction. There seemed but one thing left.

I said, turning back and barging through the excited, gesticulating group: "You had best flee to Zenicce. My enclave of Strombor will welcome you."

"I cannot—"

"Here they come!" bellowed a Deldar, leather-lunged, and we turned to the walls to repel the third attack. This time the Hamalese put in more weight, ready if we did not resist to charge home, but prepared to melt away under opposition and to let us stew a little longer. They played leem and ponsho with us.

"The confident cramphs!" snarled Jiktar Laka Pa-Re. He was wounded, a long glancing slice in his left biceps—his upper left biceps. The Hamalese were shooting crossbow bolts at anything that moved along the battlements of the palace. We had lost the kyro and had been driven back over the first of the canals. "They do not use their catapults—"

"No. Their masters do not wish to deface the palace. The place is beautiful and priceless. They fight for it, just as we do."

The Crimson Bowmen could outshoot the crossbowmen of Hamal; but their numbers were small and dwindling. Of the mercenaries with us I fancied we could rely on the Chuliks and the Khibils. As for the Rapas and Fristles and few oddments of other diff races, most of them would be gone by nightfall, slipped away to loot a little and then either hire out elsewhere or—or what else? Was not that a mercenary's life?

As for the Pachaks, until they released themselves from their nikobi, which they would not do and lose honor, they would fight to the death.

Many voices among the emperor's rump of advisers lifted in favor of flight. The Pachaks could be discharged, their nikobi satisfied, all the others could be let go. The Crimson Bowmen might stay or leave as they willed; their Chuktar kept them screwed tightly down; but. . . .

Of the people I knew in Vondium I fancied few if any would be left. Bargom of The Rose of Valka had friends along the cut and he and his family should be away to safety along the canals. The city lowered under shifting palls of smoke through which the suns struck lurid gleams of crimson and jade. The incessant nibbling attacks continued against us; men fell.

More than once I had to warn the emperor in strong terms not to expose himself too freely on the battlements. By this time we had withdrawn into the palace and taken up our positions along an inner ring of fortifications, for we were too few to man the entire cincture of walls. I remembered the way he had thirsted to get into fights before. This time the outcome might not be so jolly.

"I am fighting for my empire." He said this with a fine fierce air.

"Oh, aye? Your empire is gone, emperor. Vanished, blown away like thistledown. You imprisoned your friends, spurned those who would help you, embraced the bosoms of your enemies—"

He rounded furiously on me, and I relented, and said: "At least you let them go before it was too late. But if they were with us now—Lord Farris, Old Foke, Vad Atherston, all the others who would serve you loyally—"

"I know, I know! They were put away from me through the wiles of the queen. I know. But she repented and has she not paid the price?"

I nodded. I found I felt a great sorrow for Queen Lush.

They say speak of the devil. We looked up as an airboat flew sluggishly toward us from over the city. It staggered in flight and black smoke streamed back, so I knew the voller had been shot at with fire arrows. She made some kind of landing on a high aerial platform and the guards brought down the Lord Farris—and with him—Delia.

She looked gorgeous in her russet leathers, strapped about with rapier and dagger, striding limber and free, her brown hair magnificent under the suns. After she had embraced me she said: "Dayra?"

I touched my scratched face reflectively; but the gesture meant nothing to Delia. She regarded me gravely.

"I have seen her, my love. She is well. But there is a very great deal to tell. Can you not persuade your father, the stubborn old onker, to abandon the palace and fly to safety?"

"I will speak to him. But he never forgets he is the emperor."

"Not any more he isn't."

Greeting the Lord Farris kindly, for he was a great-hearted man, I broke the news of Queen Lush's personal tragedy. Delia touched her lips, lightly, and looked down.

"I felt she was a bad influence—many of us did. But this—will she live long?"

"Not long, I judge. She looks as though she is passed two hundred and fifty years old."

Delia shivered.

The emperor greeted his daughter, and was polite to Farris, which amused me. The old devil tried to make amends.

It was useless to look for relief. We could expect no succor in the shape of an aerial armada. From Valka was only silence. Delia said that Delphond slumbered, which did not surprise me. As for the Blue Mountains—when I told her the news her brows drew down and her eyes took on that dangerous look that indicated someone was in for it in the neck. But nothing could be done there. And Strombor—well, we faced an army of Hamalese, plus the multitudes of irregulars and the factions, all whipped into frenzy by false stories, rumors, bitter animosities fanned by Phu-Si-Yantong. We were isolated.

"The Empress Thyllis has prepared long for this," said the emperor. "She takes her revenge upon us Vallians." He rubbed his fingers together, absently, and then gripped his rapier hilt. "If only the queen were in full health, blooming like a rose—if only she were herself."

So, looking at Delia, I said: "She might be—it may be possible."

Delia shook her head; but her father rounded on me.

"Well? What mean you? Spit it out!"

"I promise nothing. But—" I tried to look at Delia; but she would not meet my eye. "I must go to my Valkan villa here in the city. When I return, we will see what may be done."

"Dray—" said Delia.

"I know," I said. "But even though I am an onker of onkers, it was you who made me go down into the pit—and more than once—to bring the famblys out."

"I remember."

177

"You cannot venture into the city, prince," said Farris. "The place swarms with looters and rioters, and Hamalians putting them down. Anyone out there—*everyone* out there—is a foe."

"I'll fly." I made up my mind. "And I'll use your flier, Jen Farris. The one I stole from Udo is a fine craft and will serve the emperor."

Before I left I took Delia aside. "Look, my heart. Make sure your father does nothing foolish while I am gone. I have warned him, and I think he understands. The flier is a good one and will carry you and him, as well as Farris, if a little cramped—"

"And you!"

"Oh, aye. I'll be back. Count on that."

The flier carried me sluggishly over doomed Vondium. For the most part the place was deserted, with stray bands of looters and rioters thieving and burning and parties of Hamalian soldiery attempting to preserve the city—to preserve it for Yantong. That truly mighty city, once proud and sublime in its confidence, lay now enthralled under the cloak of oppression. No vollers offered to stop my progress and I began to think that the absence of Hamalian skyships indicated they might be engaged somewhere over Vallia in a last supreme struggle with the Vallian Air Service. Farris would rage that he was denied that final proof of his devotion to his Air Service.

The Valkan villa was abandoned but I guessed its unkempt appearance had deterred looters. Going through those dusty halls and corridors gave me a shivery feeling; I remembered the circumstances of my last departure from here. That was prophetic; too late to realize that now. The keys were in the wall niche and the iron-bound chest opened easily and disgorged household linen and the scuffed old water bottle. This I fastened securely to my harness.

The dusty smell of the villa would have depressed me but there was no time for self-indulgence of that sort. Once we'd put Queen Lush to rights I'd make the emperor take the flier and leave Vondium. The little craft would take him and the queen as well as Delia and Farris. . . . As to whether or not I would go I was not decided. To be a wanderer on the face of Kregen, hunted, outlawed, whose destruction was avidly sought by powerful and greedy men, cruel in their strength, this was a fate of the most profound abhorrence. I fancied I knew what Delia would say.

All the animals of the villa had been released and I assumed Shadow had trotted off with them. I felt the strongest presentiment that I had not seen the last of that superb zorca.

My thoughts rattled on as I sprinted across the open space for the flier. My splendid enclave of Strombor in the city of Zenicce lay to the eastward on the coast of the continent of Segesthes. There the emperor and the queen might recuperate while Delia and I planned our next steps. We could gather the exiles. There were still men loyal. Lord Farris was one. Even Lykon Crimahan, despite the malice he felt toward me, was loyal. Maybe, now we had lost our estates in Vallia, much of his resentment of me would be finished, for he had his evil eyes on Veliadrin—along with plenty of other nobles of the eastern coast.

The voller took off sweetly enough and carried me perhaps half an ulm toward the palace. Then she went into a steep nose dive and only luck and a thick skull saved me. I went pitching out and into a canal, splashing, spouting water, flailing for the bank. The flier sank with a bubbling gurgle.

From now on the journey back would be on foot.

Well, on my own two feet I have tramped a fair old bit of Kregen.

I set off, and I loosened the longsword in the scabbard.

The way was barred in a couple of places by the detritus of fallen buildings. Naghan the Mask's fine new theatre had been gutted, I was sorry to see. The temples looked unscathed. A party of looters tried to loot my equipment; but half a dozen of them having lost blood and other inward essentials, the rest ran off shrieking.

An arrow past my ear heralded the attempt of the Hamalese army to detain me. But there were only ten of them, a strong audo, a section or so, and after three casts of my Lohvian longbow the others decided in prosaic military formula to retire to reform and seek fresh orders. They were wise—the seven who thus lived.

The going became a trifle tougher as I neared the palace and ran into the rear echelons of the besieging forces. There are usually ten audos in a pastang, ten sections in a company, and the Hamalese, notorious for the severity of their laws, organize tightly. Crouching down by a brick wall I stared out at the backs of the Hamalese. The swods and their officers moved about with the sure confidence of men approaching victory in their own time. They kept busy. I saw the glitter of their helmets and weapons, the panoply of their appearance, the square shapes of their shields. I chose my point with some care.

A pretty little flower-bowered bridge spanned a canal ahead and the Hamalese swod set to guard it hefted his stux, the throwing spear, at the poise. He whistled a cheerful little ditty I had heard many times in Iamal: *When the fluttrell flirts his wing,* and there was no passing him without question.

A fight would alert his comrades. So taking up the refrain at the point where the fluttrell flyer, discovering the buckles of his clerketer have parted and the saddle is sliding down the big bird's back, claps his hands over his eyes—always raises a laugh, does that, among flyers—I marched up with a swing. The swod eyed me and the stux lifted. He could punch a hole in a kax with that, at close enough range.

He shouted: *"Llanitch!* Halt! Stand you still, dom."

His shield bore the painted devices of the Twenty-ninth Regiment of Foot. I waved a friendly arm and bellowed: "Where away are the Fifteenth of Foot, dom? By Krun! This place confuses me even more than Ruathytu. What I'd give to be strolling through the Ghat Gate to the Jikhorkdun of the Swods."

At my familiar mention of places in Ruathytu he eased up. He should not have done so, of course. I reached him, still chattering on about Ruathytu, capital of Hamal, which I then knew better than Vondium, mentioning certain lively and low dopa dens, and smilingly took his throat in my hand and choked—only a little. I held him upright and propped him against the flower-drenched bricks of the bridge. I leaned his stux against his lorica. With a merry quip about the sylvies at The Stux and Mirvol, I saluted him and tromped on, turning down by the canal, and after a scything glance showed none of the swods cared about me, ducking down into a hedgerow of a private garden. The hedge let me through, not without a scrape or two, and I belted across the lawn and so through the house. Using houses and gardens I worked my way up the avenue, having passed into the engaged zone of the enemy.

No one had taken alarm. That swod would recover with a sore throat. His Deldar would scream at him; what his Hikdar would say would flay him; and when the Jiktar commanding his regiment spoke to him—well, I felt sorry for the swod, believe me.

Pressing on toward the palace, darting across side roads,

crossing canals and all the time keeping out of sight, I wormed close to the edge of the great kyro. A few murs more...

Three Hamalian reconnaissance vollers flew over the palace in wedge formation. They kept their eyes on us from time to time. From a propped-up varter a couple of bolts were let fly from the battlements. The Hamalians, trailing bright flags, flew on unconcerned.

They disappeared beyond the jumble of rooftops and another voller leaped up from the palace. Crouching down, I looked up and recognized her as the craft I had stolen from Udo. She swung away, going fast. Before she had time to gain height the Hamalians were back. The three closed in. Bolts flew and arrows crisscrossed the wind-streaming gap. The fliers turned and passed above my head. I saw the Hamalians clear—and saw the way the fleeing voller from the palace turned end over end and fell to a smashing destruction on the stones before the palace.

Chapter Twenty

Delia of Vallia

In the ensuing confusion as the soldiery boiled across to gape at the wreckage and the blood-soaked refuse within I was able to slip past. Of one thing I was certain. Whoever may have been in the flier, Delia was not one of that company. A Chulik offered to bash my brains out at the rampart until I rapped out the password. "Zamra!" I had chosen that. The confusion without was matched and overmatched by the confusion within.

"Dray! You have it?" Delia ran up to me, eager, alive, ready to let me have an earful for endangering myself. I shook the water bottle.

Together, we went to the small private inner room where Queen Lush lay on a pallet, panting shallowly, withering away. The emperor sat by her side, frightened even to hold her hand in case the brittle bones snapped.

The men in the fleeing voller were three certain pallans. I will not mention their names. They came to an evil end.

181

But they indicated very clearly the deterioration of morale within the palace. And, the means of flight had been snatched from the emperor. Delia bent over Queen Lush as I thought about the implications. Vondium was decidedly unhealthy right now and was like to get worse.

The fliers we saw did not drop firepots on us. Phu-Si-Yantong did not wish to destroy the palace. He coveted its priceless treasures. Of course, he could have razed the lot and built afresh and to a greater scale of grandeur; but that would not have slaked the greed in the man, of that I felt sure.

"Water?" said the emperor. "Is that all—?"

"Hush, father," said Delia, whereat I smiled alarmingly.

The withered brown lips were somehow coaxed into receiving some of the milky fluid from the Sacred Pool of Baptism of the River Zelph in far Aphrasöe. Delia poured a golden cupful, and we helped Queen Lush to lift herself, and Delia coaxed her gently. The crone moaned and slobbered and much of the priceless fluid ran down that withered witch-like chin.

"How much, my heart, do you think?"

"I do not know. But Yantong is a mighty powerful devil of a wizard. Give her plenty. Better more than less."

"You are right." Together we fed the magical fluid, sip by sip.

The emperor rocked back. He was shaking. His eyes opened wide. "By the sweet snke of Opaal!"

"Yes, father," said Delia, impatiently, "and don't jog the cup. You have wasted two mouthfuls."

For Queen Lushfymi changed. The lines and wrinkles sloughed away and her skin took on that smooth peach bloom. Dark tint suffused the stringy white hair; slowly it resumed that lustrous darkness that shone with blue-black light. Her body filled, her shrunken flesh restoring that voluptuous outline, the skeletal claws firming to the shapely hands with which she gestured so gracefully. In not too long a time Queen Lush glowed seductively before us, fully restored to beauty.

"My love—" She turned those limpid violet eyes on the emperor. Delia blinked and smiled. "How can I thank you? You have made me—made me myself again—"

"It was not me, my queen. Rather, thank the wild leem Dray Prescot—and my daughter Delia."

She took Delia's hand in hers. The reconciliation would have been most affecting; but the sound of conflict and shouting and the screams of wounded and dying men burst savagely in. I stood up.

"There is work to be done—but, emperor, we're finished here. You must discharge the mercenaries in honor and then we must leave."

"There is no airboat—"

"I shall arrange that."

He stood up and faced me. We stood looking at each other for a heartbeat. Kov Lykon and the Lord Farris—who was a kov, also—burst in. "The devils are through the Peral Gate! We must pull back—"

"I am coming," I said. "We will hold them at the Wall of Larghos Risslaca." That was dangerously close to the very heart of the palace.

"Hold!" The emperor spoke thunderously. He bore down on them all, imperious. "I may die soon. I do not know. But this I swear as my testament. Long have I held my son-in-law in contempt as a clansman and, also, regarded highly his skill at arms, his boorishness which he calls integrity. He is a Hyr-Jikai—"

"Get on with it," I said. "I'm going out there to bash—"

"Wait! Should I die, then you, Dray Prescot, will be Emperor of Vallia. Witness this testament of my will, all of you. This thing will be—will be, by my decree."

"You won't die yet, emperor," I said. And then, in the heat of the moment, burst out: "Sink me! You've a thousand years of life yet. Now—let us go and bash a few skulls."

Delia ran swiftly out with me and I turned on her and bellowed: "I don't want you fighting on the walls! Stay with your father and keep him company."

"You told him. A thousand years of life—he'll want to—"

"Later, my heart—"

That little fight proved harder than those preceding as we held the Hamalese on the walls, pulling back to the Wall of Larghos Risslaca and shooting down on the rasts as they raced with their scaling ladders. We halted them. It was hard. But the next onslaught would be harder still to halt. I went back to see the emperor. I found him gazing at Queen Lush as though dyspeptic—and realized my ill humor was affecting my judgment. I had to hold up. The emperor would live a thousand years, and with Queen Lush at his side could be kept out of my hair. The future looked promising, if we could escape the here and now.

"Those cramphs of Hamal have fliers out there," I said without preamble. "They build them well for themselves. I'll

183

"In racing curves around temples and walls, I avoided detection from the air."

fetch one. Meantime, arrange to discharge our paktuns and mercenaries. As for the Crimson Bowmen, they are mercenaries, also, and should be discharged. Make the compact that we must leave in safety, all we Vallians. Do this."

Queen Lush said: "And—me—?"

"You're a Vallian now, by intention of marriage. And we'll take Lome back for you. There is little time. And, while I am gone, emperor—stay out of trouble."

"A thousand—what did you mean?"

"Delia may explain, if she will. Just make sure you stay alive to enjoy it. With my blessings." I ran out.

Kissing Delia, I said as I let her go: "Take care of yourself."

In a much lighter frame of mind I took myself off through secret tunnels I had used before. Vondium was a buzzing hive of danger; but there at least I could strike out freely. I felt a keen pleasure that Delia's father was proving himself more human day by day. He wouldn't change, of course, so much as actually come to like me. But that didn't matter. What mattered was Vallia—and the country was in a sorry, blood-soaked state at the moment. Once Phu-Si-Yantong got his hooks firmly wedged into the country people would realize they had seen nothing yet.

Outside the palace I dodged like a grundal from bush to bush of some ornamental gardens, got across a canal, insinuated myself past a group of wounded Hamalese and so, in the guise of an irregular mercenary hired to the Empress Thyllis, set off for the fliers. They were easy enough to spot. Only at the last moment, as we lifted into the air, was there any trouble. Some old oily rags in the voller served to wipe the longsword clean.

Skimming low over the ground, taking the voller in racing curves around temples and over villa walls, I avoided detection from the air. Ahead the massive bulk of the palace lifted. I looked up.

Casting down twin shadows onto the white walls, rank after rank of fliers slanted in for the palace. I knew them.

Trylon Udo and his Hawkwas smashed in to strike the final blows.

And then, beyond the armada from the Northeast, another fleet hove into view. They were not as many. They flew the flags of Kov Layco Jhansi. He was the emperor's chief pallan. I did not give a cheer; but I felt like shouting in glee.

Among the fliers with Jhansi were many whose flagstaffs flew treshes of checkerboarded ochre and umber, the colors

185

of Falinur. I frowned, suddenly. Layco Jhansi was supposed to be fighting the rebellious Falinurese. It looked as though he was in alliance with them. I sent the voller hurtling flat out for the palace, treachery stinking in my nostrils.

All was confusion in and around the palace.

That frowning pile had become the centerpiece for all the vindictive hatred, the scheming, the vengeance, the sheer outright deviltry of all those attacking Vondium and seeking to claw down the emperor. The voller leaped across the sky. Quarrels spat toward me. Varter-driven rocks hissed past my head. Now smoke and flames rose from the bewildering maze of domes and towers of the palace. The unceasing shrilling of fighting men beat a diapason to the bright sky. The suns passed across the heavens, and cast down their mingled streaming light, and an empire went down in flames and blood.

Into a niche high along a flower-hung balcony I dropped the voller with a precision of handling that would have pleased Delia, who had taught me my flying. I leaped out. Smoke blew chokingly across from a burning roof. In a courtyard below men fought and struggled and died. I saw the colors. I raced away, leaping down well-remembered stairs, haring for Delia.

Faction against faction—hatreds and jealousies were tearing the heart out of the empire. Those colors down there—Jhansi's men fought them both, and the Hamalese fought all. It was a madness. Blood clotted the bright tapestries and fouled the priceless carpets. I raced along the corridors and so came, at last, to where Laka Pa-Re and his Pachaks fought the last great fight.

The longsword flamed, striking this way and that in the vicious yet fully controlled fighting technique of the Krozairs of Zy. Hamalese fell away. A group of Hawkwas surged up, screeching, and together, the Pachaks and I, we bested them and drove them off, running.

Chuktar Pola Je-Du was wounded, a slashing gash across his shoulder armor, where the plates hung down broken. His face showed only firm resolve.

"Pola—you have not been discharged from your nikobi?"

"No, prince. We fight to the end."

"No—that is madness. You need not be slain—from me, will you take your discharge, in all honor? Will you save your men?"

"If I do, I think you will die here."

"That is as may be, by Zair. The emperor—"

186

"He is sore wounded."

I felt the shock. "The get onker! I told him—the moment I leave him to his own devices the idiot gets himself wounded." Smoke boiled down the ornate passage and the Pachaks braced themselves for the next attack. I bellowed at the Chuktar. "Take your nikobi back, in honor, Pola Je-Du. And you, Laka Pa-Re. Take what you will from the palace in payment for your service—and my thanks to you for your devotion, in the name of Papachak the All-Powerful."

"Let the compact be unravelled," said Pola. And then he said: "And you, prince?"

"By the Black Chunkrah! I'll have a few words to say to the emperor, believe me! Remberee, Pachaks all." And I turned and belted along the corridor toward the inner apartments.

As I ran so I marveled that the Pachaks had consented to be released from the compact by me, who was merely the Prince Majister of Vallia. Their hire had been to the emperor. . . .

At the door of those sumptuous apartments Delia met me. The tears stood brightly in her glorious brown eyes; but she would not weep. Not just yet. . . .

"My father—oh, my heart! My father is dead."

I couldn't believe that.

I pushed through. Lykon Crimahan and the Lord Farris stood with dripping swords within the doorway, their faces ashen. Queen Lushfymi crouched over the body of the emperor. He had been killed by a slashing blow that had near severed his head from his body. Despite the Baptism in the Sacred Pool, he was dead. No man was going to recover in time from that kind of savagely mortal blow.

I stood looking down on him. I did not know what I felt.

Then I took Delia in my arms.

"He said—he said you are the emperor, Dray."

"That is so," shouted Farris, suddenly. He came to life. "Hai Jikai! Dray Prescot. Emperor of Vallia."

"There's no time for that," I said, savage, incensed, sullen, vindictive—anything but pleased. "We must get out of here. And bring the emperor with you. We will give him proper burial."

Delia shook her head.

"We cannot carry him and fight as well. He will lie here, and he will burn in his own palace. What more magnificent funeral pyre could an emperor have than that?"

I bowed to her wishes. He was her father.

"How—?"

"Hawkwas. We fought them off; but one did for him."

I knew.

"A bright, nervous, malicious bastard—?"

She nodded. "Yes, I think so." We hurried along the corridor past the Pachak dead who had fought to the last. "That sounds like him."

A few more words convinced me it had been Zankov. Zankov. He had slain the Emperor of Vallia. I swallowed. Carefully, I said: "Were there women with him? Jikai Vuvushis?"

"Yes—and very dreadful—renegades from the Sisters—"

"Was there one who—who fought with a sharp steel claw?"

"No."

Thank Zair, I said, but to myself.

Delia bore herself like a princess. But I watched her narrowly. The shock of her father's death would prey on her and I felt the agony for her tearing at me. I had watched my father die, with that damned scorpion scuttling, and I had been only a little lad. Delia had known her father for far longer than ever I had known mine, and the wrench, the agony, the shock must affect her far more profoundly—so I thought.

Useless to prate on about how I had warned him to keep himself safe and stay out of trouble. He had pushed to the forefront of the battle, convinced, determined. Now he was dead.

We reached a stairway leading up and a gang of Falinurese sought to stop us and we carved a path through them. Bitterness directed our strokes, anger and vengeance and sorrow. We smashed our way through our foemen and raced up the stairs.

We cut our way through a confused and struggling melee of Layco Jhansi's men fighting Hamalese. So Jhansi had sought the supreme power for himself. Ashti Melekhi. . . . Some veiled acts came clear. And Jhansi was interfering with the plans of Phu-Si-Yantong. There would be no easy path to the throne for Zankov, for all he had slain the emperor, when faced with the dark and secret ambitions of Kov Layco Jhansi.

Up onto that high balcony we stumbled and so over and down to the niche where the voller nestled.

Delia stood firmly at the controls. Queen Lush huddled on a bench, wrapping flying silks about her, weeping and weeping. Lykon Crimahan and the Lord Farris stared back and up, viciously, hungering for a head to appear over the balcony and so give them the opportunity to take one more blow at the hated enemies who had ruined all of Vallia for them.

"Jhansi," said Delia. "He is proved foresworn. He must have given Ashti Melekhi her orders to poison my father." She stopped, then, and her mouth trembled. "My father—"

"Take us up and away from this accursed place, my heart."

"Yes, Dray, my heart. We will go. But—one day—we will come back. We must return. . . ."

I put my arm around her waist as she sent the voller slanting up in the declining rays of Zim and Genodras. The Suns of Scorpio flamed along the horizon and bathed the burning city in crimson and emerald fires.

"Oh, aye, we'll return. I don't pretend to be perfect—or even particularly cut out for the job—but all Vallia is captive to Phu-Si-Yantong and the other villains now, and that is something I do not like and must, in conscience, try to alter." I held my Delia as we shot away over the doomed city. "Anyway, there are the children to consider. What's to become of them?"

"Outcasts," said Lykon Crimahan, his voice faltering. "We are outcasts, unwanted, fated to wander forever—"

"I do not," said the Lord Farris, "think so."

"But Vondium is fallen. The emperor is dead."

Farris pointed at me. "Not so! The Emperor of Vallia stands before you!"

I warmed to him; but it was nonsense. Crimahan put a trembling hand to his mouth, the realization of what he had seen and heard breaking fully into his consciousness. I saw the expression in his eyes, the shifting of the planes of his face, the dawning of painful emotions.

"That is of no consequence now," I said in my rough old sailorman's voice. "If I am emperor then I an emperor of nothing."

Delia moved in my arm and looked up at me, the last of Zim's glowing light rosy on her face.

"Vondium is doomed—but there are other places of Vallia."

"Aye. We fly to Valka. We will collect Velia and Didi and Aunt Katri, for I am utterly convinced they are still safe. If Valka has been swamped by foemen, we will seek others—"

"Strombor?"

"Aye, my heart. Strombor. My enclave of Strombor will welcome us and will love Velia and Didi as they love you." I looked away from her tear-filled brown eyes. It was in my heart to tell her that I would as lief remain in Strombor. I, Dray Prescot, of Earth and of Kregen, a Lord of Strombor. But—Vallia. That proud and puissant empire was torn and shredded from end to end. Could I, in all honor, turn my back on that agony?

And, so, I looked up. Against the sulphurous masses of smoke coiling from the burning city floated two wide-winged birds.

I knew them both.

Oh, yes, I knew them. That great hunting bird with the scarlet and golden feathers, circling high above me, was the Gdoinye, the messenger and spy of the Star Lords. And the white dove peering watchfully down was from the Savanti. So the two agencies who had directed so much of my life upon Kregen spied on me still in these last cataclysmic moments as a proud city burned and a puissant empire slid down into degradation and ruin.

The birds flicked their wings at me and circled and flew off once they were sure I had seen them. They reminded me of the continued existence of their masters. They did not speak to me.

Delia turned the voller eastward, toward Valka.

The burning city dwindled away below, great and magnificent and reduced. I would have to tell Delia about Dayra, about Ros the Claw. I did not think she knew. One thing piled on another, and the importance of each became distorted with viewpoint and time and emotions. The fate of one wayward daughter set against the death of an empire. . . . Did they balance out?

I, Dray Prescot, Lord of Strombor and Krozair of Zy, held my Delia close, close. Did anything else matter in two worlds?

"Empress—" gasped a soft, breathy voice. For a space no one took any notice. Then we understood. The understanding forced a small but significant change in my intentions. For her, I would dare anything. . . . "Empress," said Queen Lushfymi, pale, weeping, speaking through her sobs. "You will not cast me off?"

"Rest easy, queen," said Delia, Empress of Vallia.

The flier hurtled out of the smoke into the east, and at our backs the Suns of Scorpio threw a last sheeting refulgence of jade and crimson into the nighted sky of Kregen.

190

Presenting MICHAEL MOORCOCK
in DAW editions

The Elric Novels

☐ **ELRIC OF MELNIBONE**   (#UW1356—$1.50)
☐ **THE SAILOR ON THE SEAS OF FATE** (#UW1434—$1.50)
☐ **THE WEIRD OF THE WHITE WOLF**   (#UW1390—$1.50)
☐ **THE VANISHING TOWER**   (#UW1406—$1.50)
☐ **THE BANE OF THE BLACK SWORD** (#UW1421—$1.50)
☐ **STORMBRINGER**   (#UW1335—$1.50)

The Runestaff Novels

☐ **THE JEWEL IN THE SKULL**   (#UW1419—$1.50)
☐ **THE MAD GOD'S AMULET**   (#UW1391—$1.50)
☐ **THE SWORD OF THE DAWN**   (#UW1392—$1.50)
☐ **THE RUNESTAFF**   (#UW1422—$1.50)

The Oswald Bastable Novels

☐ **THE WARLORD OF THE AIR**   (#UW1380—$1.50)
☐ **THE LAND LEVIATHAN**   (#UY1214—$1.25)

Other Titles

☐ **LEGENDS FROM THE END OF TIME** (#UY1281—$1.25)
☐ **A MESSIAH AT THE END OF TIME** (#UW1358—$1.50)
☐ **DYING FOR TOMORROW**   (#UW1366—$1.50)
☐ **THE RITUALS OF INFINITY**   (#UW1404—$1.50)

**To order these titles,
use coupon on the
last page of this book.**

ALAN BURT AKERS—

the great novels of Dray Prescot